COLDWATER
CONFESSION

COLDWATER CONFESSION

A Coldwater Mystery

JAMES A. ROSS

LeVel
BEST BOOKS

Author Photo Credit: Taylor Lenci

First edition

ISBN: 978-1-68512-108-2

Cover art by Rebecacovers

This book was professionally typeset on Reedsy.
Find out more at reedsy.com

To my muse, Anne, and my remarkable sons Guy and Drew. Family is everything.

"There was a little girl, who had a little curl, right in the middle of her forehead.
When she was good, she was very, very good.
But when she was bad, she was horrid."

CHILDREN'S NURSERY RHYME

Praise for COLDWATER CONFESSION

"Like the lake from which it takes its title, *Coldwater Confession* will settle into your bones and hold there. Long after finishing the novel, you'll find yourself thinking about its setting and its characters, imagining the places that are critical to its plot: the high rocks of Pocket Island, a partially destroyed Frank Lloyd Wright house, underwater caverns, a boggy marsh that harbors secrets in its muck. James Ross has created a splendidly suspenseful story where the relationships among characters are as mysterious and intriguing as its thrilling plot. The novel's protagonists, the Morgan brothers, are extraordinarily well-written, well-conceived characters, both brilliant in differing ways, both unsettled, often contentious, yet ultimately dedicated to discovering the truth underneath what has swept into their lives. As the lives and deaths of near strangers require the brothers to put aside their differences in order to bring answers to their small lakeside community, they must also face the intersection of current events with their own family's mysterious history. As much as readers will enjoy the novel, they will exit eagerly wanting a third installment in Ross's Coldwater series."—Mark Leichliter, author of *The Other Side*

"With an explosive cast of often tragic, dysfunctional characters in this small upstate New York town, James Ross masterfully weaves a tale fueled by decades of deceit, delusions and missed chances in this action-packed thriller."—Mim Eichmann, author of *A Sparrow Alone* and *Muskrat Ramble*

"Need compelling characters and atmospheric setting? Look no further than the latest of James Ross's Coldwater mystery series, *Coldwater Confession*. I envy Ross's ability to create people and places that really stick!"—Robert Juckett, author of *Alfajiri, a novel of the Congo*

i

Prologue

Lightning blasted the top of a tall royal palm and hurled it through the windshield of the parked rental car. Cacophonies of thunder and colliding debris overwhelmed all other sound and thought. Andrew Ryan watched the swirling carnage from the window of the vacation cottage, heard his wife scream, and did nothing.

"Annnnn—drew!"

Peevish bleats, pitched to dramatize minor annoyance no longer penetrated the young man's consciousness. But the timbre of genuine terror is hard to fake, and his wife's cries eventually broke through. The swollen bathroom door yielded to his shoulder. The screaming woman careened through the opening. Behind her, a pale reptilian tail slithered through a gap where the bathtub and wall did not quite meet. A wave of adrenaline surged through Andrew's already overloaded system.

"I'm out of here," his wife shouted. But when she spotted the severed tree rising through their rental car windshield, she froze. "ANNNN - DREW!"

"It's okay," he whispered.

"There's a *HURRICANE* out there! We've got to get out."

"Not until it's over."

"But there's a *SNAKE* in there! I saw it."

"And tree limbs outside flying through the air at a hundred miles an hour."

"I CA...CAN'T STA...AY HERE!"

Andrew pressed the cottage telephone to his ear, tilted his head, and then tossed the mute piece of plastic to the chair. "It's dead," he said. His wife wilted to the floor, wrapped her arms around her knees, and began to rock back and forth, moaning softly. The sound that seeped out of her then was more ominous to Andrew than anything howling outside or coiled in a corner of the bathroom. It started as a low-pitched wail, like a Muslim call to prayer. Only it wasn't spiritual.

"Ah-yeeeee. MMmmmmm."

"Karen?" he demanded. "Did you take your medicine?"

"Ah-yeeeee. MMmmmmm."

"Karen? Did you take your Thorazine?"

"Ah-yeeeee."

Andrew lifted his moaning wife and laid her on the couch before searching her suitcase. "Where did you put your pills, Karen?"

"Ah-yeeeee. MMmmmmm."

"Karen, don't do this."

"Ah-yeeeee."

"Did you pack them?" His wife's eyes were unblinking...scared and defiant at the same time.

"I don't like the way they make me feel," she whispered.

Her husband's oath was an amalgam of despair, resignation, and foreboding. "There're some sleeping pills in my bag. You'd better knock yourself out before this gets ugly."

"Will you stay with me?"

"Of course."

* * *

Andrew Ryan lay in bed, listening to the sounds of lethal nature and mulling an ordinary marriage turned by slow degree to tragedy. Or maybe it wasn't slow, and he was just slow to notice. A file of overlooked clues lay open against the back of his eyelids:

Late for their first date, the tanned coed in a white halter-top boasted of getting caught in a speeding trap on her way there, peeling out and losing the startled cop in a tire burning chase through the residential hills. Aroused by the exotic combination of recklessness and sexuality, Andrew Ryan assumed that she was making it up. She wasn't.

Later came the serial drama of post-graduation employment disasters, masked for a time by the carnal pleasures of twenty-something life in the big city. Months between jobs lengthened into seasons. The fade from lioness to recluse accelerated.

The year the popular magazines were touting biological clocks ticking toward their final countdown, Karen announced that it was time for her to have children. She could do it all, she promised. Andrew was tempted to note that she had yet to do anything, but he stalled at the possibility that this might be the missing piece, the thing that could fix whatever it was that had gone so badly wrong.

But he was mistaken about that, too. The daily responsibilities of motherhood made no claim on Karen. Day-long trances behind her drawing table matured into nighttime hallucinations. The doctors first said it was a hormone imbalance, easily remedied by medication. But Karen resisted being "balanced," and she "forgot" to take her medication. The cops and the EMT drivers became frequent visitors at the Ryan house. They had their own professional diagnosis. Psycho and stoned have a lot in common, they told Andrew. Some of their charges simply liked how it made them feel.

Karen stirred under the blanket and reached a hand to stroke her brooding husband. "Come here," she whispered, her voice soft and come hither though the sounds of the storm had, if anything, gotten louder. Andrew slipped beneath the covers and snuggled close. Strange, he mused, that while everything else had fallen apart, this one thing still worked. No deception. No false promises. They came together like ice dancers to a music they heard instinctively. Or was he kidding himself about that, too?

"You lost weight in there," he said. "You look good."

"They should call it The Club Med for the Head Diet," she answered. "Institutional food and major drugs."

"How do you feel now?"

"Scared shitless of that snake in there, thank you. I was hallucinating them so much in the hospital that they had to strap me down. Most of the time it's kind of interesting, you know? But I really thought I was going to lose my mind this time."

Andrew looked away.

"You don't like to hear this, do you?"

"I don't like to hear you call it '*interesting,*'" he said wearily.

"I'm an artist, Andrew. How could I not?"

"Because your doctors have warned you a million times, *not* to find it interesting. Quote: 'Down that path lies madness.' Quote: 'One time too many and you may not be able to come back.'"

"I can come back any time I want," she snapped. Then, "You want to hear why they had to strap me down?" Andrew stared at her, but said nothing. "There was this long, pale slimy thing under my bed that kept trying to poke through the bottom of the mattress. It scared the living shit out of me. But you know what my doctor said it was? She said it was you, nagging at me to 'get out of the wagon and start pulling.' I suppose she got that charming phrase from one of her chats with you. She says that you should quit acting so disappointed all the time. That you're supposed to forgive me."

"I do," said Andrew automatically.

Karen snorted. "You don't even know what you're supposed to forgive me for." Andrew closed his eyes and mentally perused a fat catalog of forgivable misdeeds:

Wandering the neighborhood at 3:00 a.m. in your Victoria's Secret nightgown, ringing doorbells at the homes of neighbors with teenage boys. Maxing out on a half dozen credit cards I didn't know you had. Getting shit-faced at a dinner party with my boss and passing out on your plate. Leaving our two-year-old daughter alone in the house all day while you're out driving the interstate, lost in the buzz of your latest medication—or refusal to take it. The jumble of images collaged a multi-year sabbatical from the responsibilities of adult life, but they did not explain it.

"Of course I forgive you," said Andrew.

"Bullshit."

Karen tossed the covers aside and strode unclothed and unselfconscious toward the mini-bar. Andrew stared after her, mindful of Aristotle's aphorism about a pretty face being the best ambassador. Despite the abuse she had put it through, his wife had somehow managed to preserve the body of a twenty-five-year-old. In rare moments of frank self-examination, Andrew wondered if he would have put up with half of her crap if she hadn't. Watching her fondle a handful of mini booze bottles, he suppressed a familiar surge of frustration. "Don't," he said. "You'll just make it worse."

"I'm just having one."

"Is that likely?"

Karen looked at him straight and wrung the cap from the bottle with a closed fist. "We have to talk."

Here we go, he thought. You've had group and individual therapy twice a week for two years, and now you've just had six weeks of it twice a day. The excuses get more polished with every rehearsal. But your behavior keeps getting worse. And now there's a child. "I'm listening," he said.

Karen smirked and then opened her throat for an exaggerated gulp. "No, you're not. Nothing I say or do gets through to you anymore. You're numb. You don't feel anything, you don't see anything, and you certainly don't listen—unless it's about Maggie." Andrew's chin floated warily toward the horizon. "See?" said his wife. "Now you're listening." Andrew opened his mouth to protest and she stuffed it with, "You don't love me anymore. I know it, and so do you."

Andrew expelled a hiss of pent-up breath and asked, as if to a child who has done her sums wrong once again, "Then what am I doing here? How many men would stick with a partner through all this?"

"Oh, you're a rock, all right," she said. "Pride yourself on that. But somewhere along the way, you switched girls. You're here for Maggie now, not me."

Not somewhere, he thought, and his mind unprompted screened a tape whose every sad and scary frame he knew by heart:

Arriving home from work and finding Maggie tearing through the house in a filthy diaper, screaming for a mommy who wasn't there. Trying to calm the hysterical child while he phoned the familiar round of police, hospitals, and doctors. Father and daughter keeping vigil at the front window late into the evening. The child falling asleep in his lap hours past bedtime, awaking finally to the sound of a car scything through the mailbox at the bottom of the driveway and Karen stumbling through the front door. The child running to her mother and clutching her leg until almost the top of the stairs before losing her grip. Andrew staring, frozen as the frenzied toddler hurled her tiny body again and again against the closed bedroom door, screaming for a mommy who either didn't hear or didn't care. While through the door he could hear his wife on the phone with her latest doctor calmly asserting that she was not really sick at all and that she was not going to take any more goddamn medicine!

That was six weeks ago.

"Karen," he said, his voice almost without expression. "It's not a contest between you and Maggie. Kids her age are helpless. You have to feed them, change them, play with them—keep them away from hot stoves. None of that is optional."

"Mr. Mom!" His wife poured another miniature bottle of booze down her throat. "You think you're a better parent than me?"

"Most of the time, I'm the only parent, Karen."

"Not for long."

Goosebumps erupted on the surface of Andrew's arms and across the top of his scalp, heedless of the moist, tropical air.

"I've met someone," she announced.

"In a psychiatric hospital?" The surge of incredulous anger took Andrew by surprise, but it made no visible impact on his wife. "Some crack-head biker?"

"A cop," she said proudly. "And he's only mildly depressed." Andrew looked at his wife over the top of his glasses, wishing at that moment that she was wearing something more than flaming nail polish. "The irony is, I did it for you."

"What?"

"Motherhood. I did it for you…to keep you…"

"Right."

"You don't get it," his wife hissed. "You never have. I LOVED YOU!" she shrieked, and then grabbed her crotch like a ballplayer. "But all *you* ever loved was this!"

That's all you've left me to love, thought Andrew, while the rest of his mind split and tumbled down a dozen different paths at once. Can I afford to quit work and stay home? Can Karen get medical insurance on her own? Is my mother too old to come and help take care of Maggie until things settle down?

Karen watched the play of emotions ripple her husband's face. "Let me guess," she said. "You're thinking about me. About how you're going to fight for me and win me back, no matter what."

Her husband sighed. "I don't know what to think," he admitted.

"I'm so surprised."

A rumble of receding thunder filled the silence before he could respond. "What are your plans?" he asked, noting wearily the puzzled expression that was his wife's only response. "You haven't had a full-time job in over five years and your knight in shining armor is a patient in a psychiatric facility," he explained. "What are your plans, Karen?"

His wife opened another mini-bottle and took a defiant pull. "We're leaving as soon as Tom gets out."

"We?"

"Maggie and I."

Andrew Ryan's throat clamped shut over lungs that fought to surge their way up and out.

"She needs her mother."

"You're joking," Andrew stuttered. "You're not fit."

"My doctor says I am."

"When you lie to her! *'Yes doctor, I am taking my medication. No doctor, I haven't had any hallucinations in quite some time.'* And what happens when you crash and burn?"

"You'll come to the rescue. That's your role. Remember? 'The Rock.'"

"I'm worn out with it, Karen."

"Then you'll come for her."

Andrew sat hard on the rattan couch and waved a hand at his naked wife. "Put some clothes on, will you?"

"Oh." Karen looked around as if there might be a suitable change of costume nearby. "I guess I thought we might be making a fresh start on our romantic weekend. I thought I owed you one last chance, at least. You blew it, Mr. Perfect."

The long-time lovers stared at each other, the one numb, the other uncertain but vaguely triumphant. Then the telephone trilled back to life. Andrew picked it up. His face, which a moment ago had been flush with blood, drained abruptly and then slowly engorged again. *"Jesus Christ!"* He pressed the receiver to the side of his head and cupped the ear on the opposite side with his free hand.*"Get her to the Emergency Room!"* Whirling on his naked wife, and in a calm more menacing than fury, he explained, "It's the babysitter, Karen. Maggie found your 'candies' and ate them. *What the hell* was an open bottle of anti-psychotics doing in the nursery—on the nightstand—next to her bed?"

Karen Ryan did not respond, but the look on her face was chillingly familiar. Neither guilt nor fear. Andrew remembered it clearly from the very first time they met. "Oh, my god," he whispered. "You left it there on purpose."

* * *

Karen stared through the cottage window at the tow truck that was hauling away the wrecked rental car and at the men who had driven over the replacement vehicle, who were exchanging papers with her husband. Waves of nausea oozed through her pores in emulsions of heat and sweat. "Radio says there's another one coming right behind this," she heard one of them say. "You got maybe twenty minutes. Waiver says it's your nickel for any damage if you get caught in it." The brew inside Karen's gut heaved suddenly and her legs propelled an unwilling head toward the bathroom. With her face half-buried in the toilet, she heard thunder roll again. Then Andrew appeared in the doorway, keys to the rental car protruding from the side of his clenched fist.

"Do you have any idea how terrified Maggie must be?" he asked, in a voice that was no longer the patient instrument of reasoned persuasion she had come to resent. "Lying on a gurney, surrounded by strangers. One of them shoving a tube down her throat to pump her guts out, and no mommy or daddy there to calm her?" Karen gave him the deer-in-the-headlight mask, but nothing else. "You don't, do you?"

"Kids are tough," she blurted.

Andrew shook his head—not in disbelief, nor in resignation, but finally and irrevocably, in dismissal. Hesitating for only a moment, he pulled the door between them firmly shut.

"Annnn-Drew!"

The voice on the other side of the door was arctic. "All those times you left her alone, Karen—scared, hungry, reeking in her own filth—how long is a day, when you're two years old and Mommy has suddenly disappeared? Again."

"ANNNN-Drew! There's a *SNAKE* in here!"

"I can't let you take Maggie, Karen."

"ANNNN-Drew! Don't do this!"

"Can you feel now how Maggie must have felt? Can you imagine how she must be feeling right now?"

"A-A-ANDREW!" Karen tried to stand, but the panic that inflated her lungs had also jellied her limbs. "I'LL GO MAD!"

Her husband's voice was a frozen whisper. "But you can come back. Remember? 'Any time you want.'"

A staccato rip of lightning plunged the cottage into darkness. In the silence between the woman's screams, the sound of spinning tires on crushed shell driveway masked the hiss of something close, but unseen.

"ANNN-DREW!"

Chapter One

T om stripped off his sweat-soaked shorts and T-shirt and stood at the edge of the rocky ledge high above the freezing waters of Pocket Cove. With temperatures stuck in the 90's for most of the month, he had taken to ending his island workday with a regimen of cold water skinny-dipping, followed by a few cold beers. The ritual began with a leap from "Forty-seven"—so named by some long-forgotten liar who had declared the outcropping to be exactly forty-seven feet above the cove. When Tom leapt from it for the first time at age eleven, egged-on by his sheriff father, Thomas "MadDog" Morgan, the height and plunge felt more like a hundred feet. Jumping from it now seemed only slightly less perilous than it had then—his favorite parts being more vulnerable to trauma and hypothermia than they had been at age eleven.

Still, the sensation of moving naked through water is something Tom's body recognized as one of nature's gifts. Gazing across clear cold water that stretched uninterrupted for a dozen miles to the Canadian side of Coldwater Lake, and feeling the sway of giant beach trees behind and above him, Tom raised his arms, wrapped his toes over the lip of stone, took a deep breath and leapt.

Whoosh! Splash! Pulse pounding, sinus-clearing, gonad-shrinking *Brrrrrr!* Beyond his outstretched hands was only darkness. The icy, skin-tightening sensation felt exhilarating.

1

His body rose and drifted, suspended and numb. Goosebumps erupted along outstretched limbs. The fatigue of sun-baked manual labor eased, and the mental fog that still clouded his head after nearly a year, slowly lifted. Rolling to his back and paddling toward the dock, he counted strokes and thought of nothing. The distant buzz barely penetrated his consciousness, until a part of his mind recognized the metallic sound as an outboard engine closing fast at speed.

Dive! Dive! Dive!

The wail of marine engines bearing down at close range was seared into Tom's memory, thanks to a near-death encounter with Pocket Island's former owner who had tried to run Tom over with a stolen powerboat. Tom had survived that murderous encounter only because the boat's undercarriage was torn off when it hit a shelf of submerged rock just shy of its target. There were no hidden obstructions in the deep, clear water of Pocket Cove. And as far as Tom knew, the would be killer, Dr. Hassad, was still enjoying the hospitality of Homeland Security and could not possibly be at the helm of the boat approaching overhead. But the memory of his near-death experience was powerful, and Tom's reaction was Pavlovian. *Dive! Dive! Dive!*

Breath in a vise, he listened to screaming engines close fast and then abruptly reverse to a wave churning stop. Overhead, twin steel props twirled at idle. The long white hull to which they were attached, freshly painted and unmarked, rocked back and forth in the clear, cold water. The PT 109 charge through the mouth of Pocket Cove and the brake of reversing engine was the final clue. Tom allowed his body to float upward and surface beside the new Coldwater patrol boat. The maniac driver at the helm was Joe, Tom's brother.

"You're looking kind of shriveled there, Tommy."

Tom squinted at the familiar silhouette, backlit by the nearly setting sun. "You catch my looters yet?"

"Did better than that." Joe Morgan stepped aside and extended an arm. Tom leaned back, shading his eyes with one hand and treading water with the other. "Whoa!" his brother cautioned. "Watch your waterline." A second silhouette appeared beside Joe, shorter, sleeker, and unmistakably feminine.

2

"Charming shade of periwinkle, Mr. Morgan." Confident, musical voice. Jet black hair. Porcelain skin. If-you've-got-it-flaunt-it black bikini. Tom submerged.

There is no force or satisfaction to cursing underwater. Words feel like they sound: garbled and gelatinous. Slithering beneath the hull, he surfaced on the other side. Let the sun shine on someone else's bragging rights, he thought.

Joe and his passenger came to the other rail and continued the introductions. "Tommy, this is Maggie Ryan. She starts teaching at Our Lady of the Lake School in September. Maggie, this is my brother Tom. My *older* brother."

"Ch..ch..armed."

"Miss Ryan also paints. I found her on the other side of the island last week trying to sketch Washington's Head from a canoe. She said she wanted to do the fancy house above Pocket Cove, but didn't know who to ask. I told her I'd make the introduction."

The vision in the black bikini raised a slim white arm to shade her eyes from the sun. "You look like your turning to ice, Tom. Should I come by tomorrow when you're...?"

"D-ressed?"

Joe laughed. "I brought you another present, too, to help with the looters." At Joe's whistle, a large black Labrador bounded from the boat's cabin. "Go with Tommy!" The dog yelped twice and then leapt over the transom. "His name's Brutus. Jack Thompson says he's yours for the summer, if you want him. He'll wake you up if you have any nocturnal visitors. But he won't go after them. According to Jack, he's pretty much a coward. Mostly, he just eats and sleeps."

Tom forced words through chattering teeth. "Bonnie called."

Joe's smile flipped like a power switch. "Yeah?"

"She wants to meet me for breakfast tomorrow at Trudy's diner."

Joe raised his chin. "That's not your business, Tommy."

* * *

3

Frank Lloyd Wright didn't believe in air conditioning. For ten months a year that didn't make much difference in Coldwater. But summer on the big upstate New York lake could be as hot as August in Atlanta, and by the end of the day, the glass and concrete structure at the top of Pocket Island was stifling. Tom had taken to sleeping outside in a hammock. Tonight he put out a rug and a bucket of water for Brutus, then settled down to enjoy the evening symphony of lapping waves, clicking insects, and the whoosh and flutter of the bats that hunted them. As he listened, he thought of that other natural predator, his brother Joe, and his newest prey the teacher in the black bikini.

Joe was a year younger than Tom, large, hard, and comfortable in his own skin. In school, he had excelled at all the bone-crushing sports like football and wrestling. After junior college, he married a local girl, started a family, and went to work as a part-time deputy in the Coldwater sheriff's department. Ten years later, he was running it. Though for the past ten months, he'd been living alone in a massive log cabin that he had built in the woods outside town. His wife and children were living across the lake in Canada with her family.

Tom didn't envy Joe's life, or the mess he had made of his family. But there was a perverse integrity to the way he lived—extending even to his wrecked marriage. At times like this afternoon, when he appeared out of nowhere with a half-clad beauty and a grin that said, unabashedly: "You just don't get it, big brother. It's not that complicated," Tom wanted to get inside Joe's skull and understand what made him tick. He had no desire to adopt Joe's values or emulate his lifestyle—there was nothing about his brother's life, that Tom wished for himself. But as with any mesmerizing and inexplicable force of nature, he felt a need to understand how it worked.

Joe was reasonably well-liked in Coldwater. Men who felt differently tended to stay out of his way. Women either instinctively bolted their doors or sent him naughty pictures of themselves. He was one of those people who appeared to be doing exactly what he was meant to do with his life, even though what should have been the most important part was, for the moment, a mess. But who knew Joe's heart? Tom wondered sometimes if

4

he had one.

Closing his eyes, Tom summoned the image: black hair, porcelain skin, a figure to flaunt and flaunting it. Cool, amused voice. No wasted words. Got what she came for and left.

Haven't you already got enough trouble, little brother?

* * *

Sometime before dawn, a dream that had been getting increasingly salacious dissolved into the maw of a black Labrador with a tongue like a mop that it was using to swab Tom's face.

"Grab your end, you idiot!"

"This isn't going to fit in the boat, Mickey."

"We can lay it across the deck."

"And then what? Who are we going to sell it to?"

Tom wiped his face and eased out of the hammock, then stepped quietly along the concrete slab that ran along the perimeter of the house.

"Why don't we just grab the table saw and stuff we can get rid of?"

"We can do both, can't we? Grab your end and shut your mouth!"

Tom recognized the voices and the bickering. The Dooley brothers—members in good standing of a venerable Coldwater family of petty criminals, where specialty and trade craft are passed from generation to generation like Masonic ritual. Though as far as Tom knew, the Dooleys were all jacklighters and poachers. Burglary was as rare among them as a diploma.

"Where'd that soldier go?"

"He said to meet him at the boat in an hour."

"What's he going to do with all that stuff he brought?"

"Who cares? He said he didn't care what we do either, so long as we're back in an hour. Now help me lift this thing."

The Dooley's march through the woods made enough noise to cover Tom's and every other nighttime sound. He followed their stumbling progress at a distance, sitting quietly nearby while they tried to load a skiff tied to an overhanging tree. Between the curses and shouts to keep quiet, it was like watching the two stooges. Tom didn't bother to follow when they returned to the construction site for more pickings. Instead, he phoned in a message to the Coldwater Sheriff's office about a navigational hazard adrift off Pocket Island. Then he untied the Dooleys' boat, set it adrift, and returned to the mainland in the Grady White to meet his brother's wife for breakfast at Trudy's diner.

Chapter Two

Trudy's diner was a converted 1950's-era aluminum Airstream with a cigarette scarred Formica counter down the center and a row of swivel stools covered in red plastic in front of it. Four bench booths lined the windows on either side of the entrance, with a cash register, candy counter and cigarette machine just inside the door. Between the shelves of pies and cereals that clung to the back wall above the toasters and drink machines, a long hot griddle left just enough space behind the counter for the cook and the waitress to get friendly or irritated, depending on who was on duty.

Joe's wife, Bonnie, sat with her back to the counter at a booth farthest from the door. Her face looked like moist dough and her normally bright green eyes were washed of color. Tom slid quietly into the bench across from her.

"Thanks for coming." She smiled weakly.

"Sure, Bonnie. But tell me, if my brother happens to wander in here while we're chatting, is that going to be a problem?"

Bonnie scowled. "I didn't ask his permission, if that's what you mean. I came over this morning to pick up Luke's records at Upstate Medical. I figured as long as I'm in town, I might as well touch base with the member of the Morgan family who might still talk to me."

A teenage waitress came over to take their order.

"Just coffee," said Bonnie.

Tom felt his stomach growl and hoped that the waitress didn't hear it. When he said, "The same," she gave him a look clearly meant to remind him

7

that no one came to Trudy's for its paint remover coffee. They came for the sourdough pancakes, hash browns and eggs over easy. The coffee just came, and the less said about it the better.

When the waitress was out of earshot, Bonnie started right in. "This hasn't worked out the way I want."

Tom tried to think of something to say that would be empathetic but not enabling, and truthful without being incendiary. Joe's wife had struggled with the stresses and worry of being married to a small-town sheriff for almost a decade before finally reaching her limit. When Joe had been poisoned by some homicidal maniac the previous year, she'd pleaded with him to find a less life-threatening way to support their family. When he didn't and wouldn't, she loaded their kids into the family SUV one night while Joe was out breaking up a bar fight at the VFW, and drove over the bridge to Canada where she had family. Joe hadn't seen her or his three children in almost a year. And now, of course, there were lawyers.

The waitress brought the coffee and Bonnie wrapped her hands around the lukewarm cup, "I want to bring the kids back to Coldwater."

Tom waited.

"It's better for them to be in their own home. They miss their friends."

"And their dad, too, I imagine."

"I'm not stopping him from seeing them."

Tom held up his hand. "Sorry. I know it's complicated." Canadian custody law and visitation regulations were not enacted to protect non-Canadian, non-resident, and non-custodial American dads. Nor, as he had several times tried to explain to his and Joe's mother, do they give a hoot about non-Canadian grandmas. "When were you thinking of coming back?"

"I don't know, Tom. Your brother would need to move out. And he and I would have to get counseling."

Tom signaled the waitress. "Two eggs over hard, with bacon and a glass of ice water." He looked at Bonnie. "I'll help, if I can. But do you want my honest reaction?"

"Please."

"Ultimatums and preconditions won't work with my brother. Or anyone

8

else who thinks they have a choice."

Bonnie sat back in the booth. "I can't go on the way we were, Tom. I won't look the other way while my husband turns into the latest version of MadDog Morgan: absent father, philandering husband, and deceased cop. I'm not Mary."

"She's not exactly a role model. But what you want is different from how you get it."

"What I want, is our children back in their home, and Joe and me to start counseling."

"No. What you want is your family back. Taking the kids to Canada, or coming back to evict Joe and drag him to counseling are tactics to get you there. But the one you've already tried didn't work. And the one you're proposing isn't going to work, either. You need different tactics."

"Like what?"

"Like getting allies who Joe will listen to. You have a natural one in Mary. She went through the same thing with MadDog. She's a smart woman and Joe listens to her."

"Your mother is on Joe's side."

"There are no sides, Bonnie. We're family."

Bonnie smirked. "Are we? Mary's been pretty frank that I knew what I was getting into when I married her son. He is who he is, and it's not fair to expect him to change now."

"That's just mama bear protecting her cub. No one's the same as they were a decade ago, or as they're going to be a decade from now. What would be the point of life's hard-earned lessons if we don't learn from them and change? Our mother wants what she thinks is best for her son and grandchildren. If she sees that you want that too, she'll help, if you manage her right."

"Manage Mary Morgan?"

"Okay. Easier said than done. But working toward a common goal with a powerful ally has a better chance of getting you what you want than going it alone with ultimatums and preconditions."

Bonnie took her hands off the table. "I can't talk to your mother, Tom. She hates my guts."

"No. She's angry with you. Whether she has any right to be is another question. But it's also a distraction. Fix on the goal, get Mary to share it, and you've got a chance of getting what you want. Otherwise, Uncle Tom and his fishing buddy won't be going after Moby Dick again any time soon."

Bonnie closed her eyes and lifted her face toward the ceiling. "Luke tells that story to anyone who'll listen."

Tom's nephew, Luke, hadn't talked until he was nearly six and Uncle Tom taught him Pig Latin and helped him nearly land a salmon the size of a duffel bag. "Luke's talking okay now?"

"Some. Not a lot." Joe's wife shook her head and looked away. "Look, I hear what you're saying, Tom. But if I talk to Mary, she'll just spit in my face. What good will come of that?"

"She might. But she misses her grandkids to the point of obsession. You need to bring your goal and hers together. There's no path to what you want that doesn't involve getting Mary's support." He watched for Bonnie's reaction. "If it will help," he prompted, "I'll go with you."

Bonnie was silent for a long minute. Then she muttered something under her breath that Tom wished he had not overheard. "...wrong brother."

* * *

Easing the twenty-four-foot Grady White alongside the concrete dock, Tom scanned the cliff at the back of Pocket Cove for any sign of the marooned Dooleys. *'Wrong brother!' Sweet Jeezus, Tommy. Shut that door and nail it.*

In his surprise and confusion over Bonnie's muttered indiscretion, Tom had almost forgotten about his promise to show the new teacher the Frank Lloyd Wright house and the rest of Pocket Island. But shapely legs dangling over the edge of the seawall next to a battered aluminum jon boat were a timely and welcome reminder. Easing the Grady White behind the beat-up rental boat, he threw a line around the Samson post and started to explain over the muffled hum of idling engines about the Dooley brothers and their predicament. "They're usually harmless. But they've got a pal with them this time, who may not be. It might be wiser to do the tour later."

"Oh please, Tom, no. I've wanted to get inside that glass bauble for years."

"You grew up here?"

"Too many classes behind the Morgan brothers for either to have noticed, I'm afraid."

Tom blinked his eyes against the distraction of calm, confident smile and shapely legs. *There must be something in the air this morning.* Lost in scattered thought, he led the pretty teacher up the stone staircase to the top of the clamshell bluff that formed the back of Pocket Cove, then along the footpath that led to a hill hugging masonry and glass structure set inside a copse of beech and pine trees. Nothing new seemed to be missing, and there was no sign of anyone about.

While he showed Miss Ryan the outside of the Frank Lloyd Wright house, she shared a story that Joe had told her about him and his friends breaking into the house when they were teenagers. She confessed that she'd once tried to find a way inside, too, but balked at actually breaking anything.

"Joe likes to entertain with tales of his misspent youth," said Tom. "They're mostly exaggerated."

"As long as he doesn't tell stories about me."

An odd thing to say. Tom caught her eye and held it. "He wouldn't. Even if he knew any. Which he doesn't."

She returned his stare. "I'm not saying you're wrong. But how would *you* know?"

Tom held up an index finger and counted off the reasons. "First, my brother said that you're starting to teach at Our Lady of The Lake Elementary School at the end of the month. That means that until three or four weeks ago you were someplace else. Second, he said that he ran into you off the other side of this island last week sketching from a canoe. If you'd known him before that, he'd have brought you around already. Third, I had dinner with him and our mother the night before last. If Joe had known you even casually for more than a week, then our mother would have wormed it out of him by now and she would have started quizzing me. She has this thing about me being a bachelor and Joe acting like one."

"I'm sorry, acting like one?"

Shit. You didn't tell her?

"It's a long story. Not mine to tell."

The school teacher frowned. "Grandmother Rosemary neglected to mention that. She didn't mention anything about you being an amateur Sherlock Holmes, either."

"Do I know your grandmother?"

"Rosemary Ryan. Coldwater Junior High science teacher, retired. And, it would seem, a font of inaccurate information about the Morgan brothers."

Tom brightened. "My best to Mrs. Ryan. She was one of the good ones. And her being your grandmother means I know more about you than just my brother's lack of compromising stories."

"Such as?"

"Is this a test?"

"Call it a game. My grandmother told me you like games."

That's what Dr. Hassad had said, just before he put a 9mm Glock to my head.

"All right… to begin with, you don't live with your parents. But your grandmother is there now, probably just for a visit. Also, there's some sort of tension at home and you don't come and go from there regularly."

The school teacher drew in a breath. "And you know that, how?"

"My mother and your grandmother were friends when she lived in Coldwater. They've kept in touch. I know that your grandmother comes back to Coldwater for a few weeks every summer, because when she does, she goes up to the Senior Center to play cards with my mother and the other seniors. Since you seem to have heard some Tommy Morgan boy detective stories, then your grandmother must be in town. And she must have just gotten here, or else she would have been up to see my mother already, and Mom would have mentioned it. As for the rest, it's the canoe last week and the boat you came here in this morning. They're both rentals."

"I'm an early riser," Maggie explained. "My stepmother has rules about noisy boats before breakfast. It's easier to pick one up at the marina when I go out early." She remained silent for a moment and then asked. "How do you know I don't live at home?"

"The rented canoe. Joe said he spotted you in it one afternoon last week.

It's summer on Coldwater Lake—boating time. Your family has a waterfront home on The Point, and I assume the usual complement of nautical toys. But you're not using any of them – and not just when you go out early. You couldn't be living peacefully at home, but choose to rent one of Skipper's smelly fishing crates rather than use one of your family's boats. So you must live somewhere else and something must have happened to make it easier for you to rent than to go over to your parents and borrow one of theirs."

"I have an apartment at the Waterside."

Tom tilted his head. "That's three more things I know about you."

"Three? I gave you the name of an apartment building…not even a number."

Tom unfurled his last two final fingers. "Four: Joe didn't bring you over this morning. That means he probably wasn't in your apartment when you left – a useful piece of information. And five: My opportunistic brother would happily ferry you anywhere you wanted to go, any time of day you asked. So you must not know him well enough to be comfortable asking. That makes it certain that he has no Maggie Ryan stories to tell. Though, as I said, he wouldn't tell them if he did."

"You're frightening."

"Your grandmother once called me worse."

* * *

Tom noticed the school teacher's eyes returning to the places that had been mentioned prominently in the newspaper accounts of the Morgan brother's capture of an alleged terrorist: the steps leading to the wine cellar where Dr. Hassad kept his collection of lethal powders and Petri dishes, and to the stone hearth where he killed his lover and Tom's former girlfriend, before taking Tom on what was to have been his final boat ride. But she didn't ask any questions.

They finished the tour on the terrace where he explained that a group from the Frank Lloyd Wright architecture school was due to arrive soon. After the Wright group left he would take her across the island to Washington's

13

Head, if she wanted to do some sketching. When he had finished speaking, the canine lump on the rug next to the hammock raised an eyelid. A moment later an ear fluttered. Finally, it stood, licked Tom's hand, and nudged him off the terrace and across the short stretch of ground to the edge of the cliff. Maggie followed. Below, three men in a jon boat were clearing the entrance of Pocket Cove, heading toward the mainland.

"That's my boat!" Maggie shouted.

"Don't worry. They're not stealing it," said Tom.

"It sure looks like they are."

"That's the Dooley brothers I was telling you about, and some pal of theirs. The Dooley's aren't boat thieves; they just needed a way off the island."

Maggie looked subdued.

"They'll leave your boat wherever they've parked their truck. Joe will find it, if it's not at Skippers. He'll know where they'd likely put in."

The school teacher remained silent.

"Seriously, there's nothing to worry about. It's just the Dooleys."

Maggie allowed her gaze to follow the shrinking silhouette of the fleeing rental boat, "Grandma Rosemary said something else. But I'm not sure…"

Tom waited. But whatever Grandma Rosemary had said remained unshared.

* * *

With the Dooley's gone, Maggie set off unescorted on the path toward Washington's Head. The Frank Lloyd Wright people arrived an hour later and began by haranguing Tom about his wanting to put a 1% grade on an originally flat roof. Flat roofs, it seemed, are a Frank Lloyd Wright signature, even if they do collect water and, in the case of wooden ones, rot. In the end, Tom got them to admit that other owners had encountered the same problem and had adopted similar solutions. That settled, their leader brought up what was apparently the real purpose of their visit. Producing a roll of architectural drawings with Wright's plan for a main house that the original owner had not lived long enough to build, he asked if Tom

14

would be interested in having the house constructed under the supervision of the Frank Lloyd Wright architecture school, Taliesin West, using its student/apprentices.

Tom went over the drawings with the group leader. The main building was a one-story horizontal structure with two gull-winged extensions on either side designed to hug the contour of the hilltop. In profile, it looked like a seabird stretching its wings before settling down to enjoying the view from its perch. Tom admired the design's simplicity, but noted the center of the structure had the same problematic roofline as the guest house he was now living in. There was also a sketch for a grotto at the back of Pocket Cove where there was currently a concrete and stone dock. He asked if Taliesin was sure that the grotto was from the same set of building plans?

They would check. In the meantime, could Mr. Morgan be persuaded to consider undertaking the project?

"Consider? Sure. Spec it, cost it, calendar it and get back to me."

* * *

With an hour or so before the county building inspector was scheduled to arrive, Tom grabbed a knapsack from the house and headed into the woods. On the other side of the island, nearest its northern tip, a high hunk of rock shaped like a nautical figurehead jutted out over the water. To the town's early inhabitants it apparently resembled, in profile, the face of their revolutionary leader, complete with tri-corner hat. Today, from above, it was just a flat slab of sun-warmed granite, with an attractive female sunbathing in its center.

"Don't move," he called, announcing his presence. Maggie lifted her head from the stone and shaded her eyes. "Let *me* draw *you*."

"You do that, too?"

"Badly. But a man who can't respond to this kind of inspiration has more wrong with him than lack of talent."

Maggie patted the stone. Tom removed a bottle from his knapsack, tied a half hitch of fishing line around its neck, and flung it into the water. "If you've got a hunk of cheese in there," she said. "I'm going to laugh in your face."

"The men who borrowed your boat stole my generator. Anything that might keep in cold water, I put in this sack. Brutus is having the rest for lunch." Tom leaned back on his elbows and rested his eyes on the water. "Now tell me about this stepmother of yours. Who doesn't like noise and is better left alone?"

Maggie wrapped her arms around her folded shins. "There's not much to tell. She has health problems and irritates easily."

"So you keep your distance?"

"I've learned what ticks her off and how to avoid it. My father isn't so good at reading the signs."

"Sounds tricky."

"I can be. I never know when all hell's going to break loose over there. It used to make me wonder how two people so ill-suited for each other could have fallen in love in the first place. And if that's the result, then what's the point of this thing called love?"

Tom gazed at the open water. "Out of curiosity, what does a well-suited love match look like for Maggie Ryan."

The school teacher shook her head, unwilling to go there.

"Not that handsome fellow who lured you to my private swimming hole yesterday?"

She shook it again, this time sharply. "Your brother may have had certain recreational possibilities. But now that I know he's married, I think I'll pass."

You're not playing fair, Tommy.

"Look, I shouldn't have said anything. It's Joe's story to tell, not mine. And I'm sure he had a better plan of how and when to tell it. But since I've spoiled his timing, let me give you the headlines, so you don't get the wrong impression."

As Tom spoke, his gaze followed the dance of sunlight across the dappled water that lapped the crushed shale shoreline. "The job of Coldwater sheriff can be dangerous. Our dad was killed doing it, and Joe's had some close calls. The constant worrying got to be too much for his wife. About a year ago she asked him to quit and do something safer. When he didn't agree, she took the kids to Canada. Joe hasn't seen them since."

"How awful. Especially for the kids."

"Awful about sums it up. But my brother is never going to stop being a cop or leave Coldwater. If neither he nor his estranged wife budges, and all that's left is the legal wrangling, then your grandmother isn't wrong to consider Joe eligible. This is Coldwater. The pickings get slim after high school."

* * *

Tom returned to the house to face a county building inspector who commiserated on the flat roof problem and then wrote a citation because there was no generator hooked up to the emergency water pump. After him came an insurance adjuster who informed Tom that he needed to hire a full-time guard or else erect a chain-link fence around the island's half-mile perimeter. The pilferage wasn't professional, but something had to be done to discourage it, or the company would cancel its policy.

A busy day, hard on top of a busy night. Tom's thoughts bounced around like a tired sheepdog circling an unruly flock—all huff and hustle but mostly going in circles. The one recurring and coherent thought was that he was looking forward to taking the young school teacher back to the mainland when the day was over. But at sunset, Joe arrived in his gleaming new patrol boat, briefed Tom on the Dooleys, and then carried the young lady off into the sunset, accompanied by the unmuffled roar of twin Sea Witch engines.

Chapter Three

Andrew Ryan sat on the edge of the dock and waited for his wife to complete the return leg of her cross-cove swim. Well, not quite cross-cove, he reminded himself. The goal, not yet achieved, was for her to make it all the way to the other shore and back…and in the process, lose weight. She had been at it every evening for almost four weeks, and Andrew judged it time to offer compliments and check progress. He had a bottle of Chateau Something-or-Other chilling in a bucket by his side. It was almost dark. There was no moon. With Dee Dee you either took advantage of the rare opportunity or understood that the next fortuitous alignment of the planets would not occur any time soon.

The noise of labored wheezing reached the dock before visual sighting. Andrew followed sound and sight and waited by the ladder with a celebratory glass of wine. "Rumor has it a pretty mermaid has been cruising the cove these summer evenings." He lifted the turquoise forearm of a full-body wet suit and hauled his wife up the ladder. "I thought I'd come down to see for myself."

"*You're* home early."

"It's not often a fellow gets to see a Mermaid in the flesh." Andrew handed his wife a glass of cold white wine and rested a hand on her ample hip.

"Umm…lovely idea." Dee Dee took a swill of the wine and led her husband by the waist as if to music. He could feel the wine working, though he felt little else through the thick wet suit. "Speaking of lovely ideas…." *Oh, what a clever boy am I.*

"Why don't we get away?" Dee Dee interrupted. "Just the two of us?"

18

Andrew's feet drained of their music-less rhythm.

"I saw an ad in the Times Travel Section. We could fly to Athens and cruise the islands...get away from this sticky weather."

"Sounds wonderful," said Andrew, without enthusiasm. "But I'm chained to my desk at the moment."

"Then what about August ... or September? We need to get away, Andrew. Just the two of us. How long has it been since we went away alone?"

"St. Bart's in February?" He watched the thoughtless truth escaped his mouth followed by a cartoon image of truth replaced by a large boot.

"Fine."

"And half of it is still on my card," he added. He couldn't help himself.

"On top of Maggie's rent, I'm sure."

Andrew sighed. "She's just starting out, Dee Dee. They pay her squat. In fact, they haven't paid her anything yet. If we'd let her live *here* for a while—just long enough to build up a cushion... She wouldn't need any help."

"It's always about her, isn't it?"

It's called being a parent, thought Andrew, but held his tongue.

Dee Dee plucked her robe from the dock and hoisted it over her shoulders. "Are you losing money in the market, Andrew?"

"What?"

"Somebody called here this week about a 'margin call.' Last month, too. How can you be giving Maggie money when you're losing it in the market?"

"I'm not."

"Don't lie, Andrew. I can see it in your face when you come home at night. And you spend hours in the bathroom."

"I won't be getting a salary after the bank is sold. We'll need to live on our investments, then, until I can find another job. At my age, that could take time."

"And you've been losing, haven't you?"

"A little. But the alternative is to move out of this house and live a lot smaller. Perhaps permanently." He paused. "Do you understand what I'm saying?"

"Perfectly," she snapped. "You're gambling with money we can't afford to lose, but you won't spend a fraction of it to take your wife on a vacation." She flipped the empty wineglass into the water and strode toward the house.

* * *

Andrew stayed behind, sipping wine and mentally reviewing how he got into this marriage, why he stayed, and for the millionth time, why he should or shouldn't leave.

Dee Dee came into his life thirteen years ago when she interviewed for a job at the bankrupt savings and loan he and his partners had just purchased from the government trustee. She was six years younger than Andrew, attractive, vivacious, and clearly overqualified for the position the bank had to offer. He advised his partners not to hire her. "There's a story here," he warned. "There has to be. Look at her resume. Spend five minutes talking with her and then look at the job we're offering and what we're paying for it. It's a complete mismatch." The partners agreed and then hired her anyway.

Dee Dee Forte was not an exception to the rule that sales and marketing people know little about finance. But her people skills – especially with the regulators and the bits-n-bites crowd – bordered on witchcraft. Andrew enjoyed watching her play the comptroller for new office furniture and a larger expense account. He silently applauded her handling of the overseers from the Resolution Trust Corporation and the software gurus with the latest one-stop, savings, investing, college, retirement, and pay off your mortgage in half the time financial product. If she played him too, he didn't notice, or if he did it was with a mix of amusement, caution, and suppressed interest. It wasn't resistance.

It seemed to Andrew that the essence of Ms. Forte's talent was that she appeared to know exactly what other people sought from casual human contact. With the chip on the shoulder regulators, she would sit for entire afternoons listening to pompous actuarial-speak and taking meaningless notes. With the Beamer Borrowers, she would stroke their *nouveau* financial pretensions until they purred. His partners, who had not previously seemed to crave anything beyond a quick and unconscionable profit, acclimated instantly to her thoughtful, mature attention.

Ms. Forte seemed to match almost effortlessly the unspoken demand for validation that strangers bring to every social encounter. But Andrew's only need was for competence, preferably quiet competence. His needs outside of work were of a kind that could not be satisfied with well-chosen words and orchestrated eye contact. He did not perceive himself to be a likely candidate for Ms. Forte's special focus.

Like any mature bachelor with assets and responsibilities, it was frequently said of Andrew that he needed a wife. More importantly, his twelve-year-old daughter needed a mother. He'd been a single father for almost ten years, and over that time he had not come close to finding a consensus candidate for the unfilled position of wife and mother. He had stopped looking long ago.

Attractive, single, making good money, and never seeming to lack for a date, Ms. Forte did not appear, at first, to be a likely candidate. Nor did the thought occur to Andrew when, after a few months of working together, he noticed that it had become increasingly uncomfortable for him to be alone in the same room with her. There was no reason for him to be uncomfortable in the presence of an employee. He was, after all, the boss. But it was clear that Ms. Forte had become uncomfortable too, though she seemed to take every opportunity to come into his office and bask in that discomfort.

This uneasiness went on for a month. Ms. Forte would waft through the door with some minor marketing problem, consult him, ignore his advice, and then stay to talk. When the talk ran out, she stayed anyway. Near the end of one such session, he found himself attempting to relieve the awkward silence by talking about his daughter. Maggie. Once started, he simply kept going until there was nothing left to tell. He spoke about his ex-wife's inability to cope with the demands of motherhood and her solution of simply not performing them. He told Ms. Forte about the inevitable divorce, the custody fight that turned out to be no fight at all, and about his surprise and dismay upon realizing that his own parental skills, when put to the test, were only marginally better than the ones they replaced. Ms. Forte listened.

21

He could not stop the flow of words and did not want to.

That was on a Friday. The following afternoon Dee Dee arrived unannounced at Andrew's lakeside home, made suitable observations about its possibilities, and then took his daughter out for an afternoon of shopping. His treasured but troubled offspring left the house a pale, pubescent, spike-haired Goth and returned hours later with everything but the ruby slippers. He had never seen Maggie dressed in colors before. She had always worn earth tones, like her mother, and then in recent years metal and black. Ms. Forte had waved her wand and his daughter returned looking like a young Jackie Kennedy. The transformation was stunning.

In retrospect, it was also a greased skid. After enchanting Maggie, Ms. Forte turned her wand on Andrew, covering him with romantic pixie dust. He didn't resist. He was more than ready. They were married within a month.

A few weeks of reasonable calm—some tension around the wedding preparations, flashes of temper, several well-timed speak now or forever hold your peace revelations—and then all hell broke loose. Within another month, Andrew's twelve-year-old daughter and former Goth decided that she did not want to be a New England debutante, after all. She did not want to be well-scrubbed, polite to adults, and aloof and enticing to boys. She wanted to spend time with her father, as she had always done, camping on the Coldwater islands, hiking in the woods, paddling around the lake, and dressing how she pleased. She did not, after all, or at least not yet, want to be a lady.

Andrew was paralyzed. He had waited almost a decade for someone to come along and do for his daughter what he had been unable to do himself—turn her into a poised, self-confident young adult, aware of her own talents and the many opportunities to use them, instead of a hostile, withdrawn, MTV-watching, underachieving grunge who more and more had come to remind Andrew of her biological mother. He endorsed Dee Dee's goals, respected her determination, and was thankful for her timely arrival. But her methods—punishment, punishment and more punishment—froze his heart. Dee Dee was determined, high-handed and ultimately victorious. But the pixie dust that had briefly worked its magic on him was flamed to ashes in the process.

He never found out her real story, either; and he was still savvy enough to know that there was one. Why had she taken an abrupt turn off the career woman fast track and taken a nothing job in a small town like Coldwater? And why did she leave that job within months to become a stay-at-home mom to a hostile step-daughter on the brink of adolescence? He still did not know.

Nor did he fully understand his own role in the dysfunctional drama. Why did he stand by and let his daughter be bent to submission? Because he wanted the result? Or because he feared more the consequences of putting an unhappy adolescent through another divorce and all that went with it?

And why did he stay with Dee Dee after Maggie left for college? Was it simply to take time to recover from the War of the Ryans and to see if there was anything left between them to start over? And if so, wasn't four years long enough to know the answer? Didn't they both know already? It felt, lately, like he and Dee Dee were living on the brink of a decision already made that neither seemed able to voice; and the tension of that hesitation was fraying them both to near violence.

Then, too, the timing and consequence of the bank sale was more serious and complicated than the shorthand version he had given her. The bank's value had peaked over a year ago when he had wanted to sell and his partners didn't. He made enough of a stink then so that they allowed him to take a loan from the bank collateralized by his shares at their then higher value. But playing the market with that borrowed money and losing steadily had already halved his capital. He could not sustain further losses.

* * *

Dee Dee Ryan lay in the tub (a nightly ritual) and pondered her position. She could not see her husband through the steam on the half-wheel window, but she knew he was out there somewhere, pacing and brooding. She understood his financial explanations; she wasn't stupid. But he was clearly taking more risk than he was comfortable with, and asking her to share the consequences if things went sour was a crock. She'd done her part. Perhaps he had finally found the gumption to end a marriage that had never really worked for either of them. But characteristically, he wanted to do it without a fight. Which could only mean there was enough money still left to fight over. Good.

Then a wave of self-pity washed over her. *Why can't I ever have a relationship that lasts? Is that too much to ask? I've put ten years into this family and what do I have to show for it?* She looked down at the mounds of flesh surrounded by bathwater. *Fifty pounds!* She took a breath. *Alright, maybe I wasn't a perfect mother. But look at the mess he handed me! A mess that he and that wacko woman made. And look at how the brat turned out. Well mannered, well-groomed, well educated. What more could he expect? Shouldn't it be my turn now? Don't I get a turn?*

Dee Dee rubbed the clouded glass and looked through the window. The moon had risen bright and round, and she could see her husband at the end of the dock, pacing. The outline of a nearly empty wine bottle extended at an upward angle from his mouth. *Loser! You never loved me! You just used me to fix your mistake!*

She let her body sink low in the water so that only her face and belly remained uncovered. *All right. I'll go. But I won't go cheap. I'm too old to train another husband.* She suppressed a smile. She had told Andrew about a previous marriage, but not about the prior annulment. *He's not as smart as he thinks.*

The satisfaction of that pronouncement only lasted a few minutes, before returning to fret. In his current state of mind, Andrew might well lose everything. Over the past year, he had begun to be forgetful. He did not seem to remember anything she told him. She had thought, at first, that it was simply because he had stopped listening. Or maybe it was a sign of aging. Why shouldn't he have those too? But now she wondered if it was the stress of too much financial risk. What if he lost it all and there was nothing left to split?

She looked down at the rolls of flesh undulating in bathwater. If she was going to be single again she'd have to get serious about this diet. And first thing tomorrow, she would have to hire a lawyer. A rottweiler.

Chapter Four

Tom knocked on the door of his mother's Senior Center apartment. Bonnie stood behind him trying to look small. He pressed the buzzer and knocked again. A policeman's widow for close to twenty years, Mary Morgan had long since decided that life doesn't get much better than a quiet afternoon on the magic carpet of a moderate alcohol buzz. She could be napping, passed out on the couch with the television on, or sitting in her favorite chair listening to Big Band music. Tom had called that morning and said he was bringing a visitor in the afternoon. His mother might have gone out to lunch with her octogenarian admirer, Herbert. But as Herbert didn't like to drive late in the day, she was surely home by now. He knocked again and pressed the bell a second time. The door yanked open,

"I'm not deaf, young man."

"Hello gorgeous, got time for a couple of visitors?

Mary peered around his back. "What in god's name …?"

Bonnie stepped forward. But she did not extend a hand or move in for a hug. "Hello, Mary."

"Hrumph"

"Ask us in," said Tom.

"Why?"

"Because your grandkids want to come back to Coldwater, and you can help make that happen." He could feel his mother's face search his for the telltale sign of boy fibs. But she could no longer read him as well as she once could. He'd had a lot of practice in recent years disguising his thoughts and intentions—in courts, boardrooms, and dimly lit restaurants. His preference remained for candor, unless it was manifestly unkind or unwise. But he had learned to be unreadable if need be, even to an expert interrogator like his mother.

"Does my other son know you're here?" Mary asked over Tom's shoulder.

"I don't think so," said Bonnie.

"Am I'm supposed to keep this visit a secret?"

Bonnie looked at Tom.

"We'll trust your judgment on that," he said. "But you might want to let us in before some nosy neighbor takes that decision out of your hands."

Mary harrumphed again and then walked the half dozen steps to a galley kitchen that formed the east wall of the two bedroom apartment. She did not offer refreshment. "Why are you here?" she asked.

Bonnie took the chair opposite Mary, and Tom the one between them. "To get your help putting our family back together," he said, "By bringing your grandchildren back to Coldwater."

"My help?"

"Joe and Bonnie haven't made much progress on their own."

"Hold on, young man, The only reason this family is broken up is because she…," Mary lifted her chin in Bonnie's direction, "kidnapped my grandchildren and took them to Canada."

"And we want to see them back in Coldwater, agreed. So how do we make that happen? We can do the blame thing, if you want. But I don't think that's going to get us where we want to go."

"Don't bully me, Thomas."

Tom opened the cabinet above the sink and took out three glasses, filling two with ice and tap water, and the other with white wine from an open bottle in the refrigerator.

"Do you have a plan?" Mary asked, directing her question at Bonnie. "Or are you just going to pile my grandkids back in that nice SUV my son paid for, move back into that nice house he built, and hope he forgets that you kidnapped his children?"

"Steady, mama bear," Tom warned.

"Joe and I need to get counseling," said Bonnie.

"For what?"

"To talk about why I had to leave in the first place. About him being away from our children for days at a time, the probability of his getting killed on the job and, to be blunt, his philandering."

Mary glared at Tom. "Is this your idea of how to get our family back together?"

Distributing the tumblers of ice water and the juice glass of cold white wine, Tom pitched his voice toward what he hoped was calming and not patronizing. "My idea is to brainstorm realistic steps in the direction of the agreed goal: getting your grandchildren back to Coldwater. I don't know how far we'll get. But anything we come up with will be more than what Bonnie and Joe have been able to do on their own."

Mary pressed her lips and shook her head. "That's no plan."

"No? Didn't you go through the same things with MadDog? And didn't you try to change what you could? Of course, you did. So spill. What worked? What didn't? And what didn't you try that you wish you had?"

Mary glared first at Bonnie, then at Tom, before fixing her gaze out the window toward the fire escape. "I don't know what you're talking about, young man."

Okay. Forget calm and soothing.

"Sure you do. Don't you remember sending me to collect your husband passed out on the front lawn of someplace he had no business being, three times that summer I got my drivers license? I'm not asking you to talk about what was going on in your marriage then. I'm asking you to share what you tried to do about it. What worked and what didn't."

Mary turned away and said nothing.

"Come on, Cleopatra."

His mother's head snapped around like an unleashed pit bull's. "What did you call me?"

"The Queen of Denial."

"Don't be a smart ass."

"Don't be obtuse. I can count on the fingers of one hand the times your husband made it home for dinner, or to Joe's football games or my basketball games. Then he died with his throat cut, parked at the end of Coldwater's lovers' lane."

"He was a policeman."

"A violent, philandering, neglectful, and ultimately dead one. You want your grandkids back in Coldwater? So does everyone else. But not back to the same old, same old. That 'Me Tarzan. You Jane.' bs won't fly anymore."

Mary spoke to her reflection in the window next to the table. "Your brother should be here."

"If you think that will help get your grandkids back, fine. But Joe and Bonnie haven't made progress in a year. I'm a bachelor who knows nothing about keeping a family together. No pressure, but that leaves you. It's why we're here."

Mary took a deep breath. "When your brother finds out that you've been meeting his wife behind his back, it's going to get ugly."

"Then we'd better come up with something fast."

* * *

Hundreds of barges anchored off town beaches and parks stood ready to launch their fusillades of multi-colored rockets as soon as darkness fell. Among the waterfront communities of Long Island's North Shore and the Connecticut Gold Coast, the competition for which town put on the most spectacular display was serious business. Pilots coming in and out of the nearby New York airports complained angrily and annually about the Fourth of July bombardment. Some of the older ones said that the first hour after darkness, when all of the pyrotechnics went up at once, was like flying over Hanoi after Tet.

The two men in the white panel truck had been driving for several hours. They had failed to anticipate the holiday traffic on the New York Thruway and the bottleneck at the George Washington Bridge. The bumper-to-bumper purgatory of the Long Island Expressway was also undisclosed on the map had they had purchased at an upstate gas station.

Their directions led to Parking Lot #5 of the Jones Beach State Park, the farthest lot behind the farthest accessible beach. But the oceanfront park had filled hours before, and the access roads were blocked by police cars that refused to let more people in, except on foot. Cars sat abandoned everywhere by the side of the road. A parade of excited families streamed past in the fading light, carrying coolers and lawn chairs and herding small children toward the beach.

The heavily tattooed driver tried to turn the van, but it was blocked on all sides by people on foot and by the line of cars behind him. He pulled off on the shoulder to use his cell phone, not certain whether it was lawful in this state to use one behind the wheel. Two time zones away someone listened and then gave new instructions. The driver's passenger reminded him that they were supposed to get away quickly. He glared, turning the truck onto the scrub where the soil was sandy and the vegetation sparse. He drove slowly and carefully until they were out of sight of the road, while his passenger continued his litany of worry. This wasn't the plan. It was dangerous. They should return another time.

The driver stopped the truck, removed a metal trunk from the back, and began walking toward the smell of saltwater. As best he could tell, they were only a few hundred yards from the boundary of the state park which was directly under the air corridor that led to La Guardia Airport about thirty miles away. It was almost dark. They needed to find a spot and get ready. As he lowered the trunk to the ground, thousands of multicolored rockets erupted up and down the shoreline. In the glow of the fireworks, he noticed a small dune a few yards away with a clear line of sight to the west. He lifted the trunk and hurried toward the dune. Behind him, a small white light approached from where he had left the truck. "You left me!" His companion waved a flashlight. "And this."

"Move!"

The driver assembled the contents of the trunk under the cone of the flashlight. Then he lifted the heavy tube, rested it on his shoulder, and leaned his back against the slope of the dune. His companion scanned the sky with a pair of powerful binoculars. "Those rockets are blinding me!" he complained. "How am I supposed to pick out one light in all of this?"

"Look for one that doesn't fall!"

"I can't see anything!"

The driver yanked the binoculars from his companion's hands and held them on the horizon. The other man had been exaggerating, but only slightly. Anxious minutes passed before he found what he had been told to look for. "Look!" He thrust the binoculars into the other's hands. "The one moving towards us. Start counting and don't take your eyes off it." The driver held the long metal tube level with the horizon and lifted it by degrees in time with his companion's count. When he reached fifty, the airplane was visible to the naked eye and passing overhead. The driver adjusted the metal sight along the top of the tube, held the pin on the blinking fuselage, and fired.

Chapter Five

Rosemary Ryan, mother of Andrew and grandmother of Maggie, was staying for the summer with her son and his wife at their home on Coldwater Lake. While there, it was her habit to begin the day with the two-mile walk along the lakeshore road that led to Our Lady of the Lake Church. She had not been a churchgoer while her husband was alive. That was his thing and he was a superstitious bet hedger. But lately, Rosemary found her mind turning to thoughts put aside while working and raising children. Some of them seemed to seek the quiet of this lakeside sanctuary and to prefer being examined there.

Her son Andrew and his wife had been arguing loudly the previous evening. They were basically good people, and she loved them both. But they were miserable with each other and in their marriage. Or rather, one was miserable and the other angry, as reflected their respective temperaments. According to Andrew, when he and Dee Dee first met, each seemed the complete answer to the other's most important unfilled need. That alone should have made them suspicious of the romance.

At its simplest, Andrew had needed a mother for his out-of-control daughter, and Dee Dee wanted a family. But it was more complicated than that, and some of it Rosemary had only pieced together over time. She was sure that her daughter-in-law was older than she let on and had been married more times than she admitted. That she had never had children was obvious. It was also apparent that she had tired of the corporate grind and was ready to be taken care of, if the right opportunity came along. Andrew was ready to do that—financially. Dee Dee's mistake was assuming that he was capable of emotional care as well. He was not. And for that Rosemary blamed herself.

Rosemary Ryan had done little to restrain her late husband from imposing his will in every area of their family's life, which had left little room for any individual choice beyond stoic resentment. Only his death when their son was still a teenager freed Andrew to discover his own powers of choice and to make something of his dormant talents. But by then he had acquired a lasting habit of deference and perseverance that made it easy for him to fall into unequal relationships and stay there.

Rosemary quickly discovered that her daughter-in-law shared many of the same traits as Andrew's father...damaged by something never revealed and determined as a result to control everyone and everything around her. Her son's relationship with his second wife became a mirror of the one he had grown up with. Though Andrew eventually drew a line and defended it, early in the marriage he seemed to permit almost anything that might improve his daughter's behavior... something that unarguably needed improving. Beyond that, he resisted his new wife's assertions of dominance—which were relentless.

To be fair, as long as there was no issue as to who was in charge, Dee Dee was a charming, competent, self-sacrificing wife and mother and a faultless daughter-in-law. She not only met her family's every need, including her visiting mother-in-law's, she anticipated them. Staying with Dee Dee and Andrew for the summer could feel like a vacation at a four-star hotel. It included not only material comforts, but also restaurants, shopping, and lively girlish companionship, which was something that Rosemary had never had before and that she now looked forward to. But for her son and granddaughter, it was a tense and uncertain environment. Dee Dee's personality required constant obeisance and neither her husband nor stepdaughter were of a character or temperament to give it. Her daughter-in-law's second mistake, Rosemary believed, was in refusing to accept that reality and to enjoy what she had—which was pretty good. Dee Dee's ten-year campaign for control of all things great and small needlessly deprived her of deserved credit for an otherwise exemplary job, as well as enjoyment of its fruits. She angrily resented both of these slights.

In her own marriage, Rosemary Ryan had ultimately succumbed to a more powerful personality. Her son, by chance or fate, had found himself in a similar situation, though he actively resisted to a point just shy of marital rupture. The result was an unhappy stalemate the effects of which were sometimes apparent in the child, Maggie.

Maggie had a stronger protective parent than Andrew had had. But there was always the uncertainty of what the child may have inherited from her biological mother, Karen. Rosemary felt a powerful, intuitive sense of trouble coming. But from where, or what she might do about it, she could not tell. Easing from the edge of the pew and onto her knees, she looked up at the stained glass window and prayed for an answer.

* * *

Maggie, still in her bathrobe, lit a cigarette and poured her grandmother Rosemary a cup of Starbucks. "Don't tell Dad. He doesn't know that I smoke."

"He has his own secrets, dear. We all do."

"Got any good ones grandma?" Maggie had virtually no information about her grandmother's past. She never spoke about it, nor did Maggie's father.

"You don't get it out of thin air, dear. But as I've just come from church, I don't think I'll be sharing indiscretions this morning. Another time, perhaps."

"Then how about the rest of the scoop on those Morgan brothers? You left out the part about one of them being married."

"You're not going to pay any attention to my advice, are you?"

"The one skinny-dipping in Pocket Cove didn't look old to me. They're both hunks."

"And as different as chalk and cheese." Rosemary paused to sip coffee and gather thoughts. She was not here to lecture. Forty years of teaching had demonstrated the futility of monologue as a method of communication. She was here to be a grandmotherly ear and a resource of hard-earned knowledge. People respond to ideas, she reminded herself, not words.

"Men who stay single until almost forty have more in common with each other than they do with the rest of us. Women, too. Harder to catch... harder to get along with... some of them troubled. There's always a story." Something Andrew should have realized, she thought.

"So how are they different? What's their story?"

Rosemary smirked. More like a Grimm's Fairy Tale. "Alright. Listen up. You can draw your own conclusions.

"One day I had a double class of 7th and 8th graders working on a research project in the school library. About twenty minutes into the period there was the sound of an explosion down the hall. Somebody had put a cherry bomb in the boys' toilet. There was pandemonium for a few minutes until the teachers got together and compared notes and determined that no one had left any of the classrooms on that floor for at least half an hour. So the culprit, it seemed, had to be one of the students in the library. I brought all the students down to the cafeteria and told them to start copying their science books out longhand and to keep copying until the culprit confessed or was turned in."

"I can't believe what you were allowed to do back then. Today you'd get mugged... or sued."

"It was getting that way toward the end. But anyway, after about twenty minutes of collective writer's cramp, Tommy Morgan ripped a piece of paper from his notebook and stuck it to a wall. With a used Band-Aid, as I recall."

"What was on the paper?"

"A drawing of something called an 'earth shoe'—a clunky rubber-soled thing that was a style back then. Above it, he'd drawn a compass with a bumblebee at the center. Pretty good drawings, to be honest. Then he sat down, folded his arms, and looked out the window. 'Mr. Morgan,' I said. 'Why have you stopped writing?' Now, this is a quote. The tone of it was so arrogant, I can still hear it today. 'Because the criteria you established for stopping have been met, Mrs. Ryan.'"

"The drawings showed who did it?"

"They were clues, as it turned out. One was *who*, the other was *how*."

"What a little pistol!"

"I used another word when I dragged his sorry little hiney down to the principal's office."

"Did he fess up?"

"Not at first. The principal finally had to call the boy's father, who came roaring up to the school in the Coldwater patrol car in about three minutes flat, bubble lights flashing and siren blaring. The late Sheriff Morgan was a man who enjoyed a splashy entrance. Anyway, with his pistol-packing father looking on, this twelve-year-old *wisenheimer* explains that a cherry bomb has a short fuse and that to drop it into a toilet at one end of the hall and get back to the library at the other end before it exploded, the culprit would have to have run. And as the hall floor was tile and the library doors were open, anyone running in shoes would have made a racket that would have been heard. So the culprit must have been wearing sneakers or rubber-soled shoes.

"Then he pointed out that nobody was wearing sneakers, since they were not allowed outside of gym class. And that of the boys in the library, most had those penny loafers or other leather-soled shoes, two had hush puppies and one had 'earth shoes'. He said he had looked at everyone's shoes when we brought the two classes down to the cafeteria. One pair of hush puppies belonged to a boy who weighed about two hundred pounds and had asthma. The other belonged to the Reverend Livingston's son. Young Mr. Morgan said he didn't bother with the girls, because no girl would do something like that, and if they did, they wouldn't do it in the boys' bathroom."

"Okay," said Maggie excitedly. "Drum roll! The earth shoes belonged to... ?"

"He wouldn't say. And by then school was out and everyone else had gone home. I thought for a minute that his father was going to beat it out of him. Scary man. But...and in its own way, this is even scarier...this smarmy twelve-year-old spreads his drawing out on Dr. Ross's desk—the bumblebee at the center of a compass—and says, 'I won't give you his name. But these are his initials. Dad'll get it in two seconds, won't you, Dad?'

"I thought the father was going to brain him right then and there, but the kid had him figured to a tee. The father looked at the drawing. And maybe it took him more than two seconds, but not much. Then he looked at us with the same kind of smarmy expression as the son. He'd gotten it, whatever <u>it</u> was."

"Did he tell?"

"Of course. He couldn't help himself. Smug, like the son. 'SWB' he said. 'B from the insect. SW from the direction of the compass arrow/stinger—Southwest.'

"That's frightening in someone so young. I wouldn't know what to do if I got one like that in September."

"The brother was worse, and at a much younger age."

"Now comes the girls' shower story, I suppose."

"I wish was. Those kinds of things you can laugh about afterwards. No, the younger brother had his own style of problem solving. Not so indirect, but just as effective."

Maggie waited for a moment and then prompted, "I'm listening."

Rosemary hesitated. The decades-old memory retained a surprising strength of emotion. She could feel her facial mask flip from peeved to pained as she began speaking. "There was a supply closet at the back of the science lab. One day some supplies went missing, including vials of dye that we used in chemistry experiments. I knew they'd been there the period before, because I'd put them away myself. But when I went to bring them out again for the next class, they were gone. The only time I had been away from my desk was between periods when the students from the last class were leaving and the ones from the next class coming in.

"Well…I gave them all a little talk about honesty and so forth and then had them open their science books…"

"And start copying from the beginning!"

"That's right, dear. Writer's cramp can be an effective disciplinary tool, if you don't overdo it. You may want to remember that when you start to teach. In any event, nobody fessed up, and to tell the truth I wasn't one hundred percent certain that it was someone in that class rather than the class before it. So at the end of the period, I let them go. They had science twice a week, so I wasn't due to see them again for a few days and I wasn't sure I was going to make them keep copying out of their books. But I didn't tell them that."

"Then how did the mystery of the disappearing dye get solved?"

"With violence, I'm afraid."

"The father?"

"No. But very much his methods, I suspect. By the time the class met again, the chemicals were back in the supply closet, intact except for one vile of blue dye partially used."

"Did somebody leave a drawing?"

"No. Someone went missing. A little boy named Billy Ambler wasn't in science lab that day, or even in school for most of the week. When he returned, he had two enormous black eyes, a buzz cut in place of the Beatles mop he'd had the week before, and a deep indigo stain on the scalp beneath what hair was left."

"Oh, my god!"

"God had nothing to do with it. I can't say for certain that Joe Morgan was responsible for his classmate's injuries. But Billy Ambler would never go near him, or even look in his direction, after that. And they were in school together for another six years.

"The Morgan brothers are bright boys, the one no more than the other. But they're as different as day and night. And they were not raised to play by the same rules as the rest of us."

Rosemary waited for her granddaughter's reaction. The stories she had just shared ought to make any young woman of Maggie's age and upbringing think twice about getting involved with either of the Morgan brothers. She was sorry to puncture what were probably harmless fantasies. But Maggie was at that age where acts and indecision can have lasting consequences. If her granddaughter was too full of youth to fret for herself, Rosemary would do it for her.

But Maggie did not seem to be paying attention. Her eyes seemed to be focused somewhere beyond the sliding glass doors, where the breeze ruffled waters of Wilson Cove, while the cigarette in her hand burned down to her fingers.

"Maggie?"

The girl didn't respond.

"Maggie?"

Rosemary felt her pulse quicken. Cigarette ember enlarged toward flesh...fingers parted...the smoker murmured, "Ouch!" Her eyes blinked. "Grandma?"

"I'm here, dear. Where were you?"

The young woman's voice quivered. "I don't know."

Rosemary slid her hand across the table and rested it on Maggie's forearm. "How long has this been going on?"

Maggie raised her face and closed her eyes. "A few months."

"Have you told your father?"

She shook her head.

"What is it?"

"This. Spacing out...losing track of time. People around me talk, but I'm not connected. Then I come out of it... most of the time."

Rosemary put her arm around her granddaughter. "What happens when you don't?"

"A few times I've just fallen asleep. But just before the end of graduate school, it happened at a concert where I was with some people I didn't know very well. They thought it was drugs and took me to the campus infirmary."

"Did you tell the doctors it wasn't?"

"By the time I came around, they'd figured that out on their own." Maggie forced a short laugh. "I think I scared them. They know how to handle drugs, but they don't see a lot of psychosis."

Rosemary took a deep breath. "Is that what they called it?"

"Not in so many words. But it seems I was hallucinating and acting paranoid. I remember thinking that people from my Statistics class were trying to make sure that I failed the final so that I couldn't graduate, and that the doctor was a TA and in on the plan. It was bizarre. The doctor finally gave me something that put me to sleep for about forty-eight hours. It was a few days before I had a conversation with him where I actually understood that he was a doctor."

"Did he tell you what was wrong?"

"He said that based on what I had told him and the symptoms I came in with, he wanted to do a bunch of tests and have me see a psychologist. Then he freaked me out by talking about Karen. I started getting all paranoid again until he showed me his notes from what he called our first session... which I also didn't remember.. and where I apparently told him about her."

"Did you take the tests he wanted?"

"No. I just decided to get out of there, hang on through finals and come home."

"Are you seeing anyone now or taking any medication?"

Maggie closed her eyes, exhaled, and shook her head.

Rosemary stared at the pack of Virginia Slims beside her granddaughter's coffee cup. It had been almost twenty-five years since she'd had a cigarette, but her lungs craved one now. "What are you feeling?" she asked gently.

"I don't know."

"Mad, sad, glad, or afraid?"

"Afraid, I guess."

"Me too. Do you know what you're afraid of?"

"The same thing as you, I imagine. That I have what Karen has. That as soon as I start teaching in September, as soon as I get out into the 'real world', I'm going to fall apart like she did."

Rosemary reached for the pack of cigarettes.

"Grandma, do you know what she has? I mean the name of it. I've asked Dad a few times. But he said that his information was old and that the doctors he talked to when he was still married to Karen didn't seem sure. She's told me a couple of different things—like 'hormone imbalance from taking birth control pills.' Or that there's nothing wrong with her at all and that it was just a misdiagnosis.

"But I'm not on the pill, so that can't be what's wrong with me. And there *is* something wrong with her, it's obvious from her appearance and speech, even if it is hard to describe. Do you know what it is? What it's called?"

"Denial."

"Grandma," Maggie smirked. "I know *that*. But what's the medical diagnosis? When did it start and what were the symptoms? Is there anything they can do for it today that they couldn't twenty-five years ago? Is it something I can inherit?

"Those are fair questions, dear. If you see a doctor, which I hope you do, he or she can talk to Karen's doctor, if she still has one. I don't know if Karen will give up that kind of information, or let her doctor give it up. She hasn't in the past. Not even to your father when they were married. But I'm serious about her real problem being denial.

"Whatever Karen has is relatively mild or she wouldn't be functioning on her own all these years. To be honest, the symptoms I remember sound a lot like the ones you just described. But they were easily controlled by medication, even twenty-five years ago. Karen's problem was that she refused to accept the fact she has a mental illness – as if that's any more under one's control than a physical illness – and so she refused to take the medications that could control its symptoms. Worse, she took no responsibility for the behavior that resulted when she didn't.

"She reminds me of the young women of my generation who refused to wear eyeglasses—before contacts and all that—out of nothing more than vanity. Fine, if all you're doing is bumping into furniture. But if you insist on getting behind the wheel of a car and driving through neighborhoods with little children, who's fault is it if you run over one? Karen always blamed everyone but herself—including the victims—for not looking out. I know the illness isn't her fault. But her method of dealing with it—which was not to deal with it at all—was infuriating."

"I never knew you were angry at her, Grandma." Maggie smiled. "You've never said anything like this before."

Rosemary shrugged. "I don't like to be unkind. But you need to know the truth now."

Maggie lit another cigarette. It seemed to calm her as much as it made Rosemary fidget. "I'll see a doctor," Maggie said. "And whatever it is, I'll deal with it. But do you remember what Karen's doctors actually said? I mean it isn't schizophrenia, is it?"

41

Rosemary could hear the fear in her granddaughter's voice. "No, it's not," she assured her. "I recall one of the doctors saying that Karen's illness was a combination of biological predisposition, environment, and personality. He told your father that there was less than a ten percent chance of the predisposition being passed on to her offspring and that even the predisposition itself wouldn't be enough to trigger symptoms.

"You have a completely different personality from Karen, and you've had an entirely different upbringing. But if it turns out that these black-outs you've been having are some variation on what she has, you'll be just fine once the doctors have sorted it out. That is, as long as you're not too vain to wear glasses."

* * *

Rosemary picked up a box of protein bars at the Coldwater Market on her way back to her son's house. She wanted to have something in her room in case she got hungry at a time when it might be prudent to stay behind closed doors. Dee Dee kept a bowl of sport snacks on the highboy in the dining room to snack on before or after her evening swim. Rosemary had tried one of the bars a few days ago and liked it. But the next day she had an uneasy feeling that Dee Dee had counted her stash and noticed one missing. Scary woman.

Rosemary passed through the stone gate at the entrance to Wilson Point, lost in fretful thought about the effect on her son's already troubled marriage should his daughter become seriously ill. She thought about her deceased husband and the drinking problem he would never admit to or do anything about. The problems people cause for themselves and everyone else, simply because they pretend what is, isn't!

Chapter Six

Father Joseph Gauss, full-time pastor of Our Lady of the Lake Church and honorary chaplain of the Coldwater Rowing Club, combined vocation and avocation by taking troubled parishioners for long rows out on the lake where they had little choice but to sit still and listen to whatever he had to say. Rosemary Ryan had declined such an invitation at the end of their vague but unsettling conversation that morning after mass. The priest decided that the next best thing was to have a few words with Tommy Morgan—today.

A mid-morning tutorial for aspiring altar boys and girls had put Gauss in a bad mood. Turning adolescents into acolytes had been possible, at least in theory, when the requirement to memorize long Latin prayers weeded out the knuckleheads. But the current combination of vernacular and mixed-gender classes made anything approaching genuine spirituality impossible. Gauss felt old and out of step. The endorphin surge from hauling the wooden skiff toward Pocket Island temporarily masked the feeling. But it was with him more and more lately.

Easing the boat onto a shore of crumbled shale, he set out through the woods toward the construction site. But his rower's mental compass, adequate for flat, featureless navigation, lacked the bells and whistles required for choppy, wooded terrain, and when he arrived at the opposite end of the island, he was nowhere near where he intended to be. Spotting a chair-sized boulder, he took a seat and tried to decide what to say once he found Tommy Morgan. "Don't be an ass!" came first to mind. Likely there was a more diplomatic approach, but that was the gist of the message. He hoped Tommy would listen.

Then he said a prayer. Nothing in particular. One couldn't sit in a place like that—soft breeze rustling a canopy of leaves overhead, water lapping tunefully nearby, and small bird noises—and not feel the urge to pray. At least he couldn't. But it was human voices, not seraphim, that responded. Turning an ear, the indistinct words resolved into a single voice that seemed to be conducting both sides of an anxious conversation. *'Mustn't hear something I shouldn't'*, he reminded himself. "Hello," he bellowed and then stood up and walked in the direction of the sound.

From behind, the woman looked stark naked. Sitting on a blanket with arms banding folded legs, the only sign that she might not be entirely nude was a thin black stripe across the middle of her back that might easily have been a shadow. Gauss cleared his throat.

"Go away," she answered.

"I beg your pardon."

The woman turned. "Oh-my-goodness, Father!" She jumped. "I thought you were somebody else."

"Content to be myself, thank you. Or I'd have to leave, it seems."

"Give me a sec."

Gauss turned his back and closed his eyes, though the image of Our Lady of the Lake's newest teacher trussed in a black bikini remained screened on the back of his eyelids where he did nothing to banish it.

"Have you had lunch?" the woman asked when Gauss turned around. The original of the remembered image was now chastely hidden beneath a pair of white tennis shorts and a man's paint-splattered dress shirt. "I have a couple of ham and Swiss cheese sandwiches…and there's a bottle of ice tea at the end of that line over there."

"Intended for someone else, obviously."

"He stood me up. You probably overheard my ranting."

"It's a stressful time, Miss Ryan. Don't be unnecessarily hard on yourself."

"Summer on Coldwater Lake?"

"The end of academia and a long, pastoral summer to fret about what's coming next."

The woman's face revealed nothing.

"First time teaching?" Gauss pressed gently. "Not being sure if you're going to like it or be good at it. No Plan B if it turns out not to be what you're really supposed to be doing with your life. You should go easy on yourself at times like these. And on whomever the young man is who can't tell time."

Finally, the face moved. "You're not easily distracted, Father. And you're every bit as unnerving as I've heard, if you picked all that up from just this." She gestured at the surrounding landscape. "Or have you been talking to my grandmother?"

"A woman with worries. But not inclined to share them... at least not with me. No... More than a few young people have begun their careers at Our Lady of the Lake Elementary School. The issues are common enough. They sort themselves out sooner or later, as long as one keeps looking for happiness."

The young woman smiled. "Happiness?"

"Of course. How else do we pick a path or judge whether the one we're on is right? If we see that we're not heading in that direction, hopefully we ask ourselves why and act on the answer. The practice can demand courage at times. But the idea is simple enough."

The young woman looked thoughtful. "I'm embarrassed to admit it, Father, but I don't believe I've heard that before."

"You wouldn't unless you'd taken a theology course somewhere. We only feed so much to the schoolchildren. Wow them with the miracles, mostly. We dumb down the Sunday sermons, too... out of self-preservation."

"People would be happy to hear a sermon on happiness, Father!"

"And half would hear it as a call to hedonism and act on it. The rest would be picketing the Chancery for my removal." Gauss smiled kindly. "We have adult classes for the theologically curious. But I wouldn't recommend them for you at the moment. You have enough on your plate." He slapped the flat stone next to his hip. "Do you know the name of this rock we're sitting on?"

"Washington's Head?"

"That's right. The church teaches that God wants us to be happy. The

Founding Fathers' claim was more modest. They said that Man was endowed by his Creator with certain inalienable rights, among them the right to "life, liberty and the *pursuit* of happiness." According to them, whether we find it, is at least partly the result of our own efforts. The Founders were Enlightenment Humanists—and Protestants. But I'm not sure that their approach isn't the wiser. It requires something of us too, not just of God."

"Prayer isn't enough?"

"If it was, nobody in this town would need a snow shovel, would they?"

Maggie smiled. "Do you know a lot of happy people, Father?"

"I know a few mindful of the need to keep looking with a certain amount of discipline. But I don't believe that happiness is a permanent state...at least not in this life. What about you? Do you know any?"

"I recently met one who seems to be."

"The one who stood you up?"

"No. His brother."

Gauss shook his head. "You couldn't be more wrong, Miss Ryan."

"My grandmother said more or less the same thing."

"A wise woman... even if she is a worrier. And if I can address the thought that you're too well-bred to utter: of course, it's difficult to weigh advice from those without first-hand knowledge. But message and messenger are only confused by those who wish to be."

"You're scary, Father."

"And you have your grandmother's gift for left-handed compliment." The priest paused. "May I ask another question?"

The soon-to-be teacher shrugged and waved a wary hand. 'Depends,' the combined gestures seemed to say.

"Do you know many unhappy people?"

"Plenty, I'm afraid. My father, stepmother, grandmother—just about everyone else to a lesser degree."

"And have you detected a common thread among them?"

"Bad choices?"

"And ignorance of how they might change the current situation for the better? Or an unwillingness to pay the price? Bitter acceptance of the status

46

quo?"

"All of the above."

"Does any of that describe you?"

"I think I'm too young to have made any irreparably bad choices. And there's not much status quo in my life right now. But I wouldn't say I'm on anything that feels like the path to happiness."

"Then in the name of our Heavenly Father," Gauss intoned as he patted the rock beneath them. "And on the head of our Founding Father, I say it's both your patriotic and spiritual duty to keep looking."

* * *

Gauss found the path that led to the Frank Lloyd Wright house and followed it until he came upon its owner hanging a Tarzan rope from a giant beech tree towering over Pocket Cove. He stopped beneath the tree and wondered if his intended instruction, "Don't be an ass, Tommy Morgan," had wider implication than he'd first thought. On the walk across the island he considered whether a less confrontational approach might be best, reminding himself that in matters of the heart and loins, peremptory command has little place and less respect. Its emotions are thwarted, if at all, by stronger emotion—guilt being a church favorite.

Apart from the school teacher complication, there was also the question of what Tommy Morgan thought he was doing camped out on a mosquito plagued island all summer, and how much longer he intended to stay. He had been laid up in the Coldwater hospital for two months the previous year, after being nearly shredded by a pair of Dobermans used by the island's previous owner to discourage visitors. While in the hospital, he'd announced that he was through with Wall Street; and believing it would be a good thing for Tommy to remain permanently in Coldwater, his brother, the local sheriff, had persuaded Gauss to get Tommy involved a project to build a school on Pocket Island. Gauss knew that the sojourn was likely temporary, good for whatever time it took Tommy to figure out what he was supposed to do with his life, or at least what he wanted to do next. When the school project was halted by an environmental lawsuit, Tommy had moved out to the island, ostensibly to renovate the Frank Lloyd Wright guest house that would serve as the school administration building. What he was actually doing there, besides dreaming, drifting and pretending he was Huck Finn, was anyone's guess. No good would come of it, though, if he stayed much longer. Idle hands and so forth.

But that was tomorrow's problem. Today's was to ensure that his newest school teacher didn't become involved with his oldest protégé to the detriment of both. Gauss brooded on how to artfully avoid disaster, as he followed his former altar boy to the cliff-top glass and concrete house and sat on a stone patio sipping Beaujolais that he suspected was originally intended for someone else. "I need a favor," he finally began.

"Name it."

"I want you to befriend a friend of mine, without getting romantically involved with her."

"Will that be a temptation?"

"Only if all your parts are in working order."

His former alter boy scoffed. "Temptation like that doesn't often come to this island."

"I believe it already has."

A frown of suspicion came over Tom's face. "Is this friend of yours a teacher?"

"Not yet," said Gauss. "And not for long…unless she gets stuck in a local romance. She doesn't know who she is yet, or what she's meant to do with her life. There are family complications, which I won't bore you with. It will all work itself out. But not here. And the sooner she realizes that, the better."

Tom remained silent. Gauss left him to his thoughts. A new braided rope hung from a limb of an ancient beech tree. Remnants of older ropes, broken off at different lengths bracketed it on either side. He remembered a young Tommy Morgan arriving at mass one morning with a missing front tooth, and some story of daring-do that involved the notorious Tarzan rope on Pocket Island.

"This friend of yours," the now mature Tommy Morgan asked. "You ever get a look at her in a black bikini?"

"The vow is chastity, not myopia."

"You have no idea what you're asking."

"Oh, I think I do."

Chapter Seven

The Coldwater Veterans of Foreign Wars building was a cinder block eyesore on a prime piece of Wilson Cove waterfront—the only non-residential property along a three-mile stretch of stately Victorians with wide wrap-around porches and deep manicured lawns. A half dozen Harley Davidson motorcycles stood afternoon guard on the gravel strip in front of the club, reinforced after dark by a convoy of pick-ups and clunkers that lined the lakeshore road in either direction. Inconvenienced residents no longer bothered to call the Coldwater sheriff to complain about the tarmac gauntlet. Even if the sheriff was inside the club, which was often, he wouldn't do anything. "There's nothing unlawful about making noise in a bar," he explained to a long-ago complainant. "The town decided to let the Vets put their club here. Don't expect me to pick a fight with a dozen marines because some long-ago zoning commissioner took a bag full of cash."

But the lawfulness of the VFW had gotten louder and rowdier of late. An equidistant twenty-five miles from the Canadian border and the U.S. Army base at Fort Drum, thirty years of marginalia on the beer shellacked map behind the club pool table attested to the happy mayhem that coincidence made possible.

Fort Drum had been designated for closure in the budget wars of the mid-1980s and had survived on account of the buildup for Iraq I. Fifteen years later it was enjoying a temporary renaissance on account of Iraq II. The newest generation of reservists and guardsmen being rotated through the Fort on their way to Baghdad—young, loud, and cheerfully violent—had made the lakeside VFW their hangout. Less exuberant locals, older and bound to the place by decades of dollar beers and a bump, surrendered the bar to the newcomers and retreated to the booths along the wall to await the end of hostilities.

In the booth nearest the bar, a middle-aged patron with a name embroidered over the pocket of his faded green factory shirt, and a thinning, Grecian-formula-ed ponytail hanging over its collar, was trying to interest his female companion in the spoils of his hobby—reading files from the crashed hard drives that came in for repair to the computer store where he worked as a technician. He pitched his voice over the shouts from the bar and the collision of billiard balls from the pool table on the other side of the booths.

"A guy brought in this ancient 386! You wouldn't believe the crap on it!"

His companion showed no interest.

"Listen to me! It was your ex! Maybe there's stuff on it about you!"

"Who cares?" she mouthed.

The ponytailed man, whose shirt read "Burdock," raised his voice a few more decibels. "There's pieces of a journal came off of it too! Some of it's so old it's in DOS!"

"Perfect!" she shouted. "Old *and* boring, just like him!"

"Doesn't seem to be getting along with the missus!" Burdock shouted back, encouraged. "Cow can't stick to a diet!"

The woman said nothing. She had stopped tending to her own appearance long ago, though it seemed not to diminish the attention of men like Burdock. The concept of body consciousness no longer had a place in her life or, as far as she was concerned, any meaning in a mouth like Burdock's.

"There's shit on there about your daughter, too!"

That caught her attention. The woman leaned across the table and lowered her voice. "Like what?"

Burdock closed the distance between them so that their heads were an inch apart and he lowered his voice as well. "He doesn't think she's '*doing too well*,' whatever that means."

The woman looked hard at the little man. Burdock was at least two inches

51

shorter than her five foot ten and had a character to match his stature. "Where's this journal?"

"At work. On a CD."

"I want to see it."

"It's in pieces," Burdock explained. "Text fragments. Christ, the thing must have been a gigabyte. I think he used every word processing program made in the last twenty years and never converted anything. When the drive crashed, the file just exploded. All that's left are fragments. No dates...page numbers, just blocks of text and gibberish."

"I want to see it."

"All right. I'll print out what's left tomorrow."

"I mean now."

Burdock's voice was petulant. "I thought we were going to the trailer after this?"

Karen Ryan hooted. "You won't see this ass again if you don't get yours out there and do what I told you."

* * *

A soldier who had been sitting at the end of the bar nearest the booths followed Burdock to where he had left his truck and watched as it weaved away down the center of the lake road. He took a pad from his camouflage jacket and wrote down the license plate number and then opened his cell phone and punched some numbers. "Where did you take that laptop?" he asked. Then he explained what he had overheard and where, and then recited the license number he had copied. "I think you'd better let our friends know about this." He listened for a minute and then spoke again. "That's your problem," he said.

Chapter Eight

The night before the start of fall term at Our Lady of the Lake Elementary School, Andrew Ryan brought an apple to the new teacher's condo with a plan to wish her luck and impart some fatherly advice. Had he thought about it more deeply, he might have anticipated finding the novice teacher nervous on the eve of her first professional job. The possibility that an alcohol anesthetized wreck might answer the door had not occurred to him.

Andrew held the apple at arm's length as his eyes took in the frizzled hair, puffy face, and crimson ears. His daughter looked at the fruit and burst into tears. Andrew stiffened. He had not grown up around histrionics. But having twice married into it, he had learned that pain can be real even if its expression is exaggerated. Though he still struggled with how to show compassion without encouraging bad behavior or being manipulated by it. Meet-you-at-the-door tears put him on the defensive. The arm he wrapped around his daughter's shoulder remained tense. "What's up, Maggie-pie?" he said at last. "They can't hurt you, you know. They're only six years old."

Daughter clung to father as she had not since she was little older than the first-graders she would face the next morning. Andrew could see a half-empty wine bottle on the kitchen counter and an empty bowl of what looked to have been chocolate ice cream nearby. "Go splash your face," he said.

He filled a clean glass with ice and tap water and then waited in the rug-sized living room for his daughter to reappear. He did not like to see her using booze to cope with the ordinary stresses of adult life. Her paternal grandfather had been a drinker. And her mother had used it copiously to anesthetize her own demons. He had not had an adult conversation with his daughter about any of that.

The woman who came out of the bathroom wore a shapeless Cornell sweatshirt and no makeup. But she had brushed her hair and was attempting to smile. To her father, she looked beautiful and pitifully vulnerable. His throat tightened. "Look, Maggie, I don't want to be a scold. But be careful about the drink." His voice contained no hint of the emotion it suppressed. "You can't swing a dead cat in our family without hitting an alcoholic. It's in the genes." He added, "Looks and brains too, thank God. But they're a package. You need to be smart about it."

Maggie took a sip from the glass of ice water. "Our local sheriff says the same thing you do. That the Irish have the brains and the looks, but that they also have messed up copies of whatever gene it is that's supposed to filter booze and dilute anger. He says that's because we all came from the same crowded island where there aren't any DNA opposites."

"So we're the West Virginians of Northern Europe!" Andrew laughed. "Well, there may be something to that." He narrowed his eyes and tilted his head. "This sheriff...is he a new boyfriend?"

Maggie shook her head. "A summer keep healthy option, if nothing better comes along. But he has issues."

Andrew snorted. The women of his daughter's generation were more like men than the men of it...a bunch of lightweights, if he could judge from what came into the bank. "So this isn't love gone bad or anything like that?" Andrew opened his palm and waved it past his daughter toward the evidence in the kitchen.

"No. You hit it the first time." She hesitated. "But it's not the kids exactly... it's the whole thing. Coming back to Coldwater. Taking a job I'm not really interested in. Both mistakes, I realize now. I just didn't know what else to do after I left school. I still don't."

"You wouldn't be the first teacher that wasn't cut out for the classroom. We've all had them."

"Sister Mary Francis."

"A legend! But do the kids and yourself a favor. If you're not cut out for it, don't stay any longer than you have to."

Maggie nodded her head and leaned forward on the couch. Her expression said plainly that she was waiting for something more.

"What?" he asked.

"Coming back to Coldwater."

It was Andrew's turn to go silent.

"I don't want to hurt your feelings, Daddy," she prompted. "But coming home was just as big a mistake as pretending to be interested in becoming a teacher."

"Oh, I don't know," Andrew muttered. "There are some things you have to take care of at your age: love, work, excitement. You can find them here just as well as anywhere else."

"And stir up a pot of trouble."

Andrew grimaced.

"Mommy management," Maggie uttered the code phrase that her father had coined long ago to refer to their joint effort to deal with her stepmother's volatile temperament. "I don't want to cause more problems between you and Dee Dee. You don't need that."

Andrew felt the muscles in his face grow tight. *"Mommy management's* isn't necessary for either of us anymore. Dee Dee and I had a come-to-Jesus session after you went away to school."

"I hadn't noticed a difference."

"Well, things were quiet for a while."

"And then I came back."

Andrew realized that he had been holding his breath when he felt it suddenly escape in a sigh. They both laughed. "All right. I've been letting her get away with the put-upon drama-queen stuff again. Maybe I'm getting old. But *letting* her get away with it and *having* to let her get away with it are two different things. That part's over. And from here on, it's my business, okay? Nothing to do with you."

"Unless I want to come over for dinner…hang out in my old room…visit grandma."

"You can do any of that, any time you want."

"And feel real welcome while I'm at it."

Andrew bowed his head. "All right. All right." He raised his gaze without lifting his head so that his pupils and eyebrows were on the same horizontal plane. "I want to say something to you about this '*Mommy management*' stuff. And it falls under the heading of *do what I say, not what I do*. So bear with me and don't laugh at the old man. There're a few things I've learned the hard way."

He took a deep breath. "First, "*Mommy management*" is nothing more than perseverance and diplomacy. It's a survival mindset and it's meant to be temporary. Take it out of the crisis that spawned it, or prolong it beyond that crisis, and it's a formula for misery—especially in jobs and relationships.

"Second, I want you to give Dee Dee a break. Not because she deserves it. But because you and I need it. Take the good of her and let the rest go."

"And the good would be what? The time…"

"Stop." Andrew's voice was curt and impatient.

"You have no idea, Daddy."

"Of course I do. I was there. Biting my tongue and grinding my teeth the whole time. But for a reason."

Maggie was silent, but her body language screamed resentment.

"Do you remember anything from when Karen lived with us?"

"A swing set in the back yard. Lots of doctors."

"Do you remember your first few years at school?"

"That I was in trouble a lot."

"The only girl I've ever heard of being brought home twice by cops before fifth grade."

"And then Dee Dee came to the rescue," Maggie interrupted. "I know the story. She tells it at least twice a week to anyone who'll listen."

"And it's self-serving b.s., I know. But not in the way you think. Look, let me tell you something about Grandpa Ryan."

Maggie folded her arms across her chest. Her father had rarely spoken about his father and then only superficially. Her grandmother Rosemary never spoke of him at all.

"He died when I was a teenager, so you never met him. But he made Dee Dee look like Mother Teresa. He had an exaggerated rescue story, too. Only the rescue part was real. It was his understanding of it that was out of whack.

"Grandpa Ryan joined the Marines in 1944 right out of high school. Six months later he was stumbling out of a landing craft onto a Pacific Island beach crisscrossed with machine gunfire. For the next thirty-six days, a hundred thousand men fought hand-to-hand over a hunk of volcanic rock called Iwo Jima—the Japanese from caves and tunnels underground and the Marines from on top. There was no place on the island that wasn't covered by dug-in Japanese rocket and machine-gun emplacements. The soil was volcanic ash, so the marines couldn't even dig fox holes. By the time it was over, the Marines had lost 75% of their men and the Japanese close to 100%. That was the Japanese strategy—fight to the death. If they made the Americans pay a suicidal price for a hunk of volcanic rock out in the middle of nowhere, maybe the American government would think twice about having their military invade the Japanese home islands.

"There's probably never been a more Darwinian environment than existed on the island of Iwo Jima for those thirty-six days. And Grandpa was one of the survivors.

"I'm telling you this because, oddly enough, I never heard that part of the story from him. I had to read about it in a book. What I heard instead was all about Parris Island boot camp and a Master Sergeant Brodski. How if it wasn't for Sergeant Brodski and all the mindless humiliations he put Grandpa and other recruits through, none of them would have ever made it through the war, or amounted to a hill of beans afterward.

"I kept my mouth shut, of course. Grandpa had a pretty sanguinary way of shutting it for me when I didn't. But as far as I could tell, Sergeant Brodski was nothing more than a psychopath who enjoyed torturing teenagers. Grandpa would have me out shoveling snow without gloves on, delivering newspapers in the freezing rain, that sort of silliness. And if I so much as looked cross-eyed, he'd remind me that when I graduated from high school I was going off to Paris Island just like he did, whether I wanted to or not, and that I'd learn what real work was...blah, blah, blah. Total crap. Excuse my French.

"The point is, Grandpa had one of those life-altering experiences, but he got the lesson of it all wrong. That psycho sergeant didn't make a man out of him. He made him into a teenage killing machine—temporarily. And during one thirty-six-day period during World War II, a killing machine was exactly what Grandpa needed to be in order to survive. Whatever Sergeant Brodski's motivation, without his mistreatment disguised as training, my father would probably not have survived Iwo Jima and neither you nor I would be here. Grandpa's mistake—which I hope you don't repeat, and which is why I'm telling you this story—is that he allowed a powerful personality to get into his head and stay there long after its only useful role was over. Sergeant Brodski wasn't a lifetime role model, but he was a life-saving influence at a critical time. A naïve teenager let that experience warp the rest of his life, and an important part of mine, because he didn't understand that it was temporary and instead let it dominate the rest of his adult life where it had no use and no business."

Andrew paused for breath. He was on a roll, but he wasn't sure that he still had his audience. His daughter's eyes were looking off into the distance. "Look, do you remember the three P's?"

Maggie nodded. The '3 P's' was a predecessor theory cum strategy to 'mommy management.'

"That's all I'm saying. It's not personal, it's not permanent and it's not pervasive. Grandpa's marine sergeant didn't know Corporal Ryan from Adam and could have cared less. It wasn't personal. Whatever influence he had, lasted or should have lasted from boot camp to discharge and that's it. It wasn't or shouldn't have been permanent. And Grandpa should never have let it pervade his post-war life where it didn't belong and where it made everyone, including him miserable.

"Dee Dee is your Sergeant Brodski," Andrew concluded. "Her style of parenting was your boot camp. It wasn't personal. She would have treated any other kid the same way. It wasn't permanent either. It's over. And it doesn't need to pollute any other area of your life. You got the benefit of it as well as the pain. But it belongs in the past. Leave it there."

Maggie finished the ice water and leaned back into the couch, eyes closed and arms folded across her chest. In the absence of feedback, Andrew kept talking, struggling toward a summation and exit. "If you want to stay in Coldwater, stay. If you like this sheriff character, enjoy. And if you're really not supposed to be a teacher, get out."

* * *

Sister Mary Judith kept the door of her classroom open and her ear out for trouble. The first week of school always brought something: eighth-grade boys, some of them bigger now than the teachers, sneaking into town at lunchtime, girls rolling up their skirts and experimenting with make-up, first graders getting lost on the way back from the cafeteria. Things never settled down until the end of September. Before that anything could happen.

But Sister Judith's radar was tuned to the two's and fews: the lost child, the guilty giggle, and the whiff of drugstore perfume. Crisis rarely struck an entire classroom. But Kathy O'Hara, a pretty seventh-grader not given to tattling or known for exaggeration, appeared in the doorway of the sixth-grade class and said that it had. "Something's wrong in the first-grade classroom, Sister. They're all in there running around and screaming."

Sister Judith stepped into the hall where she could hear the commotion clearly. "Is there a teacher in there?" she asked.

"I don't know, Sister. It's Miss Ryan's classroom and the boys are all running around and some of the girls are crying."

Sister Judith ordered her class to open their Baltimore Catechisms and begin reading while she went down the hall to investigate. There were always those teachers who had difficulty maintaining classroom discipline—new teachers especially. But it was not often an issue with the younger grades. Miss Ryan did not seem to be the type that would have a problem in that area.

But it was quickly clear that Miss O'Hara had not exaggerated. "Jesus, Mary, and Joseph!" Small, blue trousered boys in wrinkled white shirts and clip-on ties twirled up and down the isles like dervishes. Plaid skirted, chalk-faced girls, huddled at their desks looking ready to burst into tears. Sister Judith took a deep breath and brought her hands together in a sharp *CLAP!* "Boys! Back to your seats!" She grabbed a nearby dervish by the ear and held him tight to her side. "Immediately!"

Scraping chairs, shuffling feet. When the noise subsided, she added, "Sit up straight. Hands on your desks." Thirty-seven pairs of small white hands (five rows of six and one of seven) did as they were told. "Do you have your rosary, Miss O'Hara?"

"No, Sister."

Sister Judith removed a rope of wooden beads from a fold in her habit and handed it to the girl, who received it as if it were a relic of the one true Cross. "Please lead the class in a Rosary, Miss O'Hara. All five decades and each of the Joyful and Sorrowful Mysteries."

"Yes, Sister."

"I'll be back before you're finished." Sister Judith looked down at the boy whose ear remained clamped between her thumb and index finger. "Come with me." Almost as an afterthought, she turned to the classroom and asked, "Does anyone know where Miss Ryan is?" A small red-haired girl in the front row raised her hand. Sister nodded.

"She said that she'd be right back."

Sister Mary Judith dragged the anonymous miscreant toward the principal's office. He said nothing—a sure sign that he had older brothers or sisters who had gone through the school before him. As they rounded the corner by the statue of the Virgin, he raised his hand and tried to turn his face toward hers—a physical impossibility given the grip she maintained on his ear. "Sister?"

"Hush."

"But Sister?"

"I said hush!"

"I have to go to the bathroom!"

Sister Judith shoved the nearest suitable door. It happened to be marked Girls, but she doubted a first-grade boy in extremis would notice the homogeneous plumbing. She waited impatiently outside. Miss O'Hara could keep the first graders busy with the Rosary for fifteen minutes, at most. The sixth graders she had left unsupervised with their Catechisms would last half that long. She knocked briskly on the lavatory door and stuck her head inside. "Finish up in there. Quick!" She waited another nanosecond and then entered.

A half-inch of water covered the tiled floor. *Now what?* Gathering the hem of her habit, she splashed around the modesty panel that blocked the view of the interior. The dervish stood beside an overflowing sink, his hands on the faucets. Above it, facing the mirror, the first-grade teacher, Miss Ryan, turned one hand over the other in the air above the basin in a motion that reminded Sister Judith of a slow-moving cement mixer. "I turned the water off, Sister," the boy said.

"Miss Ryan?" Sister Judith spoke softly. There was no response. She approached the sink and placed her hand on the teacher's arm. Miss Ryan gave no sign that she was aware of the two other people in the room. Sister Judith spoke to the boy. "Child?'

"Yes, Sister."

"What is your name?"

"Michael Dooley, Sister."

"Do you know Father Gauss, Michael?"

"Yes, Sister."

"Do you know where to find him?"

"At the rectory, Sister."

"Go there now and bring him here."

"Yes, Sister."

"And do not speak to anyone on the way there or back. Do you understand?

"Yes, Sister. Am I still in trouble, Sister?"

"No, Michael. Now, do as I've told you."

Chapter Nine

A big fire draws a big crowd: the curious, the visually inspired, the public Samaritan and the ghoul. An island fire draws a select one. You have to own a boat to join it. And often the bigger the boat, the bigger the idiot.

The Coldwater sheriff felt like a sheepdog at sheering time as he cut the thirty-foot patrol boat in and out of the flotilla of ski boats, cabin cruisers and monster cigarette boats come to watch his brother's house go up in flames. He circled the island trying to keep the flotilla from storming the beach. But several had landed before he arrived, and more piled on while he was trying to keep a pair of thirty-foot Donzis from suicide racing through the mouth of Pocket Cove.

The Donzis were Canadian according to the provincial markings on their bows. Their owners must have hauled ass down the lake when they saw the flames. Joe lifted the nine-volt bullhorn and warned them to stay clear of the island. When neither responded, he turned the four million candlepower spotlight on a pair of hairy northern butts. When he ordered the mooners to turn off their engines, they responded by flipping him the bird, pulling up their pants, and taking off in a sonic blast of unmuffled exhaust and fifty-foot rooster tail.

Joe slammed the twin throttles forward and surged after the Donzis, staying to their starboard to block a sudden turn. The two powerful racing boats continued to flee west at nearly forty knots. Joe's lighter patrol boat, with its twin Sea Witch engines, held their flank, neither closing nor accelerating. Less than a minute into the chase he felt and then heard a muffled quake like the crack of underwater thunder. The Donzis' inboard shafts had caught the shelf of submerged rock familiar to local boaters as Sunken Island, but apparently unknown to mooning Mounties. *Tant pis.*

The Donzis skidded to a halt and drifted. Joe approached the wrecks to check for injuries and to assess the potential for explosion or fire. Both drivers had been thrown clear of their boats and into the fifty-four degree water where they sat huddled, heads in hand, shivering and groaning on the shelf of rock that had torn away their boats' undercarriages. Joe turned on the spotlight and bullhorn. "Yo!! Dudley Do Rights!! You still alive?" When neither looked up or responded, he pressed a toggle on the consul behind the pilot's wheel. Twin air horns beneath the forward pulpit blasted 200 decibels of "I'm talking to you, idjits!" ear pain in their direction. The water sprites slapped palms over ears, and Joe took that as partial indication of their condition. Then he used the bullhorn again. "Anyone else on board?" Two heads shook from side to side. Retrieving an aluminum ladder from a locker under the deck and hooking it over the gunwale, Joe threw a life buoy attached to a ski towline into the water. "Hurry up and get over here." When neither man moved, Joe pressed the AOOGHA! button again. The Donzi drivers held tight to their ears. "Listen up! You can freeze your arses here until morning—if you think you'll last that long. Or you can get over here now. There's other assholes out here tonight besides you, and I'm kind of busy."

"He's hurt!" one of the boaters shouted. "It's his leg!"

Joe took another coil of rope from the locker and added it to the end of the towline. "Then get off your ass! Grab the buoy and help him over here!"

Joe waited while the marine dragsters found their butts in the dark and then hauled the tow line hand over hand while the flames from his brother's house back lit their sorry silhouettes in a gentle orange glow. Outlined as well were two small Zodiacs loaded to their rubber gunwales, putt-putting out of the mouth of Pocket Cove. Joe hauled hard on the rescue line and barked at the half-frozen Canucks to hurry up. The Zodiacs headed north. "It's broken, eh!" the first one warned. His pal in the water looked ashen. Joe looked at the Zodiacs. They were already at the tip of the island and heading out across the open lake. He reached down the ladder, grabbed a fist full of shirt, and hauled the man with the maybe broken leg screaming onto the deck.

"Shut up and sit tight," he ordered. "Hold on to something." Then he slammed the throttles forward and felt the thirty-foot patrol boat surge like a killer shark toward the fleeing Zodiacs.

* * *

Tom moved into a spare room in Joe's cabin and began dealing with the fallout from the arson of his house on Pocket Island. The environmentalists promptly amended their temporary retraining order to assert the likelihood of irreparable ecological harm due to the lack of adequate firefighting capacity. The insurance company canceled its fire, environmental and liability policies. The Taliesin West people notified him that they were coming… to what? Fret? And the managing partner of Tom's former law firm left a dozen messages asking Tom to call, urgently.

All that was to be expected. What was unexpected was his mother's nervy and evasive unwillingness to go over what they had agreed to say, when Tom arrived early at her condo for the family pow-wow that she had arranged with Joe. Three loud knocks at the door, seemingly hard enough to cave it in, interrupted his attempt to get her to engage or explain. She waved her hand in silent command for him to open the door. Then she smiled at her youngest son, resplendent in Sam Browne hat, cross-chest leather belt, tactical boots, and a 9mm Glock sticking out from a polished leather holster, as he entered and announced, "Can't stay."

"What?" said Tom.

"Some shit for brains drove his truck through the front of Tony's Liquors. I need to get down there before the neighbors clean out the place."

"Then we can do this later."

"No. I want to get it over with. I know what you want, or at least what you're going to ask. Say your piece. Then I've got to go."

Tom turned toward his mother. She lifted her chin and held his gaze.

Sandbagged. "I want my grandchildren back," said Mary.

Joe folded his arms across his chest. "Anything else?"

"The rest is none of my business."

"And I understand Bonnie wants me to move out and for us to get counseling. And she stays in the house with our kids. My source got that right?"

Tom continued to glare at Mary, who met the glare with a half-suppressed smirk.

"I'll take that as a yes."

"Bonnie wants her family back together," said Tom. "I understand she's flexible on how to make that happen. Your source," he looked again at Mary, "can confirm that."

"And what about you, brother. What do you want?"

Me? Whatever's best for you and your kids. But before he could give voice to the thought, Joe answered for him. "Right. You don't know."

"Excuse me?"

"You're excused." Joe smiled and adjusted his Sam Brown hat. "Now here's my answer. Bonnie and the kids can move back into the house. I'll get a place at the Waterfront and talk to whoever she wants—as long as I can stand him. But I'm not leaving Coldwater or quitting as its sheriff. That's final."

Tom's eyes bored into Mary's, while she held her face like a proud Mona Lisa.

"What's left of your house is a crime scene," Joe added, looking at Tom and reaching for the door. "You can stay with me at the cabin until Bonnie and the kids move back, if they move back. But if they do, when they do, we *both* move out. Got that?"

"You seem to have thought of everything."

Joe nodded to his mother and closed the door behind him.

Tom left Mary's condo in a condition suitable only for driving fast or hitting something with a closed fist. He was half-tempted to drive to the nearest airport and catch a plane to New York or London or anywhere, but instead found himself fish-tailing to a halt beside the twin stone pillars that marked the entrance to the boarded-up Pearce estate. He was pissed and wired.

Your brother's a horse's ass, he muttered to himself, and your mother's Benedict Arnold. They're tag-teaming you like you're still the clueless senior class president of Coldwater High. But this isn't about you. It's about Bonnie and the kids. Or are you missing something?

What do you want? It was a fair question, though annoyingly insincere coming from Joe. You had a ready answer for it once: financial independence, lawfully earned. But you've had that for a while. So what do you want now? Don't say: to build a school for troubled boys like the one who mixed deadly toxins in the boathouse belonging to that mansion up there. That's a tactic, not a goal. If you're going to preach the difference, act like you know it. Besides, that tactic just went up in flames. Literally. Bonnie will decide if the kids come back to Coldwater. Mary knows that. Joe… who can say what he knows or doesn't? But your loving mother and brother, formerly anxious to have you stay in Coldwater, just sent you a clear message. This is their turf, and you can get on board or go back to the big city. What are you missing, Tommy?

Chapter Ten

The last time Tom was a visitor to Coldwater Hospital and not a patient, it was to confront Joe with what he thought was evidence linking his sheriff brother to the murder of the man who put him there. This time the visit was social and the patient prettier. Tom had brought flowers, candy, and a trashy bestseller featuring a handsome ex-attorney. But every suitable place to put it was covered with crayoned get well cards, and the cushioned visitor's chair at the foot of the bed was occupied.

"Hello, Maggie. Good evening Sister." The black habited visitor inclined her head, as did the patient. But otherwise, neither moved.

"Which one is this?" asked the nun.

"He's the older one, Sister. You were talking about his house a little while ago."

"Thomas? There was a Thomas Morgan at our Lady of the Lake some years ago—with a younger brother, I seem to recall."

Tom shifted the flowers and held out his hand. "It's good to see you again, Sister Judith. Even if I haven't lived up to your early predictions. No adult convictions, anyway."

Maggie placed a fist over her mouth.

Sister Judith was well aware that the power of her presence sometimes diminished in proportion to the years her audience had been away from the classroom. As this seemed to be such an instance, she adjusted her plan and demeanor accordingly. "I'm sorry to hear about your house, Thomas. Will you be able to rebuild?"

"It's hard to say, Sister. The house was part of a plan to build a school on Pocket Island. We've run into a few difficulties, and the fire may prove to be the least of them."

"I will pray for you then, Thomas."

Maggie's fist remained at her mouth.

"Did you know that the man who built your house came to Our Lady of the Lake first?" It was a rhetorical question and Sister Judith did not wait for an answer. "Someone misinformed him that the church-owned Pocket Island. He wanted to build a grotto there...like at Lourdes. He had an idea for a new convent, too."

Tom tried to imagine a Frank Lloyd Wright-designed convent, but what popped into his head was the spiral ramped Guggenheim Museum in New York City with black-robed nuns descending the ramp on white roller skates.

"It was right after the war. With all the soldiers returning home, the pastor decided the parish would need a new elementary school before anything else. Time proved him right about that." Sister Judith pushed herself from the chair and placed a hand on the patient's arm. "I'll take your class until you return, Maggie."

"Thank you, Sister."

"But it would be best for the little ones if that were soon."

Maggie met her gaze, but made no promise.

* * *

"Why do I feel like I'm seven years old again whenever I'm in the same room with a nun?" Tom asked after Sister Judith had left.

"It's the costume," said Maggie. "That's one of the reasons they keep it, I imagine."

"It didn't seem to affect you. She didn't extract a promise to hurry back... which, I assume, was why she came."

"I wouldn't make a promise like that, just to please someone," said Maggie. "The 'little ones' will be worse off, if I go back and the same thing happens again."

"Which is rumored to be heart attack, bee sting or pregnancy depending upon the age and character of the rumor monger."

"Oh, dear!" Maggie put her palms over her face and lowered her head. Tom waited. He did not want to pry. But the fact was that no one seemed to know why the new first-grade teacher at Our Lady of the Lake Elementary School had been taken to the Coldwater hospital in an ambulance. There were plenty of rumors—most of them silly, like the bee sting, but a few that were not, including a vague "drugs." Tom's mother had dutifully passed along all of them, and one of the objects of his visit was to alert Miss Ryan to the need for her and the school to do some basic damage control. Nothing special – something like a notice in the church bulletin asking the congregation to pray for the speedy recovery of the elementary school's newest teacher, who had been suddenly felled by a mortified toe—or whatever it was. He explained his reasoning while arranging a cone of mixed flowers into a plastic beaker of melted ice water.

"The problem is I really don't know what happened," said Maggie, her voice soft and thoughtful.

Tom toyed with the flowers. She watched him as if weighing character against common sense; then after an awkward moment, she continued. "I've been fretting all summer about starting to teach...whether I should be doing it at all...whether I'm just hiding from something else that I haven't the gumption to go after." She repeated most of what she had told her father the night before school began, leaving out the part about her stepmother. "Then when school started, I went into something like anxiety overdrive. I couldn't sleep. I couldn't focus on the kids. Each day got worse. That last morning, it was as if the kids weren't even there. Thoughts kept crowding into my head and then speeding up. At the same time my body slowed down. Finally, what was going on inside was too fast to catch, and the rest of me just came to a screeching halt."

"What do the doctors say?"

She smiled. "That catatonia is an exaggerated response to first-day jitters."

"Is that what they think it is?"

"I didn't tell them enough for them to think otherwise."

69

"I used to practice law," said Tom. "Clients who didn't tell me everything usually lost big."

Maggie's voice was tired, but firm. "This is a small town, Tom. Its only hospital is a risky place to be spilling family secrets."

Clear thinking for a sick lady. Too many files: diagnosis, medication, insurance, tests, etc.—and too many people not bound by doctor-patient confidentiality, who have access and who like to gossip. He had learned the same hard lesson, but only recently. "I have a suggestion."

"Please."

"Talk to Father Gauss. He won't betray a confidence. He's got a Rolodex the size of the Manhattan Yellow Pages, and he'll know somebody who can help."

"That might put him in an awkward position. He's also the head of the school... at least nominally."

Tom turned his palm to face the ceiling. "You can't just lie here."

The school teacher looked like a butterfly pinned to a mat and her voice fell to a whisper. "It happened before, right at the end of grad school. I spent two weeks in the university infirmary."

"Did the doctors there tell you it might happen again?"

"They didn't have to."

The rest was easy enough. Though obviously reluctant, she responded to gentle question and answer. It seemed she needed to talk. "So your father doesn't know?"

"Not what happened a few months ago; and we haven't had a chance to talk about this one yet."

"Your stepmother doesn't know, of course."

"But she's been waiting for years."

Tom closed his eyes and rocked his head on his neck. "That makes sense."

She looked at him quizzically. "Did you know about my mother?"

"My mother plays cards with your grandmother. They're in cahoots. One called your attention to my birth date. The other called mine to your genetic heritage. Old ladies play rough."

"God, I hate living in a small town. I can't believe I came back here."

70

"Did the university doctors say there might be a connection to your mother's illness?"

"They don't know, since I wasn't able to tell them what she has. No one has ever told me. I don't even think my father knows for sure. But the clinic doctor said that major mental illnesses like depression and schizophrenia tend to show up, if at all, in your mid to late twenties—like now—triggered by some kind of prolonged anxiety or stress."

"So now that something has happened twice, what are you going to do? Try to keep it a secret?"

"I'm thinking about my father, Tom. He must have been worrying for years that something like this might happen. Now it has. It's going to take the stuffing right out of him."

"At first. Then he'll have a drink and get on with helping you."

"He's not that cold."

Tom shook off the barb and stored it for later examination. "If your Dad's been living for almost three decades with the possibility that you might inherit your mother's mental illness, then he came to terms with that possibility a long time ago and has likely moved on to Plan B, which is how to provide effective help, if and when it happens. In fact, he's probably the first one to go to, even before Father Gauss."

"There's more." Her voice fell to a whisper, and Tom had to sit on the edge of the hospital bed to concentrate. "It's not just physical freezing. I've been hallucinating, too."

"Here?" he asked. "It could be a reaction to something they gave you."

"No. In the girl's lavatory where Sister Judith found me."

"What were you seeing?"

"Me, mixing a batch of poison. That's why I froze at the sink. It was ready, and I was supposed to use it."

"On who?"

"My stepmother."

Chapter Eleven

Rosemary knelt by the side of her bed, a childhood habit she had returned to lately as she found herself thinking more often about her own mortality. Life is crammed into the middle years, with too much empty space at either end. Was the design as poor as it seemed, or was there a reason that escaped her?

She tried to hold the thought and use it to block the dissonant chord of marital strife that penetrated the floors, walls, and closed doors around her. She prayed that her granddaughter, who had just been discharged from the Coldwater Hospital and who was convalescing in the room next door, could do the same. But unless she had been stricken deaf, in addition to whatever else had hold of her, that was unlikely.

"Put that back!"

Andrew moved a protein bar in and out in front of his face as he tried to bring the fine print of its "nutrition" label into focus. "Twenty-nine grams of sugar."

"I said put it back."

"Gladly." He dropped what amounted to a three-dollar candy bar into a cut-glass bowl with the others.

"You haven't answered my question," his wife said.

"I thought I had. Several times. I don't know how long she'll be staying. As long as she needs to."

"And how long is that?"

Andrew shrugged. "I don't think anyone knows." He watched a bead of water teeter on the edge of his wife's bathing suit and then fall into the deep oriental carpet. Her exercise program was beginning to show results, but he was not surprised to find that he didn't care. Dee Dee had started the fight on the dock when she returned from her evening swim and they had moved it indoors by mutual consent to escape the mosquitoes.

"I'm not a goddamn nurse Andrew."

"I'm not asking you to be. Maggie doesn't need a nurse, she needs rest."

"This isn't a spa either."

"Agreed. It's a home."

"Well, I'd like some privacy in it."

"From whom?" When Andrew didn't get an answer, he pressed. "Our daughter? Me?"

"*Your* daughter."

"So we're back to that again?"

"I don't know where we are, Andrew."

Sure you do, he thought. You're on the cusp of an ultimatum. 'It's either her or me, Andrew. You have to choose.' Or some variation on a theme you've played countless times to exhaustion. You know what my answer will be. Or maybe this time it's not going to be an ultimatum? Maybe this time you've decided that you really are going to leave. But then your plans must not be quite ready yet, or you wouldn't miss the dramatic high of flinging them at me. He turned toward the doorway that led to the den where he slept.

"Don't walk away from me!"

"Is there more to say?"

"Asshole!"

"Be more precise," he said, staring calmly at his wife's trembling face. "And if you can't, then consider the possibility that I'm not." He waited again for a response and received only an angry glare. "Consider the possibility that I'm actually a pretty nice guy, and the problem is that you just wanted me to be somebody else. Or thought that you could make me into him. That all this high drama is just a long drawn-out tantrum because Dee Dee didn't get what she wanted. It's just a thought."

"You're weak," she said, answering the challenge. "And a user."

"Really?"

"You use women to fill holes in your boring life and to clean up your messes. You used that wacko first wife of yours for sex and then me to straighten out the brat that came from it. But you don't love anybody—certainly not me. You don't know-how. You think you love Maggie. But that won't survive this paper slippers gig if she finds that she likes it in La La land and decides to stay there…just like her mother."

Andrew took a long, silent breath. "You would have made a very good psychologist, my dear. Insight into other people's weaknesses is one of your real strengths. It's a shame you never use that talent to look for the truth—only for targets you can hit and spots where it will hurt most. You never turn the lens on yourself."

"Weak and a user," she repeated confidently.

"The paper slippers crack is good…a bull's-eye as usual. But do you know why?"

"Don't bore me with a lecture, Andrew."

"Not even about love? The thing you say I know nothing about?"

"Andrew…if you're going to tell me that you love me, I'm going to spit in your face."

I could tell Jekyll, he thought, she wouldn't spit in my face. But she disappeared as soon as the honeymoon was over, and Hyde came to live here instead. Hyde murdered Jekyll. She has that kind of temper.

"Andrew? You're spacing."

"Sorry, I was thinking about love. What I was going to tell you is that you're correct in thinking that how Maggie handles her illness will change our relationship. She's not a child anymore. The illness isn't her fault, of course. But how she handles it is certainly going to affect her life and mine and how we relate to each other. But not for the reasons you think."

Dee Dee rolled her eyes, but did not interrupt or turn away.

"Most parents love their children unconditionally and forgive them unconditionally—when they're children. But when they grow up, the parents may not hold them to the same standards that they hold other adults, but they do hold them to some standard. The adult child's behavior isn't met with the same unconditional love and forgiveness as the child's. There are some minimum conditions.

"What I don't understand is how you can know that, intuitively, about Maggie. And even throw it at me, as if it's some wounding insight I'm not prepared for. But not see the same thing about yourself and our relationship. That like every other adult relationship, it's conditional… based on attraction and behavior.

"If this is going to be about sex again. I'm really, really, really not interested."

Well, we know that, thought Andrew, but he bit his tongue. There was no way to know how long Maggie would need a place to rest. And rest would be difficult to find in the kind of poisonous environment that Dee Dee seemed bent on creating. Another dramatic blow-up or resentful stalemate served no purpose. It was time to bring this decade-long tension to some sort of resolution.

"Not interested in a lecture," said Andrew. "Not interested in intimacy. Not interested in sharing your house with your family. What are you interested in, Dee Dee? What exactly do you want?"

"Don't provoke me, Andrew."

"It's a simple question…and an important one. All this high drama must have a purpose. It can't possibly be just for sport."

"I *want* to come *first*, Andrew!" Dee Dee's voice was hard and sarcastic. "I want a husband who pays attention to *me*. I want to fix up this house, buy some new clothes, drive a decent car, and take a goddamn vacation!"

"And when you've had all that," said Andrew. "Which by the way you have…more than most people. Then what? Will you be happy this time? And for how long? And what comes after that?"

"You've always chosen her over me."

"It's called being a parent."

"No, Andrew. She's an adult now. You said so yourself. And if you choose her over me again, it's going to cost you plenty."

Chapter Twelve

J oe turned the Coldwater patrol car onto an overgrown dirt track a few
miles up the lake road north of town. Tall weeds swept the underside
of the car, and branches scraped its sheet metal sides with a sound like
the squeal of a dying rabbit. Dousing the headlights, he eased the car down
the track to where it ended at the edge of a weed-choked lagoon—home to
mosquitoes, snapping turtles, and not much else. The grassy bank beside
the track was an occasional and last choice lovers' lane, where in the warm
months, you could not crack a window on account of the mosquitoes, and
where if the track leading in was blocked, there was no way out. The last
Sheriff Morgan to come down here had been found dead in the front seat of
his patrol car, his tongue pulled through a nearly decapitating gash in his
throat.

Joe switched off the engine and for a while sat listening to the sounds of the
deepening night: croaking frogs, lovesick insects, clicks and groans from the
cooling patrol car engine, and the rustle of trees and bushes rubbing against
each other in the warm breeze off the lake. Through the windshield, he
could see the outline of a pickup truck, its rear wheels poised at the edge of
the lagoon and behind it a galvanized boat trailer submerged to its rollers in
green scummy water. He cracked a window and listened. A mosquito zipped
through the opening and circled the tree-shaped air freshener suspended
from the car's rearview mirror. Opening the flap on his Glock holster, he
leaned back against the headrest and waited.

* * *

A thick humming that a sleepy slap to the ear didn't stop, woke him. The horizon glowed in predawn light. The pickup truck at the edge of the lagoon was visible now, its hood and windshield dappled with dew. Joe shook his head. The humming grew closer, as if a swarm of bees was advancing down the lagoon. He knew that sound.

Swish!...the sound of brush scrapping cloth. He moved his hand to the gun under his arm. *Hmmmmm*...the swarm advanced toward the waiting pickup. *Crack!*...a piece of dry wood splintered under pressure. *Splash!*...two figures jumped from the bow of a jon boat that had come to a halt over the partially submerged boat trailer. The humming stopped.

Joe sat motionless, watching as the figures from the boat pushed and hauled it onto the trailer. A homemade noise suppressor, in the form of a wooden box fitted like a cap over the outboard motor, explained the sound of bees. He checked the rearview mirror. The outline of a tree at the side of the track seemed to bulge unnaturally from ground to about man height. Truck doors slammed and a flatulent exhaust system spewed noise and carbon into the morning stillness. Joe kept his eye on the bulging tree. As daylight grew stronger, the man-sized bulge grew limbs and a cap. The pickup turned away from the lagoon. The trailer behind it came out of the water with a sound like a giant sneaker being pulled from a mud hole. Truck and trailer covered twenty yards before the driver slammed on its brakes, grill to grill with the Coldwater patrol car.

"Shit."

Joe heard the voice but did not look up. At an eruption from the truck's exhaust, he turned the ignition key on the patrol car's dashboard. The tree silhouette in the rearview mirror sloughed its man-sized bulge, which came to a rest on the ground facing the back of the patrol car. Joe lifted the handle on the steering column, putting the car into reverse. A middle-aged man in wet dungarees and a graying ponytail stepped from the passenger side of the pickup and approached. The prone silhouette in the rearview mirror levered slightly from the ground. Mickey Dooley leaned his arms on the patrol car door. "Morning Sheriff."

Joe stomped on the gas pedal. The patrol car covered the thirty yards in less than three seconds and then crashed into the tree where the man-sized silhouette had been. Joe slid across the seat and out the passenger door. A chaos of snapping and squelching receded into the woods. From the ground in front of the pickup came a howl of pain. Joe took a pair of binoculars from the sprung patrol car trunk and scanned the woods. The squelching stopped. He dropped to his knees and ran his hand on the ground under the car, put something into his jacket pocket, and then walked back to the truck.

The injured Dooley huddled on the ground cradling one arm in the other and moaning pitifully. "You broke his god damn arm!" shouted his brother, Kevin.

Joe inclined his head toward the woods. "Friend of yours?" When neither man answered, Joe took a step toward the Dooley on the ground and poked him with his shoe where one arm held the other.

"Shii—it!" Mickey screamed. His brother, Kevin, lurched toward Joe but stopped when Joe pulled a muddy handgun from his pocket. "Your pal dropped this."

The uninjured Dooley looked at the gun in Joe's hand. "What pal?"

Joe leveled the gun at Kevin Dooley and then kicked his brother in the arm.

"Ahhhhh!"

"This isn't poaching, assholes," Joe spoke calmly over the whine of Mickey Dooley's moans. "The rules change when you start shooting at people."

Kevin Dooley leaned over his brother, who rolled from side to side on the wet ground. "I didn't hear any shots," he spat.

Joe swung the muddy gun toward the woods in the direction of the last squelching sound and pulled the trigger. *BANG!*

"I'm going to sue your ass," Mickey gasped, "Gonna sue the whole damn town!"

"Got to get out of here first." Joe held the gun level with Kevin Dooley's face and began to recite in a flat, officious monotone as if reading from an official report. "Officer Morgan was driving south on Cross Lake Road when he heard what sounded like gunfire." Joe swung his arm and fired into the woods again. *BANG!* "He proceeded down an unpaved access road known locally as Beaver Lane, where he discovered the bodies of two male Caucasians lying next to a red Ford pickup truck parked at the end of the lane. Each appeared to have been shot once in the head. An unidentified individual, perhaps wearing camouflage, was observed fleeing the scene." Joe waved the gun in the Dooleys face for emphasis. "Two 9mm shell casings were recovered from the ground near the bodies. A nine-millimeter handgun was found in the woods nearby."

The brothers looked at each other. Kevin spoke. "Morgans aren't that kind of assholes."

Joe nodded. "Didn't used to be. Used to be Dooleys just poached fish. But it seems things have changed." Mickey Dooley held his arm and winced. "Come to think of it," Joe added. "A Morgan got his throat slit down here a few years ago. Maybe another one was about to take a bullet in the back of the head here this morning." He hefted the muddy handgun for emphasis. "Maybe it's time for some Dooleys to get whacked too?"

Mickey Dooley rolled on his side and threw up.

"Besides, I don't see another way out."

When Mickey finished retching, he asked, "Out of what?"

"Mickey, Mickey, Mickey…" Joe's voice dripped disappointment. "I don't know that guy out in the woods. I never saw his face and I don't know what he's doing here. And for that, he was going to shoot me? You fellows know who he is and what he was doing. And he's out there right now listening to Mickey bawling and watching the both of you yapping with a cop. So you figure out what comes next."

"Shit."

"Lie down with dogs. Get up with fleas."

"My brother needs to get to the hospital."

Joe waved the gun down the dirt track blocked by the smashed patrol car. "Start walking."

Kevin helped his brother to his feet.

"Your pal could give you a lift. But then you don't have a pal, do you? And if you did, who's to say if you start down that track you'll make it to the other end? That's a nasty mother out there." Joe slapped his shoulder holster and jacket pocket. "Good thing I've got these. But then I need them, don't I?"

When neither Dooley responded, Joe continued. "I could be wrong. Maybe you'll be fine. I can't imagine anybody around here with reason to harm two unarmed fish poachers."

Kevin put one foot in front of the other, but his brother didn't move. "We'll pull your patrol car out with the truck," he said.

"No thanks," said Joe.

The Dooleys looked at each other. A loud crack sounded in the woods.

"That guy out there might not be a friend of yours. But he sure seems interested in what's going on here. He didn't have another weapon, did he?" The Dooleys didn't answer, but they moved to the other side of the truck, placing it between themselves and the sounds from the woods. Joe walked beside the trailer and looked into the open boat. There was no fishing equipment inside and nothing in the fish box except a thermos, two flashlights, and a block and tackle. "Not going to catch much with this," he said holding a fifty-foot length of three-strand rope.

"Boom! Ping!"

The first sound came from the woods. The second from the aluminum jon boat, where a small, dime-sized hole appeared in its side a foot from Joe's hip. Joe vaulted over the trailer tongue and put the truck between himself and the woods. The Dooleys were already in the ditch on the other side. He motioned to them for the truck keys. Mickey shook his head. Joe took the recovered handgun from his pocket and pointed it at Mickey's face. Kevin Dooley took the boat keys from his pocket and tossed them underhand to Joe's outstretched palm.

Cracking the truck's passenger side door, he slipped behind the wheel, started the engine, and put the truck in reverse. Slowly, truck and trailer moved backwards toward the lagoon. Joe motioned to the Dooleys to follow. *Boom! Smash!"* The windshield of the truck buckled and shattered. Joe jumped out of the truck and trotted beside it, reaching inside to turn the wheel when the trailer started to jackknife. When it hit the bank, the trailer flipped on its side and the jon boat slid off and floated free.

Removing his service revolver from the holster under his armpit, Joe fired twice toward the sound of moving brush on the other side of the track. He motioned to the Dooley's to get into the boat.

Boom! Ping!

Boom. Boom. Boom. Boom. Boom. Joe returned the fire and then jumped into the boat with the Dooleys. There was no need to tell them what to do next. *Boom. Boom. Boom. Boom.* He lay down a steady stream of handgun fire until the jon boat was out of the lagoon and onto the open lake.

* * *

Mickey Dooley lay in the bilge on the bottom of the boat. The fabric of his shirt just below the elbow bulged at an unnatural angle. His face was fish-belly white and his body trembled. He was going into shock. "We got to get him to the hospital," said Kevin.

Joe shook his head. "Pocket Island."

"He's hurt."

"Sure looks it."

"I'm taking us to the marina."

Joe took the nine-millimeter handgun from his pocket. "This one's still got three more shots," he said flatly.

"You're a madman."

"And your new friend… what's he?"

Kevin Dooley seethed but said nothing.

"You don't get it, do you?" Joe's voice was calm and reasonable. "I didn't need to get out of there. You did. You burn down my brother's house. You hook up with trash that shoots cops that they really don't need to. But when trash turns on you, who is it saves your sorry asses?"

"We didn't burn your brother's house."

"Bullshit."

Mickey Dooley vomited in the bottom of the boat.

"We're going there now. And you two are going to show me exactly what you were doing out there…last night, the night I set your boat adrift, the night you say you didn't burn down my brother's house, and any other night you've been out there this summer. Then you're going to tell me who you did it with…and what fairy tale they told you about what you were supposedly doing. Unless of course, it was your idea… whatever it was. But I don't think that's likely…you being Dooleys."

A wave lifted the bow of the boat and dropped it with a slap. Mickey screamed.

"I'm taking us to the marina." Kevin turned the boat to port.

Joe dropped his hand to the fuel line that led from the 25 HP outboard to the ten-gallon fuel tank under the center thwart and turned the stopcock at the top of the line. The engine sputtered and died. "You've got more gumption than your brother. I'll give you that. But that's not going to help him."

"Turn that back on."

"I don't think so." Another wave lifted the boat and slapped the bow with its trough. Mickey screamed again. "Getting rough out here," said Joe.

Kevin Dooley moved suddenly to his feet.

"Whoa! Whoa! Whoa!" said Joe. "What do you think you're going to do? And with what? You're going to fall in the water, you idiot."

"I'm going to take that gun."

"This one?" Joe took the nine-millimeter handgun from his pocket and held it over the side of the boat, opened his hand and dropped it into the water. "Or this one?" He took the handgun from the holster at his side and threw it after the first. "That was a good gun," he said.

Kevin stood and stumbled across the short space from the back of the fourteen-foot boat to the middle thwart where he braced himself unsteadily over the Coldwater sheriff and cocked a fist. Joe let him swing and miss and then shoved him halfway over the side. The weight on the gunwale tilted the aluminum jon boat almost vertical. Grabbing the Dooley by his shirt collar, Joe hauled him roughly back into the boat, which made it crash back to horizontal and Mickey in the bow scream.

Joe shoved Kevin roughly toward the stern. "Listen up. Your brother's in shock. Which isn't good. We'll get him to the hospital as soon as we finish up here."

Kevin seethed but would not make eye contact.

"That guy out in the woods," Joe continued. "I didn't get a real good look at him. Was he a tall guy?" Kevin looked away and didn't answer. Joe leaned toward one side of the boat and started to rock it. Mickey moaned and started to dry heave. Kevin let out a cloud of foul breath, which was as good as a white flag. "Six two," he muttered.

"Meet him at church?"

"The VFW."

"Army guy?"

"Civilian clothes, army haircut."

"Redhead?"

"Blond whitewall."

"So what did this Nordic jarhead say he needed two fish poachers for?"

"He needed a guide, and help carrying some stuff."

"A guide?"

"He wanted to go out to Pocket Island in the dark. He heard there were a lot of rocks in the cove and around the island."

"So how many times did you take him out there before he got what he wanted?"

"A couple of nights last month," Kevin sighed. "He brought a snorkel once and the next time a metal detector. He told us to take some stuff from your brother's building site so if someone saw us they'd think it was just pilferage."

"Did he find what he was looking for?"

"I don't know."

"He find anything?"

"He had us help him haul two metal trunks halfway across the island."

"From where?"

"Not sure. It was dark."

"Did he take them off the island?"

"Not that night. Some funnyman untied our boat."

"So what did you do with the trunks?"

"Nothing. He told us to take a hike. We went across the island to the cove to see if we could borrow a boat from your brother. But there was a dog

83

there."

"This guy ask you to take him back later?"

Kevin didn't answer. Joe took a pocket knife from his hip pocket opened the blade and held it to the fuel line. "You were doing real good Kevin. But I cut this…and blue-lips up there is going to get real bad."

"You're a son of a bitch, Joe Morgan."

"You're just finding that out? Could have saved your brother a lot of pain if you were a bit quicker." Joe held the fuel line balanced on the blade of the pocket knife. "So he had you take him out there again."

"A couple of times," Kevin admitted. "But your brother was always there with that damn dog."

"So there was a fire," said Joe quietly. Kevin didn't answer and Joe began to saw the blade of the penknife across the plastic fuel line.

"He said that would keep everybody busy," said Kevin. "And that one more boat wouldn't be noticed."

"So why'd you have to go out there again tonight?"

"The fire brought out too many boats. And too many people on the island. He made us leave and come back tonight."

"So where are these trunks?"

"At the end of the lagoon. He had us drop them off, and him too, before we came down to the trailer. That's why he didn't leave, I guess. I don't know why he shot at you. He could have waited and picked them up later."

"Maybe he didn't trust you two not to tell me," said Joe folding the penknife and opening the fuel line stopcock. "I wonder what he's going to do when he finds out he was right?"

Chapter Thirteen

"You don't look sick to me."

The Coldwater patrol boat eased alongside Ryan's dock, where a pale, overdressed Maggie Ryan lay on a deck chair, her face half-covered by the brim of a straw sunhat. She put down her book and reached for a pair of sunglasses that lay beneath the chair. "If I don't look sick, Sheriff Morgan, how *do* I look?"

"Thoughtful."

From the open window of one of the upstairs bedrooms came a clear, unmodulated screech. "I can't have her in my house! What if she gets violent? I am <u>not</u> a psychiatric nurse!"

"I can lock her up for disturbing the peace," Joe offered easily.

Maggie turned a knob on the portable radio next to her chair. The soft strains of classical music didn't mask the noise from the house, but they diluted it. "The only permanent solution is death or divorce," she said. "And her husband's not decisive enough to do either."

"I don't know," said Joe. "When the meek finally snap..."

"It might be better for him if he were meek. But he's not. He just thinks too much."

"I've got a brother like that."

"Who beat you here by a week." Maggie laughed.

"Sometimes he's not so slow. But today I'm here on official business. I need to ask what you might have seen on Pocket Island."

"Is this about the fire?"

"I have an informant who says that it was started by someone who wanted to take something off the island and not be noticed in all the confusion."

"I'm sorry," said Maggie. "I was in the hospital that night."

Joe lifted a hand as if to say, *'I don't know what to say, I'm sorry, too.'* But instead, he asked, "How about before that, when you were sketching and so forth? Did you see anyone on the island besides my brother?"

"Three poachers the first day I was there. They took my boat. But you know that."

"Did you roam around the rest of the island?"

"Around Washington's Head a little. I was supposed to be sketching. But most of the time I was just fretting and spacing out." She removed her sunglasses and Joe decided the rest of the cop questions could wait.

"You see a lot of wackos in my line of business," he said.

"If that's meant to be comforting, Sheriff..."

"No...listen...I have a theory. The wackos I see are mostly teenagers and people in their twenties. By the time they're in their thirties they're not wacko anymore – not stealing cars in broad daylight, not picking bar fights they can't possibly win. Why is that? It's not like only some of them get better. All of them do... unless they end up in jail or get killed. Why?"

"I give up, Sheriff," she said, then laughed. "I bet you hear that a lot."

"Don't flirt. Listen. When you know the families they came from, it's not hard to understand how they got wacko. Why they're worse while they're living at home and better the longer they're out of it. Unfortunately, some of them have already started making their own babies by then, and they don't think to parent differently from the wacko parents that made *them* wacko. So the cycle starts all over.

"Here's my theory. I want to try it out on a school teacher first: Wacko must be the *normal* result of being raised by wacko. Get away from that and eventually wacko disappears."

"I'm not a criminal, Sheriff."

Joe jerked his head toward the noise still coming from the house. "Yeah. But you're wacko—and it's not hard to see why. I'm just saying don't get too bummed about it. The longer you're out of here, the better it'll get. But you need to get out. Nice place and all. But that crap up there is what's likely making you wacko."

Maggie was silent for a moment, slapped in the face by a life vest of street psychology thrown to her by a married cop with the looks and physique of a Greek statue.

"Look, if you need a place to stay…"

Maggie laughed, the reverie broken. She stood and put on her robe. "My biological mother has the same thing I do. The screamer up there is my father's second wife. You have an interesting theory, Sheriff. But I'm afraid in this case 'wacko' is likely in the genes."

"Only if mama was raised by Ozzie and Harriet. If they were smacking each other around…or messing with her…or if anyone with any control over her was doing any of those things sick adults think up to make kids' lives a horror show, then all you've got is two generations of wacko behavior producing the same result. That's not heredity. I don't know what to call it…something like wacko welfare?"

Chapter Fourteen

I t was sunset when Joe left the station. The temperature on the Coldwater Bank clock read 96 degrees as he passed it on the way up the lake road. Hot, muggy darkness is not a propitious time to be exploring semi-swampland. The prospect of wet footwear, sharp unseen branches, and relentless insects can be as unappealing as the experience. But he reminded himself that while men see less in darkness, they also see differently; and the things they see in that concentrated frame are the things they sometimes miss in the wider and brighter landscape of daylight.

Like the majority of Coldwater adult males, Joe and Tom's father had been a hunter. One of the many nuggets of outdoor lore he passed on to his sons was the wisdom of waiting until darkness before tracking a wounded animal. Flecks of blood that disappear in the ocher patterns of decaying leaves, shine like rubies in the beam of a Coleman lantern. The late sheriff Morgan didn't look for poachers until nightfall either. "Why bother when the idjits can see you coming?" he'd asked. "Take away their daylight and you're even. They can't see you coming and by the time they hear you, you can hear them too. Then it's a game. Who has more patience? Who can keep still the longest? Are you still there? Or were you even there in the first place? Who are you, anyway? Sooner or later most of them move—even if it's just to sneak back to their truck before sunrise. Then you've got 'em."

Joe turned the patrol car onto Beaver Lane and shifted into low gear. Center growth grass lay flat in either direction and waffles of tire tracks on either side stood in bas-relief in the glare of halogen headlights. At the edge of the lagoon near the overturned boat trailer, Joe got out of the patrol car and retrieved a lantern, a plastic bucket, and a waxed carton from the trunk. Mosquitoes swarmed when he lit the lantern. Peering through the darkness down the sometimes lovers' lane, he thought, your mind really has to be on something else for this place not to give you the creeps.

A pair of brass handgun shells lay on the ground near where the Dooley's truck had been parked. From there, a shallow gouge led to the edge of the woods where broken ferns lay facing the missing truck and the smell of trampled skunk cabbage hovered like a ripe fart in a closed elevator. Pocketing the brass, he held the lantern over the flattened vegetation and sucked stagnant air through clenched teeth.

The trail that led through the swampy lowland was as clear as if it had been made by a plow and pavement roller. Triangular gouges in the soft earth alternated with flattened paths of crushed underbrush and pressed fern. Footprints appeared from time to time on either side of the gouge or inside the swath of pressed earth...a single set faced back toward the track.

The footprints were at least two sizes larger than Joe's own size 13's and he started to think of their unknown maker as Big Foot. Where the scrape skirted a low patch of standing water, he stopped to dip the plastic bucket and open the waxed carton inside. Then he poured the powder from the carton into the water, stirred it with a fallen stick, and poured the runny paste into a pair of treaded boot prints. When the prints were full he covered them with wet leaves and tied a strip of pink surveyor's tape to a nearby tree.

Farther on, the trail intersected a pool of stagnant water that ran into the woods in either direction. Circles of cord hung wrapped around a sapling on both sides of the pool. One had a tail that hung into the water, as if someone had strung a length of rope from tree to tree over the pool and then cut it near the end. Joe untied the shorter side and put it into his pocket. Then he gripped the lantern and bucket and jumped the ditch.

Splash! Crack!

Pungent muck poured over the top of Joe's boots. The crack of snapping wood was somewhere off in the darkness. He put the lantern on the ground and covered it with the bucket. Then he moved his lower legs from side to side and hauled with his withers. But the boots remained stuck in the muck. While he plunged his fingers into the ooze and pulled at the muddy laces, he felt something ripple through the water behind him. A long-ago memory flashed into consciousness: *SNAKE!*

Shit.

While his throat closed and his heart knocked numb against the wall of his chest, Joe waited and willed for calm to return. A cloud of mosquitoes found his ears and the succulent patch of bare skin on the back of his neck. He closed his eyes and listened. The symphony of the nighttime swamp had only two notes of interest to him: the ripple of something slithering through shallow water nearby, and the crack of parting wood. He stood motionless in the crawling mire for minutes out of time, a living buffet for airborne and aquatic tormentors. But there were no further sounds on the frequencies that mattered. The cloud on his neck feasted until it became too sated to evade his hands. He smeared a handful of insect corpses across his neck and then reached into the mud cut the laces from his boots with a penknife.

Feet and footwear made un-mucking noises like a quartet of bathroom plungers—but there was no helping it. He had heard nothing beyond the first crack off in the woods. Perhaps a dead limb chose that moment to separate from a dead host and fall of its own weight. But he'd heard nothing hit the ground—just the crack of breaking wood. And there were only so many things in the nighttime swamp that might have broken it.

Joe cut a slit in the bottom of the plastic bucket and pulled the lantern handle through it. Then forcing his feet into muddy boots, he resumed the trail, bending low so the shaded lantern lit a pie plate of swampy ground, but threw no light above the level of his toe tops. From time to time he rested the bucket and listened until the mosquitoes owned him. The gouged trail switched left and right and back again, following the higher ground and arcing wherever possible toward the lagoon. Big Foot must have been dragging something pretty heavy, he thought. The trail ended—or began— just short of where the lagoon opened onto the lake. Joe peered into the darkness and listened before tilting the bucket so that the light shone in an arc in front of him. Beneath a canopy of chokeberry vine, covered with ferns and dead branches, the light fell on what looked like a metal trunk, shaped like a student's footlocker but flattened to half the usual height,

Joe copied the letters and numbers stenciled onto the top of the trunk, as well as its dimensions, into a pocket notebook. He had no intention of trying to haul the thing back through the swamp, though when he lifted one of the straps, it moved easily. The top squealed when he lifted it open. Inside was lined with padded cloth, grooved down the center with irregular indentations. Otherwise, it was empty.

Crack!

Joe eased the bucket to the ground and squatted beside it. *Crunch! Splash!* Of the thousand sounds in the nocturnal symphony, there is no mistaking the percussion of mud-sucking boots crushing ground cover. Joe moved his hand to his armpit. Only then did he remember that what usually rode there was now at the bottom of Coldwater Lake. He reached under the bucket and extinguished the wick. 'Shit.'

Big Foot went silent as well. Joe endured a squadron of mosquito reinforcements while he struggled to organize his thoughts. What did he know? What did Big Foot know? Did anything give either an advantage that he would be wiser to realize sooner rather than later?

He had big feet.

He didn't come by car.

He isn't running away.

He's interested in what I'm doing here.

He isn't rushing in to find out what that is.

Joe took a breath. What did Big Foot know about him? If he's a friend of the Dooleys and if they told him about their conversation, then he knows a lot. He knows why I'm here. He cares. He knows that I carry a gun and he may know that I threw it away. If he was close enough to the track when I drove in, then he also knows how I got here and where I left my car. Shit!... he knows where I left the patrol car! Big advantage to Big Foot.

Joe took mental inventory of his possessions: a notebook, a pencil, a pocket knife, two feet of cord, a plastic bucket slit through the bottom, two empty ammunition shells, matches, and a gas lantern.

Crunch! Smack!

*H*e blew a wet mosquito softly out of a nostril and opened his penknife.

Crunch! Smack!

Something flew through the air above his head and crashed against a tree behind him. He remained still. Wooded debris whistled from the darkness and fell in a wide arc. *Thud! Crunch! Clank!*

"I got a dog here, asshole," said a menacing voice. "Want to meet him?"

Joe felt his heart accelerate. Not good. *Crunch! Crunch!* The sound of footsteps drew closer. He dropped to the ground and pressed backward with toes and elbows, moving away from the trunk. Then he stood and began walking cautiously in the direction of the lagoon. *Crunch!* He tried to match his steps to the rhythm of the ones coming toward him. *Crunch!* The ground dipped behind him. He shortened his steps and tried not to fall. *Crunch!* Water poured over the tops of his boots. *Crunch! Crunch! Crunch!*

Joe thought of Tom, who had been attacked last year by a pair of Dobermans in the water off Pocket Island. He'd managed to drown them both, though he'd taken a terrible mauling. Joe reached the edge of the lagoon. He had no desire to wade into fifty-four-degree water, much less dispatch a dog with a penknife—or its owner for that matter. What kind of hound does Big Foot have? Or is he full of it?

Joe strained to listen and to keep his teeth from chattering, but he heard nothing. No footsteps. No growling. Even the mosquitoes stood down for the moment. His feet grew numb and his arm stiffened from holding the bucket and lantern above the water. He eased toward shore, but he did not lift his boots from the water. At least he could count on any snakes remaining in the comparative warmth of the swamp.

This was the waiting game. He strained to hear and to stay silent and alert while distracting himself from his own discomfort. It wasn't easy. But that was the game. He thought about snakes… about the spring when he and Tommy were kids out hiking with their dad and Tommy found a copperhead sunning itself on a flat rock near the lakeshore. Their dad had stopped for a call of nature and had not yet caught up with them. Tommy went back to find him, leaving his little brother alone with the prize. Naturally, the young Joe had been reluctant to see his older brother get all that glory. But what could he do to trump something as cool as finding a monster snake? He could pick it up! Timed to his dad's appearance hand in hand with a beaming Tommy, Joe grabbed the thick, coiled serpent behind the neck as he had been taught, and hoisted it overhead. But the snake was thicker and longer than the boy realized and it easily forced an extra half-inch through the twelve-year-old's grip, pivoting its fist-sized head and sinking its fangs into the boy's knuckles.

The pain was indescribable. More than thirty years later, he could still feel it—an injection of pure Drano that made him want to rip off his hand at the wrist. Within minutes the hand was the size of a softball, and it did not go numb...not at all. From wrist to fingertip, the hand was on fire. While none of the other parts of him could move at all, and a voice inside his head began to scream, 'you're going to die.'

As his dad later admitted, it was a distinct possibility that one of them was going to expire. It was a mile uphill to where he had parked their car, and twelve-year-old Joe weighed one hundred and twenty pounds. He remembered walking no more than a hundred yards before shock overtook him and his legs gave out. He remembered too feeling that his heart was close to bursting. His father said later that he felt the same after hoisting his son on his back and carrying him the rest of the way out of the woods.

Father and son spent a week together in the intensive care unit of the Coldwater Hospital while the poison and swelling spread up the boy's arm and across his shoulder, stopping after five days just short of the collar bone. His father slept in a chair by the side of his son's hospital bed, watching college basketball and explaining to Joe in a way that the doctors couldn't, why he was sure that Joe wasn't going to die. "You got to think about what they eat, Joey," his father said. "Birds, lizards, sometimes a rabbit. That poison's not made to take down a hundred twenty pound man."

Tommy came to visit too. Joe was grateful that his older brother didn't call him stupid or anything like that for picking up the snake. None of the men did. It was as if they all understood that no self-respecting twelve-year-old boy would allow his older brother to hog all the glory—although some might have looked for a less ballsy way of upstaging him.

That week in the hospital was also some kind of journey for father and son, beginning almost as a death watch and ending as an epic near miss. Tommy missed out on that. Joe and his father talked sports into the small hours of the morning and—for the first time—girls. "I'm not going to embarrass you with the birds and bees stuff," his father said. "You can get that anywhere these days. But what I can tell you is that women are more different from us than you can imagine and that they'll mess with your head if you don't understand that." His father went on to explain a variety of differences that made no sense to Joe at the time, or for a long time afterward. Later, when he told Tommy that he and his Dad had talked about sex, older brother got all pissy and broody.

By the time they were in high school, the brothers understood simply that one took after their mother and the other their father—no harm, no foul. But at age twelve and thirteen respectively, they were still competing for the title of Heir Apparent and Clone of the King. With the snake saga, it became apparent that Joe the Younger was more likely the true heir apparent and that Tommy the firstborn would have to find another kingdom.

A nearby explosion and flash of light shook Joe from the reverie. The sky above the treetops glowed orange, followed by the smell of burning gasoline. *Took him long enough.* Joe waded onto dry ground and lit the lantern. There were new tracks around the trunk, and at one end the lining had been pulled free. All of the prints were Big Foot's. No sign of any Fido.

Joe put the lantern inside the trunk and worked rapidly. Wedging the brass shells upright behind the hinge that connected the body of the trunk to its lid, he packed his remaining matches into them so that they stood like candle wicks above the packing. Then he cut the lining into strips and packed the cloth around the lantern. The longest of the strips he threaded into the kerosene cup at the base of the lantern and tied the other end to the hinge above the match-filled shells. Finally, he threaded the matchbox strike plate between the match heads that protruded from the tops of the shells, poked a stick through the end, and tied it to the cord he had pulled off the tree in the swamp. The rest of the cord he looped over the top of the hinge and through the strap on the outside of the trunk. Then he turned off the lantern, eased the lid closed, tied the tail of the cord taut to the strap, and cut off the tail. The trunk was now a massive Molotov cocktail.

Crunch!

A beam of flashlight strobed the trees. Joe backed away from the trunk and headed for the water.

Crunch!

He waded silently until the freezing lake was up to his armpits and then rolled to his stomach and swam slowly, parallel to shore. He was still stroking when he heard the explosion of the improvised firebomb followed by a high-pitched scream.

Chapter Fifteen

Tom returned to the island to begin cleaning up the mess from the fire. Brutus rode in the bow, subdued like his companion. As they entered the Pocket Cove the dog sniffed the air and whimpered.

The roof of the Frank Lloyd Wright house was gone. The gutted shell stank of wet, rotting furniture. Tom knew that he would have to strip everything back to the concrete shell, haul the debris off by boat and be lucky to get everything done and tarped by first snowfall. The insurance adjuster had been through already, as had the people from Taliesin West. Their respective restoration estimates differed by a factor of five. Construction could not resume without additional funds and, most likely, litigation.

Brutus leapt to the dock and ran up the stone staircase to the top of the hill. Tom tied the Grady White to the Samson post and followed. Earlier in the week, he'd finally answered a phone call from Tanner Hartwell, the managing partner at his former law firm, which for transparently selfish reasons continued to treat Tom as merely on "temporary" leave. Tanner explained that a major client wanted to establish a futures market for Hollywood films. Movie studios would use it as an alternative source of financing, and the public could invest in the box office successes and failures of their favorite actors, directors, and stories. Backers of the next blockbuster film stood to make fortunes. The studios could cut a meaningful chunk out of the cost of financing and production. It was a market crying for someone to make it happen, and the client had asked for Tom.

"No," was his immediate answer. But it was delivered without the firmness designed to truly discourage. Tanner took it as a near 'yes' that only needed more convincing. "There's at least an eight-figure payout for whoever can get this past the regulators, exchanges, studios, distributors, and who knows what else. The client is looking for a proven, out-of-the-box thinker, so the project doesn't grind to a halt every few months over something nobody's thought of. That's you. Besides, it's money out of thin air—all-new, nobody taking anything from Peter to enrich Paul. We all know you have a sweet spot for that kind of thing. Whoever pulls this off is going to make a fortune."

Tom already felt sufficiently wealthy by any standard he valued or understood. But he still found himself tempted. He'd been planning a trip to London in October to wrap up some unfinished business, hoping to stay there over the winter to enjoy one of his favorite cities. But a new kind of financial futures exchange was not a three-month project—more like five years. Maybe more. If he left Coldwater now with the Frank Lloyd Wright restoration and school project in limbo, neither would get finished. His promise to Bonnie to help bring her family back together would not be met, either. Then there was Joe's increasing resemblance to their father, "Mad Dog" Morgan, the narcissistic, violent, and morally indifferent, role model of their youth. Joe's swaggering arrogance seemed lately to be accelerating down a greased slope toward menacing bullying. Would it get there? And where would it end?

Tom's gut tightened. *Who and what do you think you are? A family therapist, or a deal maker.* Wasn't a project that would return him to a world he understood and thrived in, away from one he increasingly didn't, a timely gift to be thankful for and embraced? Or was it a cowardly fade from further involvement with a people and place that he loved, but whose values, and truths he neither shared nor understood? Or was it both?

Part of him missed the Wall Street action, though he had easily dismissed the knowing predictions of his colleagues that he'd be back in six months. Why did he think they were wrong, or that he was so different from everyone else? What had months on a mosquito-ridden island, with only the company of a cowardly canine, actually accomplished? He looked around at the ash-covered debris of his torched house, and the provocative questions came fast and almost frenzied.

The firm was dangling an opportunity to make a lot of money doing something new and challenging that had not been done before. The opportunity wouldn't wait or return if he didn't say yes, soon. Kicking a piece of burnt debris across the blackened cement porch, he felt frustrated and nervy. He had never had trouble making decisions, even with incomplete information. Except for the mess he'd be leaving behind, this one seemed close to a no-brainer. What was the chance, realistically, of permanently and positively influencing the ongoing Morgan psychodrama? Zilch. *Who are you, Tommy? What do you want?*

Looking down at the shaded cove as if an answer might be hidden beneath its chilly waters, he called to the dog. "Come on Buddy. Let's go clear the webs." Man and dog trotted down the path to Forty-seven, where man stripped off his shorts and shirt and grabbed the Tarzan rope, swinging far out over the cove and yodeling expletives at the top of his lungs a la Johnny Weissmuller. Back and forth, naked and maniacal he shouted at the dog to join him before dropping gracefully into the gonad shrinking, head-clearing water. A long, calming moment later, he surfaced choking hard, his face pressed flat against a bloated corpse that strained the fabric of a turquoise wet suit.

Chapter Sixteen

It was hard to tell whether the circumstances of Dee Dee Ryan's death had anything to do with the number of mourners at her funeral or whether she actually had that many friends. But the church was packed. The Morgan brothers stood at the back and surveyed the crowd. Father Gauss preached a short homily on happiness—an interesting choice for a funeral mass—with some erudite bits about the difference between the Church's historical teaching and the views of the 18th-Century Enlightenment.

As the crowd began to scatter after the service, Tom could feel Joe slipping into his hunter mode. "What's up?" he asked.

Joe raised his chin toward a man standing across the street dressed in an unseasonably heavy suit, with a bandaged left hand and unpolished shoes the size of canal boats. "Big Foot over there left through the door by the sacristy just before Mass ended, and he's been standing across the street checking out everyone who comes in or out of the church... everyone except us."

"Maybe we're not pretty enough."

"He hasn't said anything to anyone and no one's so much as waved to him."

"Maybe this isn't his church."

"Half the town is here Tommy."

"Then an out-of-towner... I don't know...ex-boyfriend? No, too young."

"Kevin Dooley said the guy that he and Mickey took out to your island was about six foot two, two hundred twenty pounds and had an army haircut."

"The Dooley's snitched?"

"I'll fill you in later."

"And you think sweathog's bandage is from playing with matches?"

"It might be." Joe had phoned the head MP at Fort Drum and given him a description of the inflatable watercraft that had visited Pocket Island the night of the arson and the markings on the trunk that the visitors had later abandoned. The subsequent torching of Coldwater's only police vehicle had been on the front page of the Coldwater Gazette; but Joe had not made the connection for the MP's and had told no one, other than Tommy, about the rest of that night's adventure. "He still hasn't looked at us," Joe added. "We're standing on the front steps of the church for Christ's sake! How can you not look here?"

"Hey, Joe."

"What?"

"Picture Mr.—it's ninety degrees outside but I'm going to wear something brown and be inconspicuous—picture him in overalls and long, greasy hair."

Joe saw immediately what Tommy meant. The man was a Heller—one of an extended clan of local ne'er-do-wells, as violent and competent as the Dooleys were neither. Not long ago, Tom had witnessed the Heller patriarch being shot and killed by a business associate, just as the Heller was about to do the same to Tom. "What's a Heller doing here?" Joe wondered out loud.

"Casing the collection?"

"I'll have a chat with him."

"Need back up?"

Joe snorted and then trotted down the steps two at a time.

* * *

An hour later, the brothers were riding up the lake road in Joe's customized Silverado. Tom asked about the autopsy report. "She drowned," said Joe. "No sign of foul play," explaining that Mrs. Dorothy "Dee Dee" Ryan had recently begun an exercise program that involved an evening swim across Wilson Cove. "She used to be a high school swimmer. But as far as anyone knows, she hadn't been in the water for thirty years. Probably got a cramp."

"She swam all the way to Pocket Island and *then* got a cramp?"

Joe reminded him that for most of the month there'd been an offshore wind picking up after sunset when the surface of the cold, northern lake gave back whatever marginal warmth it managed to hold onto during the day. It would not have been difficult for a body to get pushed out past Pocket Island and then, when the thermals reversed during the night, drift back into Pocket Cove.

"So it wasn't a heart attack from looking up and seeing yours truly in his birthday suit?"

"No. But it might have been what caused her to swallow all that water." Joe turned the truck off the lake road onto a dirt track. The landscape was familiar to Tom, though it had been almost thirty years since he had been there.

"Never been down Beaver Lane in daylight, he said.

Joe parked the truck near the Dooley's unrecovered boat trailer and briefed Tom about his adventure with the Dooley brothers and his return engagement with Big Foot.

"You think that might have been him at the church?" Tom asked.

"He hopped on that motorcycle pretty fast when he saw me coming."

"And that bandaged hand might be from your Coleman Molotov cocktail?"

"If that was him."

"So what are we here for?"

"Souvenirs."

Tom gestured at his expensive Italian suit and English footwear and then over at the nearby swamp.

"There's a box with a pair of boots in the trunk," said Joe. "Take off whatever else you want to. Most folks do when they come down here. And bring the box."

The brothers left their jackets and ties in the truck and headed off into the swampy woods. Joe retraced his steps along the gouged trail, stopping first at a twist of surveyor's tape where he uncovered a pair of plaster footprints nearby. He wrapped the plaster casts in bubble wrap and then placed them in the box Tom had taken from the trunk. The next stop was the muddy ditch that he had failed to jump in the dark. Daylight revealed a few places where it could have been crossed more easily, but none bracketed by trees suitable for stringing a rope to help slide over something heavy. He explained to Tom his theory that Big Foot combined the contents of the two metal trunks that the Dooleys had helped him recover from Pocket Island, but that while dragging one was easier than carrying two, the heavier trunk left a clear trail and presented other challenges—such as the scummy water ditch—as well as the need to come back and do clean-up.

The final stop was a scorched patch of brush surrounding the remains of a burnt-out metal trunk.

"I'd say you got him good, brother." Tom surveyed the blackened greenery above his head.

"Surprised him, maybe," said Joe. "There wasn't enough fuel in the Coleman to do real damage. Marshmallow burns most likely."

"But he didn't stick around for more."

"One of those Zephyrs putt-putted out of here a few minutes after the explosion. My guess is that Big Foot came back for this trunk. But then had to leave it because the fire made it too hot to dump into a rubber boat and he probably thought he better get the hell out of there before someone came along to check out the bigger fire from the patrol car he'd torched."

"Why do you think he wanted the trunk?"

"I don't know," said Joe. "It's unusual though—half footlocker, half suitcase. Maybe if you know what you're looking at, it means something. Like a Tiffany's box."

Tom snorted. "What do you know about Tiffany's boxes?"

"We've both had some expensive lessons, Tommy."

Tom picked up a long stick and used it to probe the trunk's blackened interior. Little was left of its cloth lining, and the pasteboard sides were buckled and pulled away from the metal walls. "Hey, look at this." Tom pushed the stick behind the pasteboard and pried it forward. Layered against the metal like a green veneer, were a half dozen thin bricks of singed one hundred dollar bills.

The brothers looked at each other. Unspoken was the shared thought:

Just like the hundred dollar bills found by Morini's Funeral Home hidden in the lining of the suit jacket their mother had provided for their murdered father to be buried in.

Chapter Seventeen

J oe pumped the brake as his monster Silverado slipped sideways down the Ryans' tilted driveway. Windshield wipers thumped like drunken soccer fans, flinging yards of water to little effect. As he rolled down the window and stuck his head outside, the right rear tire clipped a decorative rock and the truck swung roundhouse toward the defenseless clapboard. All Joe could do was stand on the brake. The nose of the truck slid to a halt inches from the Ryans' front door.

When he could breathe again, he turned off the engine and remained motionless for several seconds. A curtain parted at an upstairs window and remained that way until Joe jumped from the truck and sprinted through raindrops to the side of the house. "Hello!" he shouted into an empty room where a kettle gurgled on top of a gas range. Hanging his dripping coat on an empty peg on the wall of the Ryans' mudroom, and placing his boots carefully on the dry mat by the kitchen door, he shouted again, "Hello!" After a few moments, the kettle began to hiss and soon after that to whistle. Rosemary Ryan appeared from the back of the house and turned off the flame. "Hi, Mrs. Ryan."

The startled woman threw her arms in the air. The sleeve of her sweater caught the handle of the kettle and yanked it off the stove. Boiling water fanned a half ellipse, and Rosemary Ryan skipped to one side to avoid the splash. Joe started forward and then remembered that he was in his stocking feet. "Don't move," he ordered.

"What are you doing here, Joseph?" Rosemary Ryan's voice sounded confused and alarmed.

"Putting my boots back on and finding a mop," said Joe. "Go back inside while I clean this up."

"I was going to make tea," she said vaguely.

"I'll fill the kettle and put it back on."

Joe found a mop in a corner closet and tea bags and a tray in the cupboard. A few minutes later he was sitting on the Ryans' lakeside porch sipping Liptons with his former junior high school science teacher and watching a cold rain beat against the mortised panes.

"Summer's over," said Mrs. Ryan, seeming to have recovered her composure. "We'll have fall when this rain is done."

"My favorite season."

"Really?" Her voice had the same tone it might have used had Joe revealed an undeclared love for grand opera.

"Every gun in town is out in the woods with their owners sitting up a tree. There's not much serious crime in Coldwater during hunting season."

"What do you call it when they shoot each other?"

"A hunting accident," said Joe. "...whether it is, or not."

Rosemary put down her tea and sat up a little straighter. "All right Joseph... I'm sufficiently recovered from the shock of finding you barefoot in my kitchen. But what were you doing there? Sneaking in or out?"

"In."

"To see my granddaughter? You should use the front door in that case and preferably call ahead."

Joe didn't bother to explain that the front door was temporarily blocked. "To see both of you, Mrs. Ryan. To ask some questions in connection with your daughter-in-law's death."

"Oh, dear." Rosemary Ryan looked away. "There isn't going to be any trouble, is there? This family has had enough of that."

Joe shrugged. "Can I ask when you last saw your son's wife alive?"

"Must we?"

"I'm afraid so, Mrs. Ryan."

Rosemary exhaled loudly, arranging her hands in her lap as if composing herself for any unpleasantness. "Dee Dee passed me in her car on the Wilson

Point Road as I was walking back from Mass Wednesday morning."

"Did she stop?"

"No, she was going in the other direction."

"Was anyone else in the car with her?"

"I didn't see anybody."

"And did you see her again that day?"

"No. She was gone all afternoon. I went up to the Senior Center to have dinner and play cards with some friends. When I came home, I went straight to bed."

"Do you know where Mrs. Ryan was going when she passed you in her car? To a friend's maybe?"

"That's possible, Sheriff. Dee Dee had a lot of friends."

"That was quite a crowd at her funeral."

"My daughter-in-law had a gift," said Rosemary. "She was outgoing, a good conversationalist, and considerate. She remembered your birthday and your children's and what schools they were going to and how they were doing. She sent thank you notes and spontaneous little presents for no reason at all. Friendship was an art with her. She was a remarkable woman."

"Did she have one friend in particular? I'd like to understand her movements on the day she died. A friend might know her plans for that day...or part of it."

"I wouldn't say Dee Dee had one friend in particular. She used to talk to Missy Miller regularly, although I'm not sure about recently. Before she started this swimming business, she used to volunteer at the hospital with Grace Oliver. Both were at the funeral."

Joe took out a notebook and wrote down the names. "And you were at the Senior Center until early evening?"

"Late evening. It was probably close to 11:00 o'clock when I came back."

"Did someone take you there and bring you back."

"Yes."

"Who was that?"

"Your mother's friend Herbert. He has a car and he can still drive at night, so he's very popular with the ladies."

When Rosemary did not elaborate, Joe added the name to the other two. "Do you know where Mr. Ryan was that day?"

"At work, I imagine. He hadn't come home by the time I left for the evening. I presume he was in bed when I returned."

"Would he have gone to bed if his wife had gone swimming and not come back?"

Rosemary looked annoyed and also pained. "I don't think he would have noticed," she answered.

"How is that, Mrs. Ryan?"

"They have separate bedrooms."

"They don't say goodnight?"

"Not as a matter of course."

Joe scribbled a note and continued. "And where was your granddaughter that day, if you know?"

"In her room."

"Did you see her or speak to her?"

"I stopped in with some snacks when I got back from Mass. We had lunch together in her room. Then I stopped in again before I went out for the evening."

"She was still in her room?"

"Yes. She wasn't having a good day."

"Did she leave her room at all?"

"Not as far as I know."

"Was there something particularly wrong that day?"

"Are you a doctor now, Joseph?" said Rosemary, reverting to her schoolteacher voice.

"Not having a good day covers a lot of ground, Mrs. Ryan. A violent argument with her stepmother, for example."

"I see. I'm sorry. I'm being testy. You're doing your job. Actually, she did have something of an argument the day before. But it was with Sister Judith, Our Lady of the Lake's school principal. She wants my granddaughter to return to the classroom, and she's being persistent."

"Hello!" The voice came from the kitchen, followed moments later by the person of Andrew Ryan. "Sheriff Morgan! Glad to see you're not hurt. More glad that your truck is outside my house and not in it."

Joe stood and extended his hand. "Your driveway's a water slide in this weather Mr. Ryan."

"Impossible. Impossible. We should have donkeys instead of cars. The one road is all the Point can really hold. Beautiful views on either side, of course, but we're all perched up here like eagle's nests. The angles are just too steep for cars—especially in this weather."

Rosemary stood. "Andrew, would you like a cup of tea?"

"Love some, Mother. I'm soaked." When Rosemary left the room, Andrew asked in a low whisper. "What's she done, Sheriff?"

Joe's answer was flat and serious. "Answered some questions about your wife's movements on the day she died. I'll need you to do the same."

"I see." Andrew's tone changed abruptly from mock conspiratorial to wearily abused. "So! No small talk. No 'Sorry for your troubles, Mr. Ryan.' Cut right to the chase."

A small part of Joe's brain acknowledged that Ryan had a point. But he had his rhythm now and he'd go with that as long as it lasted. That and the effect of the white knuckle skid down the driveway had made him nervy. "Your wife's body was found at approximately 10:00 AM on September 20th," Joe began. "Your mother saw Mrs. Ryan leaving the house at approximately 9:00 AM the day before. That's a twenty-five-hour gap. Can you help fill it?"

Rosemary returned with a cup of tea and handed it to her son. She did not sit. "Sheriff Morgan wants to know my whereabouts on the night of September nineteenth," said Andrew, reverting to his conspiratorial voice. "What do you think of that, Mother?"

"I think you should answer the sheriff's questions truthfully and treat him with respect." Rosemary turned to Joe. "Somewhere along the way my son chose humor as his preferred way of dealing with uncomfortable emotions. I suppose that works well enough in business, but he sometimes forgets that it's not appropriate to every situation." Andrew looked chastened. "I'll leave you two alone."

Joe resumed his questioning. "So...any idea where your wife may have been between nine AM on the nineteenth and ten AM the following morning when her body was found floating in Pocket Cove?"

"Idea? Sure: shopping, swimming, obviously. Do I know for certain? I'm afraid not."

Joe took his time examining Andrew Ryan's face and weighing his demeanor before posing another question. Ryan accepted the scrutiny and did not elaborate on his first answer. "Do you know anyone who might know where she went and what she was doing during that time?" Joe asked.

"No."

"Was it your wife's habit to spend entire days alone?"

"I don't think so."

"You don't know?"

Andrew sighed. "I don't believe it was her habit, no. But did she occasionally spend a day entirely by herself? Presumably."

"Did she have a job?"

"No."

"Did she have friends?"

"Lots. But it was a changing roster. I don't know the current bunch."

"Can you tell me how you spent your day on the nineteenth?"

"Work. Bed."

"When did you leave work?"

"About eight PM."

"And did you come directly home?"

"Yes."

"Was your wife home at the time?"

"I assumed so, but I didn't actually see her."

"And why did you assume she was home?"

"Her Mercedes was in the driveway."

"And you went to bed at what time?"

"Midnight."

Joe scribbled a note. "And in the four hours you were home, you didn't notice that your wife wasn't?"

"I'm afraid not."

Joe placed his notebook on the glass-topped table and leaned back in the wicker chair. "Some people might find that hard to believe."

"I imagine they lead different lives, Sheriff. Or live in smaller houses."

Joe searched the middle-aged face, intelligent, weary, the body beneath it sunk into the wicker chair, hands open. No twitches, very little muscle tension…as if the cup in its hand was filled with scotch instead of tea. "Can you explain what you mean by 'they lead different lives'? I don't want to assume."

"Are you married, Sheriff?"

"The drill is I ask the questions, Mr. Ryan."

"Yes. Normally that would be the case. But the scuttlebutt in this house is that one or both of the Morgan brothers may be 'interested' in my daughter."

Joe remained silent.

"And here I sit, being interrogated by one of them, however politely, closing in fast on the intimate details of my marriage. So I'm wondering, Sheriff, if this is really necessary. Because if not, it couldn't be more inappropriate."

"Does your job ever interfere with the rest of your life, Mr. Ryan?"

"Occasionally."

"Mine does all the time. So let's move on. You and the missus didn't sleep together, is that it?"

"No, we didn't."

"How long had that been going on?"

"Since we were first married."

"Was there a reason?"

"Sex," said Ryan. He didn't add 'duh!', but it was in his voice. "After a while, we irritated each other in other ways as well."

"Sex isn't usually a problem with newlyweds, is it?"

"You'll pardon me, Sheriff, but that's a very naïve point of view."

"Then make me smart, Mr. Ryan. I got a dead woman who shouldn't be and I'm supposed to find out why."

"Is this a murder investigation, Sheriff? There's been no suggestion of that! Or any reason to."

"Mr. Ryan, unless you die in a hospital hooked up to a machine, or in an accident with witnesses, when we find a dead body in this town we ask questions. Okay?"

"I see."

"So you were explaining the birds and the bees to me."

Andrew drew a deep breath and let it out slowly. "In a nutshell, Sheriff, my wife's concept of marital relations was once a year under the Christmas tree, whether you needed it or not. More often than that, she described as adolescent. My experience prior to marrying Dee Dee had been quite different. So I was confused, as you can imagine. I tried to get to the bottom of it. She eventually admitted that there was a story, but that she didn't trust me to tell it. Once it became clear that, for whatever reason, she was not going to change or explain, I decided that it was futile, and probably wrong, to keep pushing. Under the circumstances, sharing a bed was pointless."

"Did you and your wife ever consider discussing your differences with a therapist?"

"Therapy was another sore subject in our house, Sheriff. Almost immediately after we were married, Dee Dee went from being a happy ray of sunshine to a dark neurotic mess. And intimacy, frankly, was the least of it. I thought that she needed to see a therapist. She insisted that my daughter did and that she was the source of all our marital problems. I'm ashamed to admit that I gave in to her and sent Maggie to a psychologist. I told myself that as she was having her own problems with Dee Dee, it might help her to have someone to talk to. But it was weak. Maggie was never the problem. Dee Dee was. Her demons waxed and waned, but they never went away."

"Did you ever do any kind of family therapy?"

"A single session. When it became clear from the doctor's line of questions that she was looking at Dee Dee and not Maggie as the source of the family's conflict, Dee Dee stormed out."

"Sounds like a family in a pressure cooker. Did it ever explode?"

Andrew Ryan was silent for a long time. Joe waited patiently for him to speak. "You're very clever, Sheriff. Not at all what I was led to expect." Joe remained expressionless. "I don't see that any of this has anything to do with Dee Dee's death, which surely was an accident. But yes, the 'pressure cooker' as you call it, did explode... frequently in the beginning. Once, if that's what you're after, with more than words."

"What happened?"

"Maggie was about thirteen, as I recall. She came into town on her bicycle one afternoon and stumbled into my office hysterical, disheveled, and with one ear the size of a grapefruit. I thought she'd been in an accident.

"When she'd calmed down enough to speak, she told me that Dee Dee had hit her... obviously more than once. I rushed home and found Dee Dee waiting there...spoiling for a fight. She admitted that she had hit Maggie and said that she would do it again 'until the brat learned to obey.' I slapped her." Andrew closed his eyes. His chest rose and fell beneath his damp shirt.

"What happened next?"

"Nothing. That was the entire extent of the domestic violence, Sheriff."

"How did Mrs. Ryan respond to being slapped?"

"With words...always her preferred weapon. 'This is going to cost you plenty,' she said. Though oddly enough, things settled down after that. It wasn't a happy home, Sheriff. But as far as I know, that was the last time anyone did violence in it."

Chapter Eighteen

A ndrew Ryan's ex-wife, Karen, lived alone in a two-bedroom apartment in Coldwater Commons, a subsidized housing project on the back side of East Hill. Most of Joe's domestic violence calls came from the Commons, as did many individuals who came to the attention of the Sheriff's Department for other reasons. He parked his pickup truck where he could see the front entrance to the building and where anyone looking out of an apartment window could see him. The truck was not as instantly recognizable as the Coldwater patrol car, but it was known widely enough. Lowering the window, he listened to the cacophony of crying babies, screaming couples, and high-volume television, while he watched the building to see who fled on general principle.

No one came through the front door, though two vehicles rolled silently out the side of the lot as he locked the truck and made his way up to Karen Ryan's third-floor apartment. The walls of Coldwater Commons displayed no graffiti, and the hallways did not smell like piss. Remembering the one time he had visited Tommy in Manhattan, Joe wondered if Coldwater's sporadically employed were a better class of people than the city breed. Or since there were fewer of them with more space, maybe they had less need to mark their territory.

A tall middle-aged woman answered the door wearing men's pants and a partially open shirt buttoned tight over large breasts and belly. Her rounded shoulders and dark, stringy hair capped the bloated body of a boozer, or someone on heavy-duty medication. Joe held up his badge. "I know who you are," she said. He started to explain the reason for his visit and she cut him short. "I know why you're here, too."

"May I come in?" he asked.

"No."

Joe put his hand on the door. Karen Ryan swung her foot behind it. Pressing steadily, he quickly made it clear that the price of poor hospitality was going to be the top of her toe. "Leave it open," he said. "If there's anyone inside, get rid of him."

"I'm alone, handsome."

Joe stepped into a darkened room, crowded with more furniture than it was designed to hold and where every flat surface was covered with yellowing newspapers, old magazines, and unopened mail. The wall that separated the apartment from its neighbor was covered floor to ceiling with shelves filled with books and photographs. While not entirely unknown in the Commons, books were not a standard decorative feature. An entire wall of them was unheard of.

"Let's sit," he suggested. Karen settled herself in a faux leather recliner facing a flat-screen television and a shelf jammed with framed photographs. A plastic liter bottle of Coca-Cola sat on a table next to the chair, and an open bag of Oreos lay on the floor beside it. Joe lifted a pile of newspapers from a wooden stool and brought the stool over to face Karen Ryan. "Let's start with the basics. Name, age, occupation."

"You know my name," she said. "I'll be forty-eight next month."

Joe took out a notebook and started a fresh page. "Occupation?"

"Disability."

"Do you drive?"

"I have a license."

"Do you have a car?"

"Not at the moment."

"How do you get around…at the moment?"

"Shuttle bus. I can get to most places off of there…doctors' appointments… get my check. I got a friend with a car when I need one."

"Do you know a Dee Dee Ryan?"

Karen snorted. "That didn't take long." She pressed a wooden handle at the side of her chair which pushed the back of the chair forward and lowered the seat. "Bad knees," she explained. "You want a beer?" Joe shook his head. "Mind if I have one?" She didn't wait for an answer, and he didn't bother to give one. Over the sound of a refrigerator opening and a bottle cap being popped, she shouted. "She's the bitch that took my daughter! But then you know that, don't you?" Joe took a quick eyeball inventory of the books and photos on the shelves. Most of the photos were of a much younger Karen Ryan, some with a baby and others with a dark-haired little girl no more than two or three years old. There were a couple of ancient cheesecake shots as well...Karen Ryan at the beach...looking young and pulchritudinous. None of the various men in the photos were Andrew Ryan.

"When was the last time you saw Dee Dee Ryan?"

"See her running lights in that Mercedes all the time, don't I?"

"When did you see her last?"

"Can't remember."

"Try."

Karen took a swill of her beer. "Cutie pie...what is it you think you're going to get here? You think I hang out at the same beach club with my ex-husband's trophy wife? That maybe us girls decided to take a swim together? That maybe I grabbed those fake bazooms and pulled her under?"

"When did you last see Dee Dee Ryan?" Joe repeated.

"Tuesday last week."

"Where?"

"Kellogg's grocery."

"Did you speak to her?"

"Hardly."

"Did she see you?"

"Looked me right in the eye."

"And?" Joe pressed.

"Put a box of Atkins bars in her handbag and walked out without paying."

"Was anyone with her?"

"Someone under one of those big straw hats with a yellow ribbon around the crown. Could have been that doctor's wife, Miller. I've seen her around

115

town in a hat like that."

"And when was the last time you saw Andrew Ryan?"

"My ever-loving? I see him around, same as her."

"When did you last speak to him?"

"Five years, maybe. He answered one day when I called for Maggie, so I got through that time. Usually, he never picks up, and it's the cow that answers. Mostly she just says Maggie isn't home, or else she puts down the phone and goes off someplace but doesn't hang up. Heard some interesting stuff that way."

"Do you have any contact with the grandmother, Rosemary Ryan?"

"I send her a card on her birthday...Christmas. She sends me school photos and things like that. She knows what's right."

"Did your daughter get along with her stepmother?"

Karen hooted. "You're really fishing, aren't you?"

"Were they friendly?"

"I doubt it. She's been away at school for years though, hasn't she? Just came back."

"Have you spoken to her since she returned?"

"No."

"Mrs. Ryan, can you account for your movements on September 19th?"

"You know, everything was fine until I got sick."

"Sorry?"

"Andrew couldn't deal with that. It was like it was the end of the world for him or something. My god, it was just a simple hormone imbalance for Christ's sake! From the pill! It stopped as soon as I went off it. And for that, he stole my baby!" Karen Ryan shoved the wooden handle and propelled herself upright. "Come with me." She shuffled down the hall to an open bedroom, and he followed to where she stood at the door of a pristine room decorated in pink and filled with a tiny ruffled bed covered with stuffed dolls. A large wooden toy box sat open and overflowing in a far corner. "They're a couple of shits," she said, sweeping her arm from one side of the room to the other. "What else do you need to know?"

"I need to know where you were the evening of September nineteenth this year."

"What?"

"Where you were the evening one of those 'shits' died."

"Oh." Karen Ryan sat on the ruffled bed and clutched one of the stuffed dolls to her chest. "I wouldn't have hurt her, you know." Her eyes closed and her head moved rhythmically, her shoulders and torso following. "They made too much of that."

"Mrs. Ryan, where were you on the nineteenth of this month…Tuesday…the day Dee Dee Ryan died?"

"Eye-eeeee. MMmmmmm." The sound was a low-pitched wail, like a cry of mourning.

"Mrs. Ryan?"

"Eye-eeeee. MMmmmmm."

"Mrs. Ryan!"

"Eye-eeeee."

Shit!

* * *

Joe called the Coldwater Hospital while Karen Ryan remained sitting on the edge of the child's bed, clutching a curly-haired ragdoll and rocking back and forth moaning softly. She stared vaguely at the EMT guys when they arrived, but otherwise did not respond. She did not fight, but she did not move either, and since she must have weighed nearly a hundred sixty pounds, no one tried to lift her. The ambulance driver seemed to know her, and he tried to cajole her into coming with them. Joe left them to it while he searched the apartment.

The tops of the books were coated with a film of dust, as if they had not been handled in a long time. The framed photos were the opposite—not even a fingerprint on the glass. Joe opened the backs of the frames. Some had photos stacked one behind the other. One had a flattened and probably forgotten baggie of marijuana pressed between the photo and the cardboard backing. The ambulance driver persuaded Karen to leave the child's room.

She shuffled through the apartment and out into the hall, staring blankly at the faces of the few neighbors who had gathered outside. Joe shut the door and continued his search. *Cutie-pie, what do you think you're going to get here?* she had asked. Fair question. *I don't know*, he admitted to himself... maybe a bloodstained bathing suit? The refrigerator was empty except for condiments and a depleted twenty-four pack of Miller Lite. The freezer was jammed with frozen TV dinners. Was this what Maggie had to look forward to?

He ignored the first knock and the buzzer bleating. But then the door started to take a pounding, and he yanked it open. Someone with a dyed black ponytail and the name Dwayne embroidered over the pocket of a stained gray shirt, demanded: "Who the hell are you?"

Joe reached into his jacket and produced a badge.

"What did she do?"

"She was taken ill. Are you a friend of hers?"

"Yeah, sure. But what are you doing here? Somebody gets sick you just come in and nose around?"

"If you're a friend of Mrs. Ryan's, I've got a few questions for you." Dwayne remained silent, standing just outside the door. Joe gestured toward a couch covered with newspapers. "Come inside and find a place to sit." The man stepped into the apartment, wary and truculent, and made room for himself among the newspapers on the couch.

"Let's start with how well you know Mrs. Ryan."

"I see her a couple of times a week."

"Are you a boyfriend?"

"Something like that, yeah."

"How long have you known her?"

"A year maybe."

"Did you ever know her to go swimming or boating?"

From the smirk on Dwayne's face, Joe might just as well have said 'wine tasting.'

"Do you know anything about her family?"

"She's got a daughter that she talks about all the time. And an ex out on

118

Wilson Point married to some bitch." Dwayne's eyes opened a bit wider and he looked at Joe. "That's why you're here. The wife died a few days ago."

"You didn't read about it?"

"Karen told me."

"When did she tell you?"

"The day it was in the papers, I guess."

"When was that?"

"Last Wednesday, I think. At the VFW."

"When was the last time you saw her before that?"

"The day before…same place."

"What time?"

"I don't know. I came in at ten. She was there already. We left around one."

"What was she wearing?"

Dwayne paused and closed his eyes. "I don't know," he said finally. "Same shit she always wears."

"What did she say was in the papers?"

"That 'the bitch' drowned or something. Fell out of a boat."

Joe scribbled in his notebook. A phone rang in the kitchen… and rang and rang and rang and rang. He waited for a machine to pick it up or the caller to get discouraged, but neither happened. "Don't leave," he ordered and left the room to answer it. The voice on the other end was as surprising as it was familiar. "Maggie? No, she's not here… I'm afraid she's been taken ill… Coldwater Hospital… Yes… I'll come by and fill you in later."

Dwayne's grin was wrapped around both ears when Joe came back into the room. "Like father like son."

"What?"

"You're one of the Morgan boys, aren't you? The ones whose daddy got his throat slit."

"Be a careful asshole. You were doing good until then."

"I'm just saying," said Dwayne, showing stained irregular teeth. "That your daddy was a lady's man. too. Dicey, though, you go dippin' in the wrong honey pot."

Without thought or hesitation, Joe backhanded the man twice. Then, when the man gasped something that included the word "lawsuit," Joe let both hands fly. He didn't stop until the little bone behind the knuckle of his middle left middle finger went 'ping' and Dwayne lay at his feet, blood seeping from mouth, nose, and one rapidly swelling ear.

Chapter Nineteen

J oe left Dwayne crouched in a fetal position and continued to search the apartment. He copied information from the labels on the plastic vials in the medicine cabinet and dropped one into his pocket. Then he went through drawers, lifted mattresses, and removed the old marijuana stash from behind the beach photo of a young Karen Ryan and some guy in a wet suit. Searching Dwayne's pockets, he removed a folded manila envelope and replaced it with the baggie of grass and a plastic vile of prescription pain killer. Then, while he waited for Dwayne to return to consciousness, he slit the envelope and read through the papers inside. There were four dated document fragments, excerpts from a journal of some sort, all about Maggie.

When Dwayne started to move, Joe got a glass of water from the kitchen. "Sit up," he ordered. The man's eyes lolled from side to side and then came slowly into focus. Joe handed him the glass. "Drink this."

"You hit me."

Joe wrapped Dwayne's hand around the glass and asked, "What's your last name, Dwayne?"

The man on the floor looked as if he wanted to say something rude but not at the risk of another beating. "Burdock," he muttered.

"Occupation?"

"Computer technician." Burdock lifted the glass and sipped. The muscles of his face and torso contracted as if the water had scoured something raw and tender.

"How old are you Burdock?"

"Fifty-three."

Joe scribbled a note. "Getting mighty long in the tooth for this kind of thing."

"What kind of thing?"

"Assault. Burglary."

"Bullshit!"

"I pulled out your pockets while you were napping." Burdock slapped his chest where the envelope had been, reached inside, and found a baggie and a plastic vial.

"These aren't mine." He dropped the baggie and vial on the carpet.

"That's what makes it burglary," said Joe. "The pills make it ten years." Burdock opened his mouth and then shut it. Joe noted the ascendancy of brain over emotion and encouraged it. "Good choice," he said. "There's a chance you might get out of here without bracelets." Joe opened his notebook. "Address?" Burdock gave it. Joe held up the envelope he had taken from Burdock's pocket. "And where did you get this?"

"Off a computer that came into the shop."

"Do you know the name of the customer?"

"Andrew Ryan. Karen's ex."

"Has she seen these?"

"Not yet. She's seen some others."

"Pages from a journal?"

Burdock grunted.

"When?"

"Last Sunday. More on Tuesday."

"And where are those pages now?"

"She has them."

"Do you have copies?"

"On a disk at work." The upper half of Dwayne's face contracted in pain. The bottom half sank in sullenness.

"That's Percodan," said Joe, gesturing toward the plastic prescription bottle on the floor. "Take one, it'll make you feel better." Dwayne opened the bottle and swallowed two pills. "Keep the rest. You'll need them if you want to

122

sleep tonight."

"This isn't right," Dwayne muttered.

"Assault. Burglary. Possession of a controlled substance." Joe held up the envelope of papers. "And this." Burdock looked confused again. "Did you read it?"

"Some," he muttered.

"Did you read any of the other documents you copied for Mrs. Ryan?"

"I read them."

"More about her daughter getting beaten by her stepmother?"

"The stuff I gave her on Tuesday, yeah. The first stuff was just about him not getting laid."

"And what part did Mrs. Ryan seem interested in?"

Burdock nodded as if he finally understood. "The daughter."

"Not happy?"

"Nuclear."

* * *

The doctor on shift at the Coldwater Hospital Emergency Room pocketed his stethoscope, unstrapped the blood pressure cuff from the sheriff's arm, and told him to remove his shirt. "It's my hand," Joe protested.

"I'll get to that. Your neck looks like the day after a mosquito wedding feast. We've had two cases of West Nile in Coldwater this summer. I want to see the rest of you, take some blood ('*so did they*,' thought Joe), and give you a shot of antibiotics. I don't think your constitution is up for another major hit, Sheriff. Not after abrin poisoning last year."

"Who told you...Dr...." he read the name from the plastic tag on the doctor's blue tunic. "Tran?"

"I've read your file, Sheriff. Or rather files. They're rather voluminous for a man of your age. Though perhaps not for someone in your profession."

"And you read all of it just to treat a banged-up hand?"

The doctor shrugged. "Carelessness can have fatal consequences in both our professions, Sheriff."

An hour later, Dr. Tran returned with a set of x-rays and a plastic cast. "You've got a hairline fracture of the third metacarpal. Keep this on for a few days and the fracture will mend itself." He wrote a prescription and gave that to Joe as well. "I don't want to wait for the lab results before starting you on antibiotics. When I see insect bites in the hundreds the odds are that at least one is virulent."

"Conscientious." Joe meant it as a compliment, but he could see that the doctor was troubled. "What?" When Tran remained silent, he pressed. "You got that reluctant bystander witness face, doctor. Whatever it is, spit it out."

The doctor closed his eyes and his face became still, almost as if he were praying. "We had a case in here last week." His voice rasped as if his throat had suddenly lost a great deal of moisture. "An apparent drowning. It caused some disagreement among the staff."

"I'm familiar with the case."

"At the peer panel review, our chief allergist questioned the initial diagnosis of drowning. The deceased had water in her lungs. But not as much as is usually found in a drowning victim. And the throat was almost closed. The allergist asked the panel to consider the possibility that the deceased asphyxiated, rather than drowned. That started a somewhat heated debate. In the end, the panel voted not to amend the initial finding—unnecessary trauma to the family, with no obvious significance, even if an alternative might theoretically be possible."

"And that troubles you?"

"As a medical professional, yes. My colleagues were clearly outside the scope of their competence in choosing to close off further inquiry based on non-medical assumptions."

"How might Mrs. Ryan have asphyxiated?"

Dr. Tran folded his hands. "An allergic reaction. Perhaps to something in the water. There are a number of possibilities."

"And not all of them accidental?"

"I'm afraid not."

Chapter Twenty

Joe left his truck at the top of the driveway and walked down to the Ryan house. An unsmiling Rosemary Ryan observed his progress from the kitchen window and took her time responding to his knock. "Maggie's resting," she announced, opening the door only part way. "She's not having a good day. Please don't upset her."

"May I come in?" asked Joe. Rosemary frowned. Joe pushed on the half-opened door and squeezed past. "Is there someplace we can talk?" With undisguised reluctance, Rosemary led the way to the sun porch at the back of the house. Joe took a seat on a wooden glider facing the water and a distant figure beneath a large straw hat dozing in a redwood lounge at the end of the dock. He began without preamble. "Was your daughter-in-law allergic to anything, Mrs. Ryan?"

Rosemary startled. "Well, of course. Everyone who knew her knew that. What's this all about?"

"What was she allergic to?"

"Please answer my question, Joseph. What is this all about?"

"With respect, Mrs. Ryan, this is my classroom. I ask the questions; you answer them." He looked calmly into the face of his former junior high school teacher and watched it move like data on a sign curve, alternating between caution and offense.

"Don't bully me, Joseph. I'm no Billy Ambler."

"'Take out your textbooks and begin copying from chapter one,'" Joe recited. Rosemary's face rippled. "Bullying is an effective tool when your target knows you can get away with it. I learned that from a very experienced teacher."

"And what are you're trying to get away with today?" Rosemary harrumphed.

"Whatever it takes to get answers to my questions."

"I see."

"I thought you might. Cops and teachers have a lot in common, don't they? They can't afford to lose the upper hand...ever. Lose it once, and maybe you can hang on to the paycheck, but you're finished as an effective professional."

"That's a remarkable insight, Joseph."

"And one that bears no grudges Mrs. Ryan—not that I thought you were worried about that. But I do need to know what your daughter-in-law was allergic to."

"Is it important?"

"It could be."

"Then as far as I know, the answer is restraint, men, pollen and peanuts... if that's helpful."

"Go on."

"I assume this has to do with her drowning? I have a theory about that, though it's not likely to be what you think. Do you want to hear it?"

"Please."

Rosemary looked out the window at the flat, still water, as if giving herself a moment to gather her thoughts. "Well, as you know," she began, "I come back to Coldwater to visit my son for a few weeks every August and September. For the last twelve of those summers, Andrew has been married to Dee Dee. She and I got to know each other well over that time. Lots of girl talk... about her childhood, early marriages, and things that I'm sure she never told anyone else, including her husband. Early on I came to realize that my daughter-in-law was not the Superwoman everyone thought her to be, and that in fact, she was a fragile, damaged human being. Tragically so.

"I'll let you use your imagination for the specifics, but suffice it to say that by the time the young Dee Dee escaped her father's house, she was an emotional cripple, with no use for men except to manipulate them, and no tolerance for any kind of authority or restraint. But she hid her demons well—especially from herself. She was no dumb bunny. She knew she had them. But she couldn't quite face them or even allow herself to acknowledge precisely what they were. Some people find it less painful to be angry than honest.

"The woman my son married was attractive, outgoing, and seemingly keen to help with a difficult, and some might have said impossible, parenting situation. A prayer answered, or so it seemed. But it was an act, and it proved to be an unsustainable one. The woman who drowned a decade later was the worn-out shell of a person who could no longer maintain an impossible pretense—angry, obese, and alienated from everyone who had been attracted to the act but not to the reality. To be fair, I don't think many people could have reformed the Maggie of thirteen years ago—my son in particular—and certainly none had volunteered. But the methods Dee Dee used were not the ones that brought her success in the workplace or that initially attracted the circle of former friends that you saw at her funeral. Her principal tool was the one that I suspect had been used regularly on her: punishment.

"As you've pointed out, Sheriff, punishment is an effective behavior modification tool. But its regular use comes at a price no family can pay and call itself happy. I'm surprised that my son permitted it. His father was a bully, and I know that any kind of abuse sickens him. He's weak in that respect...always hoping things will get better. And poor Dee Dee...she really did love Andrew in her own damaged way. She dealt with Maggie in the only way she knew how, even though I'm sure she knew it was wrong.

"It takes passion and energy to be a tyrant, Sheriff. You can't ever let your guard down or care what your subjects think of you. Dee Dee didn't have that kind of strength, and she cared very much about what people thought of her. Maggie eventually conformed, under duress... like a prisoner waiting for a chance to escape. Andrew simply withdrew, ashamed of his own weakness I suppose. In recent years, he and Dee Dee could hardly stand to be in the same room with each other. Which is sad when you think of it—discomfort in another's presence being the same sure sign of both the beginning and end of a romance."

Mrs. Ryan was on a roll. Joe let her run.

"Dee Dee was through as an effective professional to use your analogy, though my peace-at-any-price son kept her on the payroll. Once she realized her demotion, my daughter-in-law let herself go, surrendering to the comforts of overeating and minor illnesses. A few years ago she started having to carry an inhaler, then refused to stay away from the things that caused her to need it. She seemed committed to a slow, self-inflicted decline. Then suddenly, a few months ago, she began a strenuous exercise program, not as any reasonable person would, slowly and, given her weight, under a doctor's supervision. She did it unsupervised and unrestrained. Swimming by herself across Wilson Cove, at night, heedless of the cold, the boats, and the realities of an aging, overweight, and out-of-shape body. I don't know what new demons drove her to change course from slow decline to headlong rush for the exit. But she was clearly in some sort of hurry, and to hell with anyone who might suggest a more sensible approach. It was almost as if she was swimming away from the unhappy mess she had created here…or trying to bring it to a rapid end, one way or the other. That she got herself killed in the process might not have been her preferred outcome. But it was a foreseeable one. The only thing that surprises me, is that it took all summer."

* * *

Joe left Rosemary Ryan repeating her warning about Maggie's fragile condition and made his way to the dock. A thick September air lay over the shoreline, humid and breathless. The glare off the water was intense. He found Maggie stretched out on the same deck chair, and in the same overdressed outfit as on his last visit: long sleeve white shirt, skinny jeans, and wide-brimmed straw hat.

"Sister Judith sent me," he said, seating himself in a weathered Adirondack chair beside her.

Maggie moved her face to one side and lifted the brim of her straw hat.

"Ha! A Morgan! I haven't seen one of those lately."

"The other one found a gray hair in his comb last week. He's still recovering."

"Well, so am I. And you can tell that to Sister Judith…if that's really why you came."

Joe shaded his eyes and spoke to the upturned face. "I'm here to ask some questions about your stepmother."

Maggie reached for a colored beach towel and wrapped it around her shoulders. "I'm not going to like this, am I?"

"Probably not." Joe opened his notebook and plowed ahead. "Was your stepmother allergic to anything?"

"Earth, air, fire, and water."

"Any specific types?"

"Grass, pollen, strawberries, dairy, cat hair…. It was a long list, and it got longer every year. Why?"

"Did she have any close friends?"

"Lots."

"Any male friends?"

Maggie hesitated. "Admirers. I wouldn't call them anything more than that."

"Did your stepmother socialize with anyone from the Fort, or know anyone there?"

"Dee Dee wouldn't have been caught dead with anyone who drove anything cheaper than a Lexus. Her friends were almost exclusively other rich women."

"And the ones that weren't?"

"'Noblesse oblige.' She'd give my old clothes to the cleaning lady, help her friend's *au pair* get a green card, that sort of thing. She usually wound up firing them. But before that, they treated her like Eva Peron."

"Were any of these women married to soldiers?"

"Could have been. But I wouldn't know any of the recent ones."

Joe flipped a page in his notebook. "How did your father and stepmother get along?"

Maggie winced. "Joe...is this necessary?"

He nodded.

"I don't have anyone else to compare them with."

"Parents of your friends?"

"Not many of them fight in front of their children's playmates."

"How did you and your stepmother get along?"

"Joe! I was in the hospital when she drowned. Why are you asking all this? What could it possibly matter?"

"I understand that she used to hit you," Joe pressed. "Did you ever hit her back?"

Maggie stood and faced him. Her body and hands shook. "Grandmother was right. You are not a nice man."

"Did your stepmother cheat on your father...or vice-versa?"

"Go to hell!"

Chapter Twenty-One

Karen sat in a folding chair behind a cafeteria-style table and listened to her lawyer argue that she was no longer a 'danger to herself or others.' The hearing was a formality. She had not hit anyone or cut herself, and she had pretended to take all the medications that they forced on her. If the hospital did not let her out, Legal Aid would sue them. She would sign papers promising not to sue and acknowledge that she was leaving the facility 'against medical advice.' A promise that her lawyer reminded the panel was unenforceable if she was, as they believed, impaired. She gazed at her attorney's curly dark hair and pale, smooth skin. He was maybe thirty. While they were preparing for the hearing, Karen told him he was cute. But he seemed not to hear. He was shy. Not like the last one. But she couldn't use that one again unless she paid his bill.

Karen couldn't remember much of what had brought her to the psychiatric facility this time. Usually, there was some sort of build-up over a period of weeks, and then only after she had been off her meds for a while. This one came on all of a sudden, which had not happened in a long time. She wasn't sure what day it was. But she remembered that Dwayne was supposed to tell her something about Maggie. If it were not for that, she would have stayed in the hospital for some R&R. Why not? The food was good and they had decent cable. She had left a message on Dwayne's machine before the hearing to tell him to meet her at the VFW.

The hearing took three hours, most of which she didn't listen to. When it was over she asked the young lawyer to give her a ride downtown. He seemed reluctant and she told him again that he was cute. She felt calm and a bit lightheaded. That was the Prozac. She had held the Thorazine under her tongue and spit it out as soon as no one was looking. It made her feel fuzzy. There was nothing wrong with her mind. They had no right to just shut it off like that. She put her hand on the lawyer's thigh as they drove through the hospital gate and she was pleased when he didn't push it away.

* * *

Burdock was a no show. A few beers helped Karen remember what it was he was supposed to show her. That sick sow had beaten Maggie! And that spineless loser had let her! She could kill them both.

A lonesome reservist sitting at the bar watched Karen's reflection in the mirror behind the bottles—a woman alone, waving an empty long neck and talking loudly to herself. Usually, you had to drink straight through to closing time to see something like that. Karen looked up and caught the soldier staring at her in the mirror. She got up from the booth and walked steadily toward the empty stool beside him. "Buy you a drink?" he asked.

"Let's get out of here," she said bluntly.

"I'm game."

"What's your name?"

"Roger."

"Okay, Roger-dodger. Let's party."

Roger wanted to start partying right there in the parking lot, but Karen said that she knew a nice spot just outside of town. She gave him directions. Up the lake road, over East Hill, and then out Route 13 past the farms and state forest that filled the empty space between Coldwater and its neighbor to the north. "You live out here?" Roger asked.

"Nope."

"Not a yakker, huh? "I like that." He took Karen's hand and placed it in his lap. She left it there but told him to watch the road. A few minutes later she told him to turn onto an unpaved farm road that ran between fields of standing corn and ended in a fallow lot where an ancient trailer sat on a foundation of cement block. Two rusting Crown Victorias sat next to the trailer, one on blocks and missing its doors and hood, the other more or less whole. No light came from inside the trailer, only the sound of an open aluminum door banging gently against its metal skin.

"This it?" asked Roger doubtfully.

"Belongs to a friend of mine."

"Doesn't look like your friend's at home."

"Car's there." Karen pointed out. "Maybe he's just passed out."

Roger heard the 'he' and started to wonder whether his new friend meant the same thing as he did by 'party.' "Why don't we just party here?" he said reaching for her shirt button.

"Don't you want a drink?"

"Later."

Karen reached for the door handle. "I want one now." She pushed the door and stumbled out of the car and onto dew slick grass. Moonlight covered the rounded top of the metal trailer, its opened door banging arrhythmically in the convection of moist air rising from the cooling fields. Karen slipped on the wet grass and went down heavily. The soldier watched through a windshield fogged from his breath. 'This isn't worth it,' he muttered to himself, turning the key to restart the engine. Karen hoisted herself up and staggered to the trailer. At the steps, she turned around and made an impatient 'come-on-will-you!' gesture toward the car. Roger turned on the headlights and defogger, and then put the car in gear. Through the clearing windshield, he could see clearly into the open trailer where a motionless body lay in a pool of blood just inside the banging metal door, surrounded by pulled-out drawers, scattered papers, and overturned furniture.

Chapter Twenty-Two

Rosemary Ryan was dummy so she left the table and went out to the sun porch to look at the stars and have a cigarette. She was smoking again, which she did not care to do in front of the others. Andrew had graciously offered to chauffeur her friends to and from the Senior Center for a girls' night of cards. He seemed to have shed ten years in the past ten days. All Rosemary's women friends had complimented him on how well he was holding up. Maggie seemed a lot steadier too. It was just Rosemary, the born worrier, who looked like she'd been partying with Mick Jagger. The interview with her former pupil had started it. She couldn't sleep. Joseph Morgan was going to be the "R" in relentless until he got what he was looking for.

When the hand was over, one of the ladies joined her on the porch. "We're taking a break," she said. "Barbara has to give herself a shot."

"Getting old is depressing."

"Beats the alternative."

"Sometimes I wonder," said Rosemary.

Mary Morgan sat beside her old friend and put her hand on her forearm. "This has been a hard summer for you. And I know my son's not making it any easier."

"He's doing his job," said Rosemary graciously.

"Well the sooner he finishes, the better. He's got another dead body to deal with now. And that one's no accident."

Rosemary could sense that her friend was dying to talk about the man found beaten to death in his trailer, and the coincidence of Karen Ryan being the one who found him. But Rosemary didn't feel like obliging. According to the newspaper, Karen Ryan and some soldier from Fort Drum had discovered the man while he was still alive, but the hospital ambulance didn't get there in time to save him. Rosemary could sense that there was going to be more trouble. How could there not be?

"Dee Dee's drowning was an accident," Mary probed. "A fatal beating's another thing."

Rosemary nodded and said "Hmm."

"It's a good thing Karen had that soldier with her."

"Hmm."

"Well, he was the boyfriend or something. The man who died. It's a good thing she wasn't alone when she found him."

"I missed that," said Rosemary, being drawn in despite her intention not to. "That wasn't in the paper."

"And she is a mental patient," added Mary. "Some of them get violent."

Rosemary turned to her old friend. "I understand why you don't like Karen...I sympathize entirely. I can still get pretty angry with her myself when I think about everything that happened. But I doubt she's capable of killing anyone. If she were, she would have surely taken a crack at my son Andrew before now."

Mary looked disappointed.

Rosemary put a hand on her friend's arm. "I hope my family can avoid being connected to more tragedy, Mary. My granddaughter isn't well enough to handle that. Whatever you can do to discourage silly rumors...well, I'd be grateful."

* * *

Joe spotted Dee Dee Ryan's Mercedes parked in the shade of a Japanese maple facing the entrance to the Coldwater Psychiatric hospital. He waved to the woman slouched behind the wheel and hidden behind a pair of designer sunglasses...black hair, porcelain skin, and a wide-brimmed straw hat. He parked the Silverado in a tow-away zone and went inside to break some more rules.

Karen Ryan had voluntarily recommitted herself to the Psychiatric Center, which was a prudent move. Some of his druggie sources liked to check themselves in when things got too uncomfortable on the outside—which was prudent in their world as well. Only prudence wasn't a symptom of mental illness as far as Joe knew.

Nurse Judy Duffy greeted Joe with a bear hug like a vise grip. Six foot two of hard muscle, soft chest, and a face like Jaws, her oft-proclaimed fantasy was to lure the Coldwater sheriff into the padded discipline room and have her way with him. "Got an empty bed on B Wing today," she said, pressing iron fingers into soft flesh for emphasis. "How about it handsome?"

Joe could feel his sciatic nerve trying to escape into the muscles of his backside. "Love to Judy," he grimaced. "Why don't you start without me, and I'll stop by when I'm through with Mrs. Ryan."

Nurse Duffy released her grip. "Oh her!"

"She behaving herself?"

"If she knew about the bed in B Wing, she'd have one of those teenage coke heads in there right now."

"Thorazine not slowing her down?"

"Only when she takes it… which is never for long.

"How is she now?"

"Stressed, but not psychotic," say her doctors. You can talk to her. But I wouldn't believe anything she says."

"You don't like her much."

"She's not a girl's girl, Sheriff. No meeting you halfway. And she's not going to allow anything we say or do to get through—unless she can twist it to support her line that there's really nothing wrong with her. She's frustrating as hell." Nurse Duffy removed her hands from the sheriff's hips. "But then nobody who comes here is easy."

Joe found Karen Ryan shooting pool in the rec room, watched over by a middle-aged male nurse. Joe told him that Nurse Duffy wanted to see him and that he would stay with the patient until somebody returned. Karen leaned over the felt table and worked a cue stick through her closed palm, her half-open shirt framing an across-the-table shot on the eight ball to the corner pocket. She'd lost weight after a few weeks away from her regular vices. None where it did any harm. The male nurse gave Joe a wink and left the room.

"Andrew killed both of them," said Karen, barely looking up from the shot.

"Could be," said Joe. "Problem is how and why."

"Beat the shit out of him, is how!" she said, sarcastically. "Drowned the other one."

"Need more than what's in the newspapers."

Karen withdrew the cue through the circle of her thumb and forefinger. "Come with mama." She returned the stick to the rack. "Let's see if I've got what you need."

Karen led Joe down the hall toward the patient rooms. "Met some acquaintances of yours in here," she said, making conversation. "Sounds like you've been having some trouble lately."

"I like to think of it as job security," said Joe.

Karen's room was small and tidy, like a dorm room at a girls school…a single bed, desk, chair, and table lamp…a telling contrast to the unkempt apartment she called home. Opening a backpack that hung from the bedpost, she withdrew three unlabeled computer disks. "Dwayne got these from Andrew's laptop. It's all business stuff from his bank. I can't understand it, but it's why Andrew killed him."

"Want to explain that?"

"Look, Sheriff, the entire time I was married to Andrew Ryan, he could barely keep a job and pay the bills. Now, look at him! He's worth a gazillion dollars. The Andrew I knew never had the ambition to make any kind of money, much less the talent to do it. So he either lucked onto something or he stole it. Dwayne said there was something on these disks about what Andrew is doing with the bank. I just wouldn't know what to look for."

"Did your ex-husband know that Mr. Burdock had copied files from his computer?"

"Well he's dead isn't he?"

Joe took a deep breath. "Mr. Burdock said something about a journal, too."

Karen glared at him. "That's private," she snapped.

"And not very flattering to your ex-husband or his wife."

"Andrew is a violent man, Sheriff, and mean as a pig. He once locked me in a room with a snake. Did you know that? They poisoned Maggie against me… with lies… they got a court order so I couldn't go near her school… I never saw her in a school play, or a field hockey game. I didn't even get to see her graduation! Like what was I going to do… fart or something? They did it just to be mean."

"So where are the rest of the records Burdock took off Mr. Ryan's computer?"

"I told you. They're private."

Joe shook his head with exaggerated slowness. "I got two dead people, Mrs. Ryan. If you're right about what's on these," he held up the disks, "it won't do any good if I don't have the rest. It's too easy to add things… change things, cut things out. I'm going to have to have them all checked by an expert. None of it's any good if anything's been added or there's anything missing."

Karen stood still for a long time before opening the backpack and removing two more disks. "I'm going to want these back. They're mine." She put the disks in Joe's hand and stood close.

"Ahem!" Nurse Duffy filled the door, arms folded across her chest. "Patients are not allowed on this corridor during recreation period, Mrs. Ryan! And visitors are not permitted on this corridor at all, Sheriff."

"Flash her your badge, handsome."

"Mrs. Ryan is helping me with my inquiries," Joe explained.

"In her bedroom?"

"Some inquiries require privacy."

"Take the Sheriff to the visitors' room," Nurse Duffy ordered. "And help him with 'his inquiries' there."

Karen gave Joe a soulful look. "Tough guy," she muttered.

Chapter Twenty-Three

*I*t would start to get cold soon. Then the first snow would arrive. Five months a year, the lake was the heart-center of town. But from November on, only the hearty ice-fishermen ventured near its frozen waters, while the rest of the town retreated to their homes and bars to hibernate until Spring.

We all make mistakes...Dee Dee especially. But the harm is seldom confined to the maker, and too often the impact endures. Benefits, if any, are minor and rare.

Dee Dee had so much good in her, even if the train wreck to come was always visible. Her death was not necessary. But the good of it could be seen already. I didn't choose. It just happened.

* * *

Joe agreed to meet the Army investigator at the Coldwater VFW. Asked how they were supposed to recognize each other, Sergeant Boyd said that he had been told that the Sheriff looked like his father. That would be enough.

The man who stepped away from the bar appeared to be in his late thirties, about five foot eight, one hundred sixty pounds, whitewall haircut starting to gray. He held out his hand, "Gene Boyd," he said. "Fort Drum CID." He suggested they move to a booth. "We have a lot to talk about."

Joe suggested that Sergeant Boyd produce identification. "You may know me, Sergeant, but I don't know you from Adam." Boyd handed Joe a laminated card the size of a driver's license and Joe read it aloud, 'J.e.n.o.t' "Army can't spell Gene?"

"It's the French spelling, Sheriff. My family's from Niagara Falls."

139

"Thought that was still ours." Joe finished reading the military-speak on the card and made note of the six-letter acronym followed by the parenthetical (Reserves). "So what do you do when you're not in the Army, Gene?"

"Security at the Oswego nuclear power plant."

"And they pulled you away from that to do what?"

"Control pilferage at Fort Drum."

"We must be losing some pretty lethal stuff if they're pulling guards off a nuke plant."

"They're not losing anything on my watch."

Joe nodded. "Okay Gene, this is your meeting. What did I find that got stolen on somebody else's watch that maybe I should be interested in?"

Sergeant Boyd leaned forward and folded his hands on top of the plank table. "From the markings and your description, I'd say that you came across a 1980's era transport case for a shoulder-fired missile." He waited for Joe's reaction.

"Did you guys use the islands for target practice or something back then? Your own little Vieques?"

"You would have heard about it if we did. But a lot of stuff 'went missing' from the Fort in the 1980s. My colleagues back then weren't supposed to ask too many questions, because it was our guys taking it and sending it to the Mujaheddin fighting the Soviets in Afghanistan."

"So how did this trunk get on Pocket Island? And who do you figure decided to take it off now?"

"From what I understand, a couple of these islands were used as staging points for the transfer of the ordinance being sent clandestinely to the Afghanis. Basically, our guys would take the stuff out there and wait until somebody came down the lake from Canada to pick it up. Someone must have left a transport case behind… maybe threw some bushes over it or something. Then someone else wandering out there this summer may have found it. Interesting souvenir, but I doubt there was any ordnance inside. Our guys might have ditched a trunk to save room on a boat or something. But trust me, they would never have left a missile behind. And even if they did, it wouldn't work after all these years. Just in case, though, I've been asked to make sure there isn't anything else on that island that might have been accidentally left behind."

Joe pressed. "Are you sure this thing that probably isn't there, definitely wouldn't work after all these years? I've got rifles at home more than a hundred years old. They work just fine."

"The older model stinger missiles were powered by lithium batteries and gas, and the later ones some sort of silicon chip that degrades after a few years."

"Then I shouldn't worry about some kid picking up something that'll blow him to kingdom come?" Joe looked disbelievingly at the Army investigator.

"As I said. It's doubtful anything is there. And if there is, it won't work."

"Fine. Then I won't worry. If it's okay with the owner, I'll take you out there tomorrow."

"If it's okay with your brother," said the sergeant, "I'd prefer to go alone."

Joe leaned back in the booth and crossed his arms across his chest. "Okay, *Jenot*. How does a half-Canadian army reservist know me, my brother, and our dad? You some sort of long-lost relative?"

"You were in the papers a few times last fall, Sheriff. So was your brother."

"And how do you know MadDog?"

"Sorry?"

"Our father. You said over the phone that you'd heard that I looked like him and that's how you'd know me."

It was Sgt. Boyd's turn to pause before responding. "I worked with him briefly when I was in the regular army stationed at the Fort."

"How brief?"

"A single day."

"He must have made quite an impression. What did you work on?"

"This, I think."

Joe lifted his chin and took a deep breath. "I'm not going to like this, am I?"

Boyd shook his head. "Like I said, I was regular Army then. Same job, pretty much. Figure out who's stealing what from the Fort, and if they're not officers, stop them. The problem is everything that goes missing in the Army is "stolen" and you spend a lot of time looking for the colonel's cat. I was getting kind of fed up with that part of it and I put in for a transfer. I guess that pissed somebody off, because the next thing I knew, instead of a transfer I got this hot potato about stolen stinger missiles. I got orders to contact local law enforcement and figure out how the stuff was getting off the base and where it was going to. That's how I met your father."

"For one day, you said."

"That's right. I called him up and met him at some diner in town."

Joe nodded. "Trudy's. That's where he hung out."

"Biggest son-of-a bitch I've ever seen. Hands the size of dinner plates. That's why I figured I wouldn't have any problem recognizing you… if you looked like him. You do a little, just not quite that size.

"Anyway, I told him what we had, which wasn't much. He listened, didn't say much, paid for my lunch, and then told me to forget it. He said that I was about four years too late. That whatever was 'missing' had been missing for a long time and was long gone, and that somebody had sent me on a wild goose chase. Which was pretty much what I had suspected in the first place. This was Iraq I, mind you. The Soviet occupation of Afghanistan had been over for a couple of years. Somebody was just yanking my chain… or, finishing up old paperwork. 'Theft investigated. No recovery.'"

"So then what?"

"So a couple of days after our meeting, I read about him getting killed. I'm sorry. And I figured that maybe there were some genuine badasses in this town and that maybe I should go back to looking for the colonel's cat and mind my own business."

"So you never followed up?"

Boyd shook his head. "The way he got killed didn't look like Army business. But it did look like something the Fort wasn't going to want me to get mixed up in. I figured your dad was right…the missile thing was just someone yanking my chain because I bitched too much. Him getting killed put an end to the coordination with local law enforcement angle. So I just went back to looking for 'stolen' cats until my tour was up."

142

"So what are you doing here…now?"

"Someone who identified himself as Sheriff Morgan from Coldwater called the Fort last week with some numbers that match a stinger missile listed as 'stolen' about fifteen years ago. I got orders to make sure it got stolen to the right place."

"Who's ordering you?"

"The U.S. Army, Sheriff. That's all I can tell you…and frankly, that's all I know."

Chapter Twenty-Four

Tom put the computer disks that Joe had gotten from Karen Ryan back into their cardboard wallets and went outside to clear his mind. He had been staying in Joe's cabin for the past few days trying to decide what to do next—with Pocket Island and the charred shell of a Frank Lloyd Wright house, with the insurance company, the Taliesin people, the attractive but troubled young woman who Fr. Gauss had asked him to befriend but not romance, the now or never offer from his former law firm to return to a career that he may have walked away from too soon, his promise to help Joe's wife find a way to reunite her broken family and, most troubling, his mother's and brother's inexplicable undermining of that goal.

Little brother's mountain lair was a quiet place to sort the pieces, hike in the woods and think. A three thousand square foot hunting lodge bordered by several thousands of acres of state forest, no neighbors, and plenty of space to wander inside your own head. Tom had once questioned Joe about how he had managed to pay for his Lincoln Log fiefdom and all the sophisticated electronics that protected it while the owner was out writing parking tickets, or whatever small-town cops did to earn their keep. The feds had asked the same question when Joe failed to welcome their investigation of a poxed corpse found floating in Coldwater Lake that an autopsy revealed to be riddled with a toxin more deadly than anthrax. But when Joe delivered the alleged terrorist, wrapped literally in a blanket, they stopped asking. A small-town cop who pads his pension as opportunity permits is no threat to national security, and Homeland Security, et. al. were grateful for Joe's quiet help.

Tom had not pursued that question either, as he assumed the money came from the same source as the cash found by Morini's funeral home in the lining of the suit their sheriff father was buried in. Tom had asked directly only once because he was angry and there was a woman involved. But he asked himself now, as adult siblings sometimes do, what he really knew about his brother.

That he lived his job was obvious. There was no serious crime in Coldwater despite its long history of casual cross border commerce with its neighbor to the north—runaway slaves during the 19th century, booze during Prohibition, marijuana in the '60s and '70s, cocaine in the '80s, and now...most likely a bit of everything, including discount pharmaceuticals for snow belt seniors. Joe had once reminded Tom that he was not the DEA or the INS and that his job was simply to keep Coldwater safe. He looked upon the local criminal class as weeds in his garden and dutifully uprooted the violent and ambitious. The rest he left alone unless they got out of hand. That casual law enforcement philosophy might sound lazy or even suspicious to some, he'd said. But he challenged Tom to consider what would happen if he tried to take local law enforcement to another level. Coldwater was never going to be big enough to afford more than one full-time cop, with the occasional part-time deputy and dispatcher. If he locked up everyone who deserved it, what came along to take their place might not be as easy to keep in line as the Dooleys, the Cashins, and the Hellers. He didn't need to remind Tom of what happened to their father the year he decided to jail nearly the entire motley crew of local bad boys. A hard bunch from across the lake wasted no time swooping in to take their place, and Coldwater's only cop was dead within a month.

Aside from the bio-terrorist threat the year before, it had been a long time since Coldwater had had any serious, or even non-indigenous, lawbreakers. Tom wondered if that told him anything he didn't already know about his brother. That he was smarter than their father was obvious. That he worked harder and seemed to enjoy it more was also clear. The apparent gap between Joe's assets and means was visible only in the scale of this woodsman's hideaway. Even that hadn't changed in the five years since its construction, which suggested to Tom, if not financial discipline, then perhaps a one-time windfall rather than a corrupt annuity. Joe had never expressed a desire for a lifestyle beyond what he already enjoyed. Maybe he got lucky once, figured he deserved it, and left it at that.

An acrobatic red-tailed hawk circled overhead above the field that sloped toward the lake from the back of Joe's cabin. Tom watched it hunt for a while before turning his thoughts to the present. It had taken him a full day to read through the computer files that Joe had gotten from Karen Ryan and her boyfriend, Burdock. Reading them had made Tom feel like a voyeur in more ways than he could describe. The journal fragments were beyond depressing. How could a man like Andrew Ryan be so effective in business and so ineffective at home? How could he wallow in indecision year after year, but daily organize his finances as if he were joining the witness protection program?

Joe had asked Tom to check the disks for anything that might flag financial trouble. Most of the spreadsheets were personal rather than bank-related—daily reconciliation of assets minus liabilities, after-tax, divided by two. Typical divorce planning. The only connection between the company and personal financials was a loan from the bank collateralized by the stock in it that Ryan owned. The personal balance sheet showed that the value of the bank stock had fallen thirty percent over the past six months, while the investment of the loan proceeds had lost almost half. The bank's most recent balance sheet was three months old and had no similar adjustments. If the figures on the personal financial statement were accurate, Ryan's loan from the bank was underwater and the bank itself worth a lot less than it had been when he took out the loan.

But the discrepancy between the personal and corporate records wasn't unlawful. Accounting rules don't require a private bank to make after-tax, three-places-to-the-right-of-the-decimal-point-in-case-I-get-divorced-tomorrow updates to its balance sheet. And though the personal and corporate documents painted two different pictures of Andrew Ryan's financial health, it was obvious which one was the more accurate. Individuals and businesses that get out over their financial skis often have no idea how they got that way. But Andrew Ryan had a daily fix on every step and every cent.

So what does that tell you, Tommy?

The answer, whatever it might have been, was interrupted by an onslaught of sound and light to rival a Rolling Stones concert. The panel of bubble lights above the sliding porch door strobed a paralyzing crimson, and 200 decibels of Ah-OOGA! Ah-OOGA! blasted from twin speakers mounted to the wall above Tom's ear. Metal boxes below the eves swiveled toward the driveway and locked onto a black Silverado grinding slowly up the gravel driveway on chest-high oversized tires. Tom punched a series of letters and numbers into the security pad beside the door and waited for the noise and lights to fade. Master was home.

A few days as his brother's house guest had yet to acclimate Tom to the owner's habit of nightly testing his home security system by breaking into it. "No neighbors, no complaints," Joe had explained. "I don't see a lot of light and hear a lot of noise, I don't get out of the truck. And I don't walk into some wacko with a chainsaw when I open the front door." But he had given Tom the code to turn off the pyrotechnics so that Tom wouldn't have to hold his hands over his ears until Master had taken off his galoshes.

While Joe went through his end of the day routine, stowing his gun in a drawer next to the desktop computer and fast-forwarding through the day's videotapes connected to the motion-triggered outdoor cameras, Tom decided it was time to have the conversation that could not be put off any longer: about Bonnie and the kids coming back to Coldwater and the piece of family theater at their mother's condo which he had come to think of as *Mary's Ambush*. The longer they avoided the subject, the more awkward it was to share space and meals. But all Tom could think of to say was, 'You're being an ass, brother, and you can tell that to Benedict Arnold.'

Part of Tom wondered, too, whether he had the right to say or demand anything. Could he reasonably assert the moral high ground in a space where he had no experience? Wasn't that hubris? I'm smarter than you, so listen up while pearls of wisdom fall from my mouth and provide timely guidance to the lost and confused Morgan clan? If you don't know what to say, Tommy, shouldn't that tell you something?

Joe seemed untroubled by these or any other, concerns. He showed no sign of discomfort, unless swagger and provocation were some kind of misdirection. He'd said his piece and set his terms. Whatever would be, would be. Tom didn't understand that attitude or the values it reflected, any more than he'd understood their father's. But silence and inaction didn't seem right. The log hideaway above Coldwater Lake had the feel of a villa on the slopes of Pompeii just before the volcano blew.

Joe produced a bottle of wine from the kitchen, declaring its provenance to be "Chateau Hassad," referring to the former owner of Pocket Island who had tried to kill Tom and poison half the town of Coldwater less than a year ago. "Got the whole cellar for you."

As far as Tom knew, the former biochemistry professor who had persuaded a researcher at a Coldwater biotechnology lab to help him pass vials, powders, and Petri dishes to other 'scientists', was still enjoying the hospitality of Homeland Security and a new career of helping them with their global inquiries. The wine cellar of the Frank Lloyd Wright house had been bare to the walls when Tom purchased the house and island out of foreclosure. He assumed the feds had taken all the contents and were still "testing" it all, one way or the other.

"How'd you sneak a cellar of wine past the FBI?"

"The Dooleys did," said Joe. "While Mickey and I were bringing in Professor Hassad, Kevin was out there stripping the place bare.

"In a snowstorm?"

"Yep. I confiscated most of the good stuff: twenty cases of wine, a bunch of rugs, and paintings. If the Dooley's had a bigger boat, you wouldn't have lost so much in the fire. What's left is in storage. I was going to surprise you when you finished fixing the place up."

"I didn't know I was going to buy the house until a few months ago."

"That's when I made the Dooley's give back what they hadn't already sold." Joe uncorked the bottle and filled their glasses. "Before that, it was just stuff they took from some psycho megalomaniac who tried to poison half the

East Coast. I thought they were being kind of patriotic actually." He lifted his glass and examined the contents. "This is safe to drink, right?"

Tom shrugged. "Hassad had some pretty nasty stuff in that cellar. But if Kevin and Mickey have already cracked a bottle or two, I guess it's safe."

Joe looked thoughtfully at the amber liquid and took the glasses and bottle from the table, returning with two cans of Genesee Lite. "I don't think the Dooleys are wine drinkers."

Over beer and pasta, Joe briefed Tom about Sergeant Boyd and the provenance of the metal trunk that had survived a fifteen-year burial on Pocket Island only to be cremated on the eve of its disinterment. The subject of Bonnie, the kids, and Mary the Betrayer didn't come up.

"The story's bullshit," Joe concluded, producing a manila envelope and handing it to Tom. "I pulled that off the internet this afternoon: everything you always wanted to know about stinger missiles. Sergeant Boyd says they wouldn't work after all this time. But according to this, there are places that will fix them for a price."

Tom listened, but made no move to take the envelope. "This sergeant says he met Dad just once, the week before he got killed...? That he told Dad about ordnance gone missing from the Fort, and that Dad told him he was too late?"

"That's what he said."

"But you don't believe him."

"I don't think he ever met MadDog. Laid some bullshit on me about him having hands the size of dinner plates. That computer geek Burdock was hinting around that he knew the old man, too. Must be something in the air."

"When did you meet Burdock?"

"When I went to Karen Ryan's apartment to find out if she could remember where she was the night her replacement drowned. She threw some kind of fit while I was there. Burdock arrived after the ambulance took her away. He was a real wise ass."

"Is that why he got dead?"

Joe rubbed his left thumb over the swollen middle knuckle of his opposite hand. "All this bullshit about MadDog, all of a sudden. Burdock didn't get that from those journal fragments. I read them. The guy was a computer dumpster diver, poking through the machines that came through his shop. But he might have picked up something from another computer that came in for repair."

"What did he say about Dad?"

"Same old crap about him being a swordsman."

Tom's gaze returned to his brother's hands. "You hit something?"

Joe smirked. "Autopsy says his skull was crushed, Tommy. Not even MadDog could hit that hard."

Tom recalled the time Joe had come to his rescue in a high school fight, where the boy who was having the better of Tom until Joe arrived got taken away in an ambulance. He wondered if his little brother's capacity for spontaneous violence had acquired any restraint as he'd gotten older – and bigger. "Who else did you ask for an alibi for the time of Mrs. Ryan's death?"

"The husband, the daughter, the grandmother, and the ex—so far. I've got a couple of friends of the deceased lined up for tomorrow."

"And how about Burdock? Who has an alibi for the time somebody crushed his head in?"

"The guy who was with Karen Ryan when she found him is coming in day after tomorrow."

Tom leaned back in his chair. "So you've got a murder where you're not doing anything until the end of the week, and an accidental drowning where you're on your way to interviewing half the town?"

"That's what I like about my job, Tommy. I get to set my own priorities."

"Which says that you either know who killed Burdock already, since you're not doing much about it, or that you don't care."

Joe shrugged. "There's only one of me Tommy. I got two dead people, a torched house, a blown-up patrol car, Big Foot, and some spook from the Fort making up stories about our snuffed father. I could use some help."

"What happened to the two new deputies the town said you could hire?"

"Town Council's dragging its feet. Bonnie says the one cop thing is permanent and I'm the only one who doesn't know it. That's why she left." Tom's harrumphed and Joe pretended not to hear. "All hell is about to break loose, Tommy. I can feel it. The town will come around on more help. Part-time anyway. But in the meantime, I'm swamped."

"No."

"Even though that computer geek said it was Maggie who killed her stepmother."

"She was in the hospital, Joe."

"Is that right?" Joe took a sip of his Genesee. "I can't keep track. She might have whacked Burdock though. I might have to bring her in."

Joe's tone had shifted from bantering to bullying in an easy nanosecond and that helped Tom make up his mind. "I'm going back to New York."

Joe wrapped his fist around the Genesee can and raised it a few inches off the table. "So screw the love life? Forget someone burned you out of your house, shot at your baby brother? Fools all of a sudden dropping hints that they know what really happened to MadDog? Bonnie and the kids coming back, if the lawyers haven't changed her mind." Joe looked at Tom and swallowed a mouthful of beer. "You'd be leaving behind a shit-load of unfinished business, brother. That tends to mess with people's heads."

Don't go there. Tom spoke in a steady, emotionless voice. "The law firm's offer is 'take it or leave it now.' The school project is a pile of ashes. Literally. It will take serious fundraising and politicking to get it going again, if it's still doable. The project my firm wants me to take on is a chance to raise serious money while the other pieces sort themselves out. I can't stay here and do nothing. And to be honest, your 'I'm the boss around here' act is exhausting my patience."

Joe crushed the empty can and threw it over his shoulder in the direction of the kitchen sink. "Man, you can polish a turd, Tommy. You've made your pile. If you need to add to it, fine. But wait a month. Put that puzzle cracker of yours to work on something that matters."

"Like how a middle-aged, overweight asthmatic who decided to swim across Wilson Cove in the dark, in fifty-four-degree water, might have gotten herself in trouble?"

"It doesn't pass the smell test."

"It doesn't smell at all, Joe. I spent time in that water a little while ago. Remember? It damned near killed me. And I've got a pretty good ticker."

"She was wearing a wet suit, Tommy. And we've both read the journals."

"No, brother."

"What's in those numbers?" Joe pressed.

Tom hesitated. *You can buy a few weeks. Maybe you can still help Bonnie and Joe find some middle ground. Maybe, maybe, maybe....* He let out a long cloud of breath. "Alright. Two weeks. But then I've got to go."

"A month."

"No."

Joe remained silent.

"The answer to answer your question," said Tom, "is that Ryan borrowed money against his shares in the bank and then lost a huge chunk of it playing the stock market, while the bank shares themselves lost a third of their value. Basically, two-thirds of Andrew Ryan's net worth went puff in the last six months, and he's a banana peel away from insolvency."

"Would a fat insurance policy help?"

"It might ease the pain. But big drawdowns happen to traders who play the market the way Andrew Ryan does. It's part of the game. Big scores too. Neither matter much in the long run. A hit like Ryan is taking now only hurts if you have to cash out and can't play anymore."

"Like if his play money gets tied up while his wife's divorce lawyers pull his ass through the meat grinder?"

"If they tied up his trading accounts, he'd be finished."

"Give me three weeks."

"Two. And don't push me."

Joe ignored the warning. "You going to leave that school teacher who thinks your manhood is a charming shade of periwinkle hanging out there like that?"

"She's off-limits, Joe. I made a promise to a priest."

Joe snorted. "And I just did a round of bad cop on her to see if she was holding back anything on her dad. Besides, if Bonnie comes back..."

Tom smiled. "I'm glad to hear you say that."

"You made a promise to a priest. I've got two dead bodies, and my job is to find out how they got that way. So maybe we both forget about the pretty teacher, for now."

"For now?"

Joe's voice became hard. "*If* Bonnie brings my kids back to Coldwater, I'll do what I said. But I don't need your 'help' fixing my family. You got that?"

"Our family, Joe. And like I said, all this pissing on the high bushes is getting old."

"Then get your head out of my business and put it to use where it might actually do some good. Some Big Foot asshole tries to ambush me in a swamp. Some old fart mouths off he knows something about Dad and he gets his skull beat in. The new girl in town shows interest in the Morgan brothers and her stepmother ends up a floater. Maybe she's a wacko, but maybe somebody spiked her Kool-Aid. Just put that puzzle cracker of yours to work to make sure nobody else gets dead, okay? And keep your nose out of what's none of your business."

"You're spooked."

"Damn right, I am. MadDog was a pro. He didn't get taken out by any amateur. There's stuff coming out of the weeds that I'm not getting, connections I can feel but not see. Getting shot at by people I don't know, for reasons that I don't know either. That kind of shit always ends badly."

Tom folded his hands and looked at his brother. It was not like Joe to ask for help, much less go on and on about it. Either this was serious, or he had added coldhearted manipulation to his bag of professional tricks. There was no way of knowing, and no way he could return to New York without being sure. "Two weeks. And I'll lay off the family stuff. *For now.*"

Joe opened his mouth. But the only sound that came out was the muffled growl of a frustrated predator. Tom returned the conversation to dead bodies. "Okay, what do you want me to look into, other than Ryan's financial records."

"Do you know about lying doctors?"

"I've deposed a few."

"Good, because they're not all on the same page about Karen Ryan's cause of death." Joe recounted his conversation with Dr. Tran and the doctor's report of a split among the medical review panel.

"Fine. Get me the papers, if there are any."

It was a victory of sorts, but Joe didn't smile. "I guess I'll owe you one."

Tom didn't smile, either. "You'll owe me two. The other one's still helping Homeland Security with its *inquiries*. Remember?"

Chapter Twenty-Five

Mary Morgan spread makeup over the purple blotch on her cheek. She had fallen again and didn't want her sons to know...or at least not Tommy. Her foot caught the side of the dealer's chair at her evening bridge game the day before, and she fell as she stood up from the table. It could have happened to anybody. But she was sure that her abstemious older son would attribute it to the three glasses of wine she had at lunch and the cocktails and other refreshments she had had during the evening. At first, the girls had wanted Herbert to drive her to the hospital for an x-ray, but the revised consensus was that Herbert driving at night might add to the risk of further injury. Mary used his arm instead to get back to her apartment, and rewarded him with a peck on the cheek at the door.

A policeman's widow for fifteen years, Mary Morgan had long ago settled into creature comforts and the companionship of friends her own age. Her only worries came from Joe's broken marriage and Tommy's avoidance of the institution. It didn't help that her sons kept falling in lust with the same woman. First, it was the biologist who was killed by the man who had owned Pocket Island. Now rumor had it that the Morgan brothers were pursuing Our Lady of the Lake's newest schoolteacher, Rosemary Ryan's granddaughter. Of course, Joe had agreed to let Bonnie move back into his house with their kids, and for her and Joe to get counseling—whatever that meant. But if Bonnie didn't accept that her husband was the man she had married and that he wasn't going to change, then there wasn't much chance of a permanent reconciliation.

Then there was Tommy. It was long past time for her elder son to settle down. Though not with the offspring of Karen Ryan, to be sure. But a friendship with the daughter might have some uses. The school teacher must have girlfriends her own age, and Tommy needed to be where the chickens were. He wasn't going to meet any swatting mosquitoes out on that island of his.

He would be here soon. Mary applied some pasty camouflage, hurriedly and somewhat clumsily. A natural beauty, she'd had little use for makeup until well into her sixties. Then, when she finally gave in, she discovered that she didn't have the patience to use it properly. The result that looked out from the mirror seemed like something made up for a Halloween ball. She reached for the glass of Chablis on the top of the toilet and stuck out her tongue. Tommy would know anyway, no matter what she did. Both boys would. Very little got past the Morgan brothers. It was in the genes, she supposed.

Closing her eyes, she felt the chill liquid warm her core. For all practical purposes her older son was a teetotaler. The family tended to extremes—cops and robbers, priests and sinners…although there seemed to be some overlap in the latter category these days. Well, at least Tommy had the sense not to get preachy about his healthy habits. She wouldn't stand for that. Piety was the worst sin of all, she'd always thought.

Taking another sip of the calming liquid, she closed her eyes. Only then did she become aware of a buzzing sound coming from the other room. *Oh, dear. The doorbell!* How long it had been whining while she'd been standing there muttering to herself?

* * *

Entering the apartment, Tom gave his mother a wary smile, a soft hug, and a careful kiss on the cheek. "Napping," he asked?

"Powdering my nose."

He held her at arm's length. "You're looking good. Let me take you to lunch."

156

Mary felt her freshly painted face pinch in exasperation. "It's three o'clock in the afternoon! I've had my lunch. Besides, you said on the phone that it was important."

Tommy put his hand under her arm and steered her toward the couch. "It is."

"Would you like something to drink? Wine...?"

"I'm fine."

She sat down and waited.

"It's about Dad."

Mary could feel the muscles in her face tighten.

"I know this is a painful subject, so let me jump right in and get it over with."

She took a shallow breath. "Go ahead."

"If I remember correctly, the state investigators concluded that Dad was likely killed by Colombians who had moved in on the Hellers and their pals after Dad locked them all up."

"That's what they said."

"Did you ever think that they might have got it wrong?"

Mary folded her hands on her lap. "What's this about, Tommy?"

"Joe asked me to help him with the Burdock case."

"The man Karen Ryan found dead in his trailer?"

"That's right."

"How could that possibly be related to your father?"

"I don't know yet. But it seems Burdock may have told a few people that it wasn't Colombians who killed Dad. Now he's dead. There may be no connection. Burdock may have been full of hot air. But did you ever have second thoughts about the official version?"

"Of course," she said, bringing her attention back to the past. "It seemed so unlikely. But then so did your little adventure with Miss Pearce and her professor friend. There's always trouble when we get foreigners around here."

"Do you have any ideas now about who might have done it?"

"Not really. Your father was on a tear that year. I told the BCI that the Hellers were unhappy with him. But they said that the ones likely to have done something about it were all in jail. I suppose they were right. Your brother looked into it as best he could at the time. If there was any whispering since then, I'm sure he would have heard it."

Tom propped his hands under his chin. "Did Dad ever get involved in any investigation over at the Fort…or with any people from the Fort?"

"Is this still about that dead man?"

"I don't know yet."

Mary could feel herself scowl, as if her face was determined to say what she wouldn't. "Your father never talked about his work… at least not in the later years. When we were first married, of course, when it was all new." She held her head to one side. "Would you mind getting me a glass of wine from the kitchen? For yourself, too, if you want one."

Tom returned with two small glasses and put them on the table in front of her.

"Go on," she said.

"Was Dad ever in a psychiatric hospital?"

She reached for the glass. Though her eyes remain closed, her fingers wrapped around the stem without difficulty. Raising the glass to her lips, she took a long sip and then held the calming potion in her lap. "He was in the Coldwater Hospital once or twice when you were away at college. They threw everyone in together back then: drunks, druggies, psychos. Every once in a while your father would get depressed. He always drank a lot. Everyone did back then. But when he had the *blackass*, as he called it, usually in the winter, sometimes he just drank nonstop. Before he was killed, one of his binges put him in the Coldwater Hospital."

"Do you know if Karen Ryan was there at the same time?"

Mary fixed her son with a cold glare. "No, I don't," she lied.

Chapter Twenty-Six

"**D**ee Dee had a tongue like a staple gun," said Missy Miller, one of the names that Joe had gotten from Rosemary Ryan and passed on to Tom.

Tom shifted his weight in the coffee shop chair and took mental notes. Missy Miller was the deceased Mrs. Ryan's best friend, according to Rosemary. But Tom had yet to hear a flattering word. Her theme was vague. It seemed that Dee Dee Ryan was more complex than most people realized. Not Swiss watch complex. More like tangled knitting.

"Two months ago I sent my cleaning lady to her," Missy continued. "Olga had been with me six years…spoke English…no family over here. I never gave her name to anybody. I still don't know why I gave it to Dee Dee. I should have known better. Within a week she had the poor woman frazzled right out of her green card. Later, I got a postcard from Prague: 'I am so sorry Mrs. Miller. I can not work for your friend, blah, blah, blah. I must have rest.'"

Tom surveyed the salon-bronzed limbs, diamond-cinched ankle, unmarked tennis whites, and matching athletic accessories. The slim, dark-haired wife of Coldwater Hospital's head of thoracic surgery could have been thirty-five, though Joe's notes had her ten years older. When she paused to wet her hardworking whistle, Tom lobbed in only his second question. "How did you and Mrs. Ryan become friends?"

"We married men with bratty children," she answered. "And met outside the principal's office when one of them smacked the other. I forget which. Instant bonding."

159

"An unusual basis for a friendship."

Missy shrugged. "We had a lot in common—workaholic husbands, stepchildren from hell. Fun careers abandoned to be stay-at-home moms to someone else's botched experiments. Neither of us sure that we hadn't made the biggest mistake of our lives. We were lunatics back then."

"And you stayed friends?"

"Off and on. Mostly 'on' once the kids left. The cleaning lady thing... I don't know, it's not an exception, but it's not a big deal either. Dee Dee could be exasperating. She couldn't help herself really. She could be the best friend someone could ever have when she wanted to be. It's hard to explain."

"Couldn't help what?"

"Being a perfectionist, I suppose. Dee Dee could never cut anyone slack. Not even herself. If there was something to criticize, she jumped on it. There were no molehills with Dee Dee, only mountains. Smudged silverware, crunched fenders they all got the same reaction. She could be absolute hell on service people."

"So what made her the best friend someone could ever have?"

"Sometimes," Missy corrected. "Well, for starters, she listened. She was thoughtful. She anticipated what you needed before you even knew that you needed it. And she was always there when you did know you needed it. She actually paid for Mary Grogan's apartment and lawyer when Mary was divorcing that shit she was married to. The woman didn't have a cent. Don't tell Andrew," she added hurriedly.

"How did Dee Dee get along with her stepdaughter?"

Missy paused. "Well, as long as the daughter was perfect and didn't have any opinions of her own, fine I guess."

"Meaning they didn't get along?"

"No, actually they did."

"And how did a brat become a perfect mute and have no opinions of her own?"

"Dee Dee broke her." Missy paused, and Tom felt her watch for his reaction. There are few kept secrets in Coldwater, and the Morgan brothers' potential romantic interests were not likely among them. "I know that sounds harsh,"

Missy continued. "But there's no other way to put it."

Tom hesitated before asking. "How she 'break' her?"

"Same as you'd break a dog or a dancing bear," said Missy. "Punishment." After another pause, she added, "And ridicule. Cutting her off from her father. Telling her she was as screwed-up as her biological mother. Withholding affection and then parsing it out only when the girl began to conform. Whatever it took to get the result Dee Dee wanted."

"How did the father take that?"

"Andrew is a wuss."

"He didn't step in?"

"I'm sure he tried. But trying isn't enough, is it? At some point, I suppose Maggie realized that Andrew wasn't going to come to her rescue and that she was going to have to protect herself or perish."

Tom looked away.

"Not pretty," Missy confirmed.

"Did any of Mrs. Ryan's friends tell her that she might be acting too harshly?"

"We all tried. She just cut us off. Mary Grogan spoke to Andrew, I know. And even the school psychologist told Dee Dee to back off."

"But she didn't."

"No. And finally, Maggie just gave in. Started getting good grades, started being polite to adults and teachers, became popular with the other kids, breezed through high school, and got into Cornell." There was a tone of astonished resentment to the recitation. "While my little reclamation project told his father to go screw himself and then enlisted in the Marines."

* * *

Rosemary Ryan's other reference told the same story but with somewhat more sympathy. "Andrew is a good man," said Mrs. Oliver. "But watching him try to raise Maggie on his own was like watching a slow-motion train wreck. He had no clue how to parent an angry, frightened young girl. They were both lucky that Dee Dee came along."

"You knew Andrew and Maggie before he remarried?" Tom asked.

"It's a small town, Mr. Morgan, Everybody knows everybody."

Tom dropped his chin in acknowledgment. Grace Oliver owned the storefront newspaper store in the middle of Main Street, next to the Italian deli. She'd been behind the counter when Tom was growing up, and she was still there today—ageless and observant. He asked how she had come to be friends with Mrs. Ryan.

"She came in one day and complained about the girlie magazines. Made some snotty comment to a boy who was standing there looking at one."

"So you became friends?"

"Gave her a piece of my mind, first. Chasing away customers! 'You want to pay my fuel bill this winter?' I asked her. Besides, I didn't have a choice back then. If I didn't display the distributor's entire line, I didn't get the Sunday newspapers. And that's my bread and butter. Different distributor now. I can say no to some of it, if I want to."

"So what did you and Mrs. Ryan have in common?" Besides a quick tongue, he mused.

"Volunteering at the hospital. Reading to the patients, that sort of thing. I bring some of the unsold magazines up there once a month. Dee Dee was good with the patients. She had the gift of conversation. She was tough though, which you need to be if you do that kind of work. Or at least she gave the impression of being tough."

"Did you see much of her and her stepdaughter together?"

"Not at first. I had to chase the girl out of the store a few times before Dee Dee came along. She was uncomfortable coming in after that, though she came with her father every once in a while when he came in for his Sunday Times. I got to see more of her after Dee Dee turned her around."

"How long did that take?"

"A few years. The girl didn't give in without a fight."

"That must have been hard on both of them."

Mrs. Oliver peered thoughtfully into the middle distance before answering. "I only heard Dee Dee's side of it, of course. She used to rail something awful about that child. Wanted to send her to boarding school at first. But

Andrew wouldn't hear of it. Dee Dee had one foot out the door most of the time."

"But she stayed."

"For all the thanks it got her."

Tom waited.

"It took a while for Maggie to get the perfection act down," Mrs. Oliver continued. "And it was an act, believe me, even if she didn't know it. Dee Dee knew. But by then she was worn out and just hanging on until the girl left home."

"Hanging on for what?"

"Her own time with Andrew. That's what she talked about anyway. She got it finally. But I don't think it made either of them happy. Too much residual pain and not enough in common. They were good for each other in some ways—propped up each other's weaknesses. But as for what they wanted, two people couldn't have been more different. Dee Dee wanted a social life and travel. Andrew hated both, loved his house and never set foot outside Coldwater except on business."

"Why do you think they stayed together?"

Mrs. Oliver shrugged. "Beats me. While Dee Dee was going through the wars with Maggie, she talked constantly about leaving. But after Maggie went off to college, I never heard her mention it once."

"How did she feel about Maggie coming back to Coldwater?"

"I don't know. I didn't see much of her the past few months. She stopped coming to the hospital about then. And she never came to the store after that one time."

"Do you think she might have had a friend?"

Grace Oliver peered at Tom over the top of her readers. "What do you mean?"

Tom had told the newspaper store owner why he had come, why he wanted to ask a few questions about the dead woman's relationships and habits. But it seemed only now that she put any meaning to his explanation. He could feel the wall go up. "She didn't like her husband," Tom noted. "She didn't like her life. She seems to have stopped all her habitual activities and seeing

163

any of her usual friends in the weeks before she died. But she didn't hang around the house. So where was she? What was she doing? And with who, if anyone?"

The newspaper lady looked at him reproachfully. "I don't speculate about that sort of thing."

Chapter Twenty-Seven

The boat ride to Pocket Island was chill and choppy. The thin drizzle that had been falling all morning showed no sign of letting up. Fall had arrived fast and it felt like winter could not be far behind.

Sergeant Boyd had brought along a snorkel and wet suit, saying that he wanted to look in the water around Washington's Head. He explained that most of the islands near Coldwater were little more than glacial slag heaps of granite and shale, and that the shale often eroded beneath the harder granite leaving fissures and caves. A Washington's Mouth had featured in a few of his Canadian grandfather's stories about informal exporting during Prohibition. It might be a coincidence, but Boyd wanted to check it out.

Tom and Joe told the sergeant about a caved-in Civil War ironworks on the west side of the island. Neither had been inside since they were twelve and thirteen respectively. But they thought it might be worth investigating if Boyd was trying to find a spot where two footlocker-sized trunks might have remained undisturbed on the island for more than a decade.

Joe pulled the patrol boat alongside the concrete dock at the back of the cove and secured the boat lines to the Samson posts. The dock and stone steps that led from there to the top of the cliff were cow-pied with clumps of wet fallen leaves. Drizzle built toward thin rain. At the top of the cliff, Tom suggested they split up. Joe and Boyd could check the water below Washington's Head and Tom would try to find what might be left of the ironworks. They would meet back at what was left of the Frank Lloyd Wright house.

"You bring a flashlight?" Joe asked.

Tom shook his head.

"Matches?"

"Nope."

"Lawyer," Joe muttered, opening his backpack and removing a rolled-up towel. "There's a pair of swim trunks in there, if you decide to get adventurous. But don't crap in them, if you get stuck."

* * *

Twenty-five years ago the entrance to the old Civil War iron mine had been a vegetation-less patch in the middle of a pine grove where nothing grew in the slag that spilled from the side of the hill like dirt from a gopher mound. What was left of the entrance had been a boy-sized crawl space beneath a slab of fallen rock that jutted from the face of the mound no more than boy-waist high. Tom stumbled through the dripping pines to the top of the island and then north along its central ridge until ancient memory told him that he had gone far enough. Turning west he looked for a gully. Five dripping minutes later he found the mine.

The clearing looked smaller than he remembered. Thin yellow grass had made the beginnings of purchase in the hard gray slag. But the familiar slab of wet granite still stuck out from the side of the hill like a low salute. He walked over and peered beneath it. Inside looked as he remembered, damp, dark, and small.

Twenty-five years ago, the damp part ended just a few yards in, blocked by a section of collapsed ceiling and a pool of cold, ocher water. If a boy were hardy, or foolhardy, he could hold his breath and shimmy beneath the collapsed roof and come out on the other side where twenty feet of reasonably dry tunnel ended in a pile of fallen shale. Tom and Joe had smoked their first cigarettes in there, purloined from their mother's purse.

Slipping the flashlight from the roll of towel, Tom ducked his head under the overhanging rock and started to crawl. The air felt wet and chilly. He turned on the flashlight and pointed the beam along the tunnel walls, floor, and ceiling. No graffiti, cigarette butts, paper wrappers, or (thank god) animal droppings, and just a few spider webs. Either god's creatures cared not at all for this place, or some wood fairy cleaning lady was coming in on a regular basis. Tom crawled toward where the tunnel's ceiling met its floor and blocked further progress. A three-foot pool of black water separated the last dry patch of floor from the collapsed rear wall. The beam of the flashlight barely penetrated the water.

Tom had always wondered how his younger brother had figured out that a boy could immerse himself in that cold, uninviting puddle, slither through it and under the collapsed ceiling, and come out safely on the other side. He'd never said. Or rather, when pressed he claimed that he had gotten the idea from a National Geographic television special. But Tom knew that was bull. He figured Mad Dog must have known about this place and told Joe during their snakebite bonding.

Unrolling the towel again, he examined its remaining contents: a single pack of matches and a small candle stub sealed in a sandwich baggie. There was no bathing suit. Tom looked at the stash and at the pool of iron-colored water. The phrase 'let's not and say we did' came to mind. This is stupid, he thought. If there had been a section of the tunnel so far that was too narrow to pass one of those metal trunks, he could turn back with a clear conscience. But there wasn't. He tried to remember how much room there was in the short underwater stretch beneath the collapsed roof. It must have been at least boy-sized. All he could remember was that it was cold.

Spreading the small towel beside the pool, Tom anchored it with the candle and baggie of matches, which made it look like an offering. *I can't believe I'm doing this.* He hadn't had to remove his clothes the last time he tried to slither through this underwater tunnel, not even his PF Flyers. But he could see that it might be a prudent thing to do now. If he was going to crawl blindly through an underwater passage that may or may not be wide enough for his now manly physique, there was no sense getting his clothes hung up on some sharp protrusion and having to hold his breath until he figured out how to get loose.

Stripping to his underwear and boat shoes, he grimaced his way into the dark pool until his feet touched bottom and the cold, ocher-colored water lapped at his groin. Then he put the baggie with the candle and matches in his mouth and plunged into the dark. Sliding backwards into the pool, he held his breath and felt above and in front of his head for the lip of rock and the nubs and cracks behind it that were the rungs on the upside-down ladder that led to the next chamber.

Shitttt....brrrrrrrr!!!

He half expected to feel his shoulders, back, or butt flay against rock. But the opening was man-sized too, and if man-sized, then big enough for one of the trunks Joe had described. Gasping for air, he came out the other side unscathed and spat out the baggie. The air in the pitch-black space was stale and smelled of sulfur. Feeling along the edge of the pool until his fingers touched dry ground, he opened the baggie and removed the pack of matches and the candle, while an unhelpful little voice in his head whispered, 'don't drop them!!' He could feel his heart pound, and a spontaneous expletive echo like a canon shot in the enclosed space. Something fluttered, but he knew that wasn't possible. Then he realized it must be the baggie, flagged by his breath. By feel and memory, he opened the book of matches, stripped one out, closed the flap, and scraped the head of the cardboard match along the roughened strip. The cardboard strip burst into flame. Payoff for skills acquired in a misspent youth. He put the match to a candle and held it above his head.

The open space beyond the pool was approximately twelve feet long, three-feet wide, and slightly less than that tall. It was also empty. Tom hoisted himself out of the pool and crawled along the tunnel just to make sure. No graffiti, cigarette butts, candy wrappers, or any other sign of human visitation. The wood fairy cleaning lady had been here too.

There was no room to turn around, so he crawled backwards, carefully examining the ground beneath his face. It was packed smooth and unmarked save for his own hand, knee, and toe prints. When his feet touched water, he rolled to his back, eased into the pool, and then turned and set the candle on the ground along its rim. No sign of metal trunks, no stinger missiles, no sign of human visitation whatsoever.

He held on tight to that thought while his teeth began to chatter and the candle flickered brightly against the close, rough stone.

* * *

Sergeant Boyd looked like a five-foot-eight voodoo doll dressed in a wet suit made of broken brown glass impaled and hung from every inch of the thick rubber wetsuit that covered him. There was a minimum of blood, but the army reservist looked exhausted, and Joe, though unbloodied, looked troubled.

"There's a cave under Washington's Head," Boyd reported. "Well, more like a crack. With a lip on either side that could probably hold a stack of boxes. But there's nothing there now except a lot of old broken glass."

Joe pointed to a curved brown shard with some writing and a partial label wedged in the frame of the underwater light Boyd clutched in his hand. "Looks like a piece of an old booze bottle," he said.

Boyd plucked the shard from the lantern and handed it to Tom. "Here... souvenir. Seems like your island did a bit of business back in the day. Finish that house and maybe you could do tours."

"No metal trunks down there?" asked Tom.

Boyd shook his head. "I don't think anyone would have used that hole in the wall to store anything for very long. From all that glass, I'd say that it gets pretty rough down there when a storm comes up. The opening's too close to the waterline. It looks like somebody lost a few cases of bootleg before they figured that out. I don't think this," he waved a hand over his glass studded torso, "was just grandpa dropping the occasional bottle."

"So where does that leave us?"

Boyd shrugged. "Cold, wet, and hungry. And me having to make a report." He turned to Tom. "Did you find anything?"

"Nothing."

* * *

Later that night Tom and Joe went over what they had and what they had

169

added to it that afternoon. "We've got one empty trunk," said Joe, "that according to Sergeant Boyd once carried a pair of shoulder-fired missiles, one missing trunk (according to Mickey Dooley), a disintegrating wad of one hundred dollar bills all dated pre-1990, Big Foot and an unexplained arson."

Tom added the unrelated (?) accidental (?) drowning and unrelated (?) fatal bludgeoning. "That's a lot of unexplained and unrelated mayhem for a little town like Coldwater."

Joe added the hospital allergist's speculation about asphyxiation.

"And somebody's been in our old smoking room and cleaned it with a toothbrush."

"You told Boyd that you didn't find anything."

"That's right. Not a thing. But do you remember the last time we were there?"

"You threw up."

"Right. And what did we leave behind?"

Joe shrugged. "There was so much smoke in there by then, I could hardly see. Couple of soda cans. Half a watermelon. Bunch of cigarette butts. You tried to scratch a girl's name on the wall with a rock."

"Did you ever go back there after that, or tell anyone else about it?"

"No. I figured it'd still be smelling like your puke."

"Well, it's clean now. Not even a handprint in the dirt."

"You think that means something?"

"It means you didn't find that back room after watching some National Geographic special."

Joe laughed. "Dad told me about it."

"No kidding. And someone probably told him. So there's more than Morgans who know about that place—just like Sergeant Boyd's little glass palace under Washington's Head rock—only someone's been using it since little Tommy and Joey were down there smoking themselves green. And they've gone to a lot of trouble to make it look like no one has ever been there at all."

"Keep going."

"Well I don't think it's Huck and Jim, do you?"

"Would one of those trunks fit through there?"

"With room for half a dozen more."

Chapter Twenty-Eight

The windshield of Joe's truck was covered in frost the next morning. The pallid sky and hint of rain were a bleak reminder to Tom that he could have been in London eating meat pies and dating women who talked like Princess Diana. As they rode into town, Joe asked him if he'd found anything enlightening on the disks Burdock had created from Andrew Ryan's crashed hard drive, other than the financial stuff Tom had already explained. "What about the wicked stepmother stuff?"

"Nothing that would link Andrew Ryan to the Burdock killing. And nothing to suggest he planned to do in his wife—even if someone with a bit more testosterone might have already. I can't picture this guy doing anything to anybody. He's a tortured mouse."

"Talk to him anyway. See what kind of in-law you might be getting."

"Not happening. I promised a priest."

"You can go to confession."

* * *

The Coldwater Savings Bank was a two-story stone building, painted white and sitting alone in the center of a small blacktopped parking lot. Its neighbors were a gas station and a sporting goods shop on similarly sized parcels. Tom stopped at the first desk beyond the brass framed glass doors and asked to speak to Mr. Ryan. The woman behind the loan officer sign lifted a pair of glasses from her chest, addressed him by his first name, and asked after his mother. "Mrs. Shore," she whispered helpfully.

Mother of (?), an ancient corner of Tom's brain stirred fitfully. *You used to play baseball with him and his jerk cousin.* "How is Gary?" Tom heard himself ask. The name came smoothly from the prompting place and the mother's grateful face told him it was right.

"In the reserves," said Mrs. Shore. "He's stationed up at the Fort for a few months… something hush, hush … I get to see him now and then."

"Well, tell him I still have his thing and that it came in handy."

"Should I ask what that means?"

"Definitely not."

The mother of his old sandlot companion made a brief call and then led Tom through a waist-high brass gate and a tall mahogany door. Beyond was a set of carpeted stairs that led to a second-floor office that took up a large corner at the back of the bank facing the lake. Andrew Ryan looked up when Mrs. Shore appeared and stood when Tom stepped out from behind her. Ryan directed him to a small grouping of furniture in the far corner. "Do I need a lawyer?" he asked quietly.

It was not a question Tom had anticipated. "I haven't a clue," he heard himself say. "Do you want one?"

The bank owner remained silent.

"Look, I popped in here unannounced," said Tom. "I appreciate your seeing me, but you don't have to. I'm just helping my brother with the financial stuff someone stole off your computer. Spreadsheets are not my brother's area of expertise."

"Spreadsheets? I'm sorry. This isn't about Dee Dee?"

Tom shook his head. "No. It's about a guy who made copies of files from your computer."

"Here at the bank?"

"Your personal p.c. The one you had repaired recently at Lakeside Computer."

Andrew frowned. "I see. The computer screen went blank all of a sudden just a few weeks ago. I don't know where it went to get fixed. My secretary takes care of things like that."

"So you weren't aware that an employee of Lakeside Computer made a copy of your hard drive?"

"No. I wasn't. Isn't that illegal?"

"Including all of the bank and personal financial records on it, as well as a personal journal?"

Ryan sat with his mouth open, momentarily stunned.

"Or that the guy who made that copy was found dead in his trailer a few days ago, with his head smashed in?"

Ryan shook his head, his face Ivory Soap white and his hands trembling. "I don't know anything about that."

"I'm sorry," said Tom. "I'd assumed my brother had spoken to you about this and I was just here to follow up with some financial questions."

Ryan took a deep breath. The color returned to his face, and his hands stilled. His voice, when he spoke, was firm. "Mr. Morgan, I don't mean to be rude, but are you and your brother job sharing now?"

"I'm just pitching in, Mr. Ryan. As long as Coldwater thinks it can muddle along with just a one-man police force, I'm willing to give Joe a hand with the financial stuff when he asks."

When Ryan did not respond, Tom continued. "Peeking into people's computer files was apparently this dead guy's hobby. Yours weren't the only ones he had in his trailer, but they were the ones with financial records from the town's only bank. So my first question is whether there was anything on them that might have inspired one of your customers to bash in the deceased's head?"

Ryan shook his vigorously. "There were no individual depositor records on that computer, Mr. Morgan."

"Yes, it seemed to be mostly quarterly financials for the bank. Can you think of who might be upset by someone having that information?"

"Myself and my partners. It's confidential and proprietary."

"There was also personal financial information on the disks. Combined balance sheets for you and Mrs. Ryan, going back some years."

"My personal records, yes. I keep everything on the same machine. I don't have another."

"Then I'm wondering if you could help me out with something. I couldn't quite reconcile the value of the bank stock on your personal balance sheet with the information in the bank's financials."

Ryan grimaced. "And what might that have to do with the death of some nosy computer repairman?"

"I don't know. But when my brother asks me if anything in the copied records caught my attention, I have to say it was the difference between the value of the Coldwater Savings Bank as reflected in the bank's financial statements and the value you put on it in your own personal records."

"The bank records are accurate, Mr. Morgan. My personal records are conservative."

"By half, I'd say."

"That's a fair estimate."

"Any particular reason for recording it that way?"

"I don't like to count my chickens before they hatch."

"Fair enough." Tom took a wallet of CDs from his jacket pocket and handed them to the bank owner. "These are copies of the files that the dead man took from your hard drive. You might want to check them against the ones on the machine that you got back from his shop. Techies can get pixyish. He might have changed something. If he did, please call me."

Ryan held the disks and looked thoughtfully at Tom, who asked as he stood to leave, "Would it be possible for me to get a print-out of the bank's current balance sheet before I go?"

Ryan looked uncomfortable. "Would you think me rude if I said no? That information is highly confidential."

"Of course. And if the dead man just changed a few random numbers to be a jerk, that's one thing. But if he made any subtle or sophisticated changes, he would have needed specific direction and probably help. That could lead to who killed him."

"I see. Would you mind if I look for any discrepancies first?"

"Suit yourself. But I don't know how long my volunteer gig is going to last. After that, Joe's going to have to get some accounting firm in to look those things over." Tom gestured at the disks in Ryan's hand. "And there's more on those disks than just numbers."

175

"I was wondering when you were going to mention that."
"I was hoping I wouldn't have to."

Chapter Twenty-Nine

As Tom and Joe were trying to decide, over pizza, whether Andrew Ryan was missing a Y chromosome or two, the man from Taliesin West called to remind Tom of his responsibilities to architecture and to inquire what he was doing about them. Llewellyn said he was calling from Montreal and that he would like to drive down to Coldwater the following day to take pictures of the current state of restoration before the weather turned.

Tom told him that the roof was tarped, the insurance company had taken all the pictures anybody was ever going to want, and there was no point in starting any restoration work until spring and until somebody cut somebody a large check.

"Well, that's something I'd like to talk to you about, as well," said Llewellyn. "I may have found a sponsor willing to pick up what the insurance company won't, and maybe even fund the construction of the other house in the plans that I showed you. They're pretty excited, and they've asked for pictures of everything: the guest house, the site for the main one as well, all of the shoreline, and anything else of interest."

Tom asked if the benefactor had a name. The professor demurred but agreed to meet Tom at Skippers marina before first light the following morning. Joe remarked that the Frank Lloyd Wright groupie had better get all the pictures he needed now, as a plastic tarp wasn't going to keep anybody out of the torched house this winter and those nice stained-glass windows had exactly zero chance of being there next spring.

* * *

Wisps of vapor rose from the surface of the lake and hovered a few feet above it, as if waiting for a wind to carry them off or the sun to warm them back into a liquid state. The only sounds that crossed Tom's ear were the purr of the outboard motor and the whoosh of cool water streaming past the hull. Not even the birds were up yet. In the predawn light, Pocket Island looked like something from an old, illustrated copy of The Last of The Mohicans.

Llewellyn asked to get close to the island so that he could get pictures of the shoreline as the sun came up behind them. Tom eased the boat into the shallows and steered it along the shore. The Taliesin man took a log-nosed camera from his bag and began to methodically fill an entire flashcard. When he had finished, Tom eased the boat onto a crescent of shale gravel between two arching beech trees and hopped onto the shore where a battered aluminum jon boat lay partially hidden behind a twisted blowdown.

Goddam Dooleys! Tom pulled branches aside, put his weight on the stern of the boat, and heaved it into the water. Then he spotted a small black Zodiac farther down the shoreline, tethered to a branch of an overhanging beech tree. He waded into the water and untied the nylon tether, pushing the rubber pontoon until the little craft spun out from under the trees and drifted away from the island.

Tom called his brother as he made his way back through the woods and told him about the two boats adrift off Pocket Island. "Just a flare gun," he said when Joe asked if he had anything on board that might discourage further bad behavior.

Llewellyn looked worried when Tom arrived back at the boat and eased it away from the shore. "What's going on?" he demanded.

"Neither of those boats is mine," said Tom. "And one of them matches our sheriff's description of a boat he saw leaving here the night your national treasure got torched."

"Shouldn't you call the police?"

"I just woke him," said Tom. "He'll be out once he's had his breakfast. Do you still want to go up to the house and snap pictures? Or do you want to wait for the cavalry?"

"I've been asked to get as many photos as I can at first light." There was no trace of enthusiasm in his voice.

Tom started the engine and steered the boat around the point and along the western shore of the island and into Pocket Cove. No sunlight had yet penetrated the thick canopy of giant beech trees that surrounded the cove. He took the flare gun and flashlight from the boat and led Llewellyn up the leaf-covered steps to the burned-out restoration site.

Though sunlight had yet to crest the top of the island, there was enough ambient light to see what was left of the torched house. The blue tarp that covered the cement and glass walls looked festive to Tom, like a medieval fortress decked for a fair. But Llewellyn ran his hands over the darkened concrete and moaned for long minutes about senseless desecration. Tom tried not to listen, but as the professor droned on, he grew impatient. "It's an island!" Tom growled, "Within spitting distance of a town and an international border. No one lives on it eight months a year. What did you expect?"

Llewellyn made no response.

"Listen to me. If this 'sponsor' isn't planning to live here full time, or hasn't figured security into his budget, then he might as well save his money. Or is he willing to fund major repairs every spring, in perpetuity?"

"I don't know," Llewellyn admitted.

"Just so we understand each other, professor… I'm not willing to sell to just anybody."

"Actually, this sponsor didn't say anything about buying," Llewellyn answered. "Just about helping to finance the rebuilding."

"No strings?" Tom's tone was dismissive. "Look, I've got family here; I grew up here, and for the moment I live here. If the Rockefeller Foundation wants to buy this place to protect an architectural treasure, that's one thing. But if it's Reverend Moon or some idiot who can't even keep the local graffiti artists off it, then no deal—at any price."

"Mr. Morgan I do not have a buyer for your island. All I have is someone tentatively willing to contribute to the restoration of this house and perhaps to fund the construction of another, using students from Taliesin West. That's all we talked about."

"In exchange for what? Tom demanded.

"I don't understand," said Llewellyn.

"I didn't buy this island just to let some stranger squat on it," Tom answered. "Not even in a Frank Lloyd Wright dream house. If you've got a buyer, I'm going to need a clean biography and an attractive number. If all you've got is someone who wants to build on my land and not buy it, then I need more than that—unless of course, this 'sponsor' is willing to build exactly to those specs you found and turn both houses over to me when they're completed, no strings attached. If that's the deal, then I'll take care of the security problem myself."

Llewellyn demurred. "I would be surprised if that's what he had in mind."

"You don't ask a lot of questions when someone waves a checkbook, do you?"

"Taliesin West doesn't have that luxury."

"But it thinks it can sell lots on islands it doesn't own?"

Llewellyn made a helpless gesture.

"You've got…" Tom clamped his teeth and looked away as if there might be a thesaurus handy in the canopy of ocher leaves above their heads. "Temerity."

Llewellyn spread his palms in surrender. "I did nail down the providence of that grotto drawing," he said, helpfully. "It's definitely Frank Lloyd Wright's, and from the same set as the plans for this building and the one that was never started. And I found two more grotto drawings that go along with it."

Tom thought of the shoreline opening Boyd had discovered and of the collapsed tunnel in the middle of the island that someone had scrubbed to look like it had never been visited. "Did you bring them?" he asked wearily.

The professor smiled and removed several folded sheets of paper from his shirt pocket. "You know if we could find these locations, it might add to the value of the property. I mean if you decided to complete Mr. Wright's vision."

Tom examined the drawings. One looked like the Founding Father after a tracheotomy. The other could have been a hole in the side of a hill almost anywhere.

"I know one of these spots." Tom handed the drawings back to Llewellyn and tapped a finger on one. "It doesn't look like this of course... but that rock formation is not too far from here."

"Would you show it to me?"

He led the professor into the pines where the outline of a path had just become visible, and where root and branch reached into the half-light to tug and claw at whatever passed. They walked in silence, one moody and distracted, the other hopeful but edgy. After several minutes Tom stopped and gripped Llewellyn by the arm, simultaneously raising a forefinger to his lips. The sound of muffled footsteps and labored breathing drifted through the trees. Tom reached into his jacket pocket and placed his fingers against the grip of the flare gun he had taken from the boat. The footsteps and breathing grew louder and Tom's grip on Llewellyn tightened. One bent-over figure emerged from the trees, followed by another.

Tom waited until the figures were closer, huffing and heads down. "Hello Mickey," he said when the lead one looked up. "It's been a while." Tom lifted the flare pistol so that it was even with the man's chest.

"Whoa Morgan! No need for that." Mickey Dooley raised a plastered arm and waved it in front of his chest. The man behind him drew up alongside and squinted at the gun in Tom's hand. "We were fishing, that's all. Had some engine trouble and came ashore until it got light enough to fix."

"It's light enough now. What brings you up here?"

"Some asshole took our boat," said the other Dooley.

"And you think they hauled it up here? A half a mile through the woods in the dark?"

"Just going to high ground to get a look around," said Mickey. "Maybe they took it around to the other side of the island."

Tom extended his free hand toward Llewellyn and kept the flare gun centered on the Dooley's chest. "Mickey, Kevin, this is Professor Llewellyn. He teaches at an architecture college founded by the guy who built my house. He's a fanatic about preserving the buildings his idol left behind." Tom waved a hand toward the Dooleys. "Professor, this is Mickey Dooley. The silent one is his brother Kevin. They're the ones who torched Mr. Wright's irreplaceable architectural masterpiece."

Silence. And more silence. Birds that had also been quiet until then seemed to find their wings and voices at the same time and they began to flit and trill among the pines. Finally, it was Kevin who spoke. "That's not a real gun."

"It'll do in a pinch," said Tom.

Llewellyn appeared to be trying to read Tom's face in the dim half-light. His own had the look of a man about to wet his pants.

"I've got some business with these gentlemen," Tom said to Llewellyn, without taking his eyes from Kevin Dooley. "Just keep to this path until you get down to the water and then turn north. It's about a ten-minute walk after that."

Llewellyn jerked his head once and began to move rapidly downhill. When he had disappeared into the pines Kevin Dooley spoke again. "Two against one now," he noted.

"Hard to say," said Tom. "I saw an empty Zodiac drifting by a little while ago. Whoever came in it must be around here someplace. Unless you two were fishing out of a rubber raft, which I kind of doubt."

The brothers exchanged quick nervous glances.

"I thought maybe it was that army pal of yours. They seem to have a lot of those rubber boats." He waved the flare gun at Mickey's cast. "He's got a bum arm, too, I hear. Probably not looking to swim home." The brothers remained silent, exchanging head shakes and glances but no words. "You boys are still friends, aren't you?"

"You don't know what you're talking about," Kevin growled.

Tom raised the angle of the flare pistol until it cleared the tops of the trees. "I know you and Zodiac man need a way off this island. You find him for me and I'll give you all a ride back to town. He finds you...well, I don't know. Might depend on whether you're still friends or not." Tom lifted his arm above his head and squeezed the trigger.

Whoosh!! A streak of crimson light arced from Tom's hand and finished in an explosion of white that blew apart above the trees and fell back to earth and water in colored fragments. "You're either rabbits or hounds today, fellows. You might want to figure out quick which it is. Game just started."

Chapter Thirty

Tom left the Dooley brothers exchanging meaningful twitches and started down the path taken by Llewellyn. A half-hour later he found the professor squatting on the gravel below Washington's Head, his back against a pile of angled rock and his arms crossed over bent legs. He might have been meditating, but the look on his face was far from peaceful. When Llewellyn became aware of Tom's presence, he scrambled to his feet. "Are you all right?" he demanded. "I saw the flare..."

"I'm fine," said Tom.

"I'm still shaking." He extended his arm to prove it. "Did you shoot...?"

Tom shook his head.

"Thank God." Llewellyn placed a palm on his chest and lifted his face toward the treetops. "Where are they?"

Tom shrugged. "This is an island. They're not going anywhere."

"I mean...are we safe with them roaming around up there? That one looked pretty nasty."

"Safe as any other day."

"I see your point now."

"Do you?" Tom didn't feel like sparing the professor's feelings. "What do you really know about these islands, Professor?"

"Not enough, apparently."

"Do you think Wright knew anything about them when he decided to build here?"

"He was in his eighties, Mr. Morgan...and short of money. He built wherever his clients wanted."

Tom nodded. "And that was when?"

"Nineteen fifty-two."

"Probably the only decade in a hundred years when Pocket Island wasn't an active base for some kind of criminal activity."

"What?"

"Think about it. Canada is only a dozen or so miles that way." Tom stuck out an arm like a weather vane. "Before the Civil War, they used to hide slaves out here. In the twenties, bootleggers on both sides warehoused their inventory right under this rock. I remember bales of marijuana floating ashore in Wilson Cove when I was a kid, there was so much dope running through here then."

Llewellyn looked pained.

"Your man built his house in the middle of a hood's highway, professor. He built during a recession, that's all."

"What are you saying?"

"That we both made a mistake. Wright in building here, and me, who grew up here, forgetting where here is and what that means. Thinking that I could come back and make Treasure Island into Walden Pond …and never mind about the pesky pirates."

"I can't tell that to a sponsor!"

"He or it will find out eventually. After a few million bucks and a few winters of break-ins and arson. That is, if this 'sponsor' doesn't show up for a visit at the wrong time and get himself hurt."

"I'm just trying to help you out," said Llewellyn.

"No, you're not. You're trying to save a misplaced lemon with a leaky roof. And you don't care whose money you spend doing it, because there's always another deep pocket somewhere who can be schmoozed into funding the game for another inning."

"It's a work of art!"

"It was. Now it's just a glass and concrete shell with a tarp over it. By spring it won't even be that."

"You can't simply let it go to ruin!"

Some fundraiser probably said that to Sisyphus, thought Tom. But before

185

he could share the insight, the sound of an approaching outboard engine made it irrelevant.

"Yo!" Came the shout from the bridge of the Coldwater patrol boat. "You okay?"

Tom lifted his thumb.

"You shoot somebody?"

"I gave some light to the Dooleys, so they could find their butts in the dark. They're around here somewhere."

"Not anymore. I passed a Grady White hauling for Skippers. I think they found their butts in your boat."

"Thanks for stopping them."

"I had to slow down for a swimmer... make sure it wasn't you."

"Where?"

Joe nodded toward the locked cabin. "In there. Recuperating."

* * *

Llewellyn said little on the way back to the marina, and there was no noise from the other passenger in the cabin. The professor said a brief and shaky goodbye as he hopped off the boat at Skipper's dock and then hurried to his rental car. As soon as Llewellyn was out of sight, Joe restarted the engine. "I'm taking our pal back to the island. The three of us need to talk."

"What's wrong with the station house? Other than it's warm and you can get a cup of coffee across the street."

"Interruptions," said Joe. He eased the patrol boat away from the dock and headed out onto the lake. Past Pocket Island he turned north and when the island was out of sight and the lakeshore indistinguishable from the horizon, he turned off the engine. A stiff wind blew from the east, bringing with it a low, gray blanket of clouds. Small waves rolled the boat from side to side in a bilious cadence. Joe rapped a boat hook on the cabin door and shouted. "End of the line, sergeant. Everybody out."

The military man emerged slowly, his right hand cupping his left elbow while his torso sought the door frame for balance. A rectangular flap of rubber hung from an exposed shoulder revealing damaged flesh in patriotic hues of red, white and blue. His face looked like it had been in a nasty bar fight, but Tom had no trouble recognizing it.

"You always dress in rubber, Sergeant?"

Boyd stared dully and said nothing.

"Feeling better yet?" asked Joe.

"What happened?" asked Tom.

"Sergeant here went left, I went right. Boat doesn't come with brakes."

"Sergeant?"

Boyd remained expressionless.

"Your flare went off while I was still in the marina," Joe elaborated. "Then a Grady White blew out of the cove as I got to the island. But you weren't driving it. I hauled ass after whoever it was, and just about run over this." Joe jerked a thumb toward the silent frogman. "I slowed down thinking it might be you and that they might have chucked you overboard. The sergeant and I got our docking signals mixed."

Boyd coughed, spat blood, and spoke. "Bullshit."

Tom looked at his brother.

"You okay?" Joe repeated.

Boyd grunted.

"Fine then, let's start. What were you doing out in the middle of the lake?"

"Swimming."

"Where to?"

"Shore. From that island."

"What were you doing there?"

"Tailing two guys in a jon boat."

"All the way from the Fort?"

"From the lagoon where they launched it."

"The one where some army guy torched my patrol car? What were you doing there?"

Boyd paused for breath and stayed paused.

"You getting winded?" Joe asked.

Boyd said nothing.

"So what you were doing down lovers lane in your little rubber outfit? You a pervert or something?"

"Army business."

"What kind of Army business?"

"The kind I don't discuss with civilians."

"How convenient." Joe reached for the triangle of torn wet suit and gave it a quick, hard tug, exposing a long patch of goose flesh. "It's a long swim to shore from here, wise guy. And the water's freezing."

Boyd looked at Tom, who folded his hands behind his head and looked at his brother. "Neither of us is a national security risk, Sergeant. You know that. You should answer the sheriff's questions, if you can."

Boyd said nothing.

"Or come up with a better reason not to," Tom offered.

"Stand up Sergeant!" Joe ordered. "Or whoever you are."

Boyd didn't move and Joe yanked him to his feet by his injured elbow. "How big were Dad's hands?" Joe tossed the question over his shoulder as he backed the frogman toward the stern of the boat.

"Same as yours more or less."

"Munchkin here says they were like dinner plates." Joe jabbed an iron finger into the hematoma that bulged through the tear in the sergeant's rubber suit. "Said that he noticed them when he and Dad had a bite to eat at Trudy's... when he says he told Dad about some missing Army property." Joe jabbed a finger once more into the bloody swelling. "Then Dad got his throat cut."

Boyd winced but said nothing. Pressed backward over the stern, possibly he couldn't.

"Joe!" Tom cautioned.

"Army business!" Joe pressed his torso over Boyd's and blasted a shout into the injured man's face. "Who slit my daddy's throat is Army business?"

"Joe!"

"It's our business, mister! You're going to get that straight now or get off my boat."

"Joe!" Tom repeated.

"What?" Joe growled. "You want to go swimming too?"

"Settle down. I think the sergeant understands he owes us an explanation. There must be a lot he can share without violating an oath."

"Who gives rat's ass about his girl scout oath?" Joe jabbed his finger hard into the sergeant's shoulder.

"The sergeant cares. And he needs a minute to organize his thoughts so that he can tell us what he knows in whatever way he's permitted to. I think he understands that we have a right to know."

"Say something, shorty!"

"Pull me up."

Joe reached for the throat of Boyd's wet suit and hauled him upright to sit balanced like Humpty Dumpty on the boat's narrow stern.

"What can you tell us about your meeting with our father?" Tom asked.

"What I told your brother. That's all."

"That the army sent you looking for some missing ordinance, and that our father said that you were on a wild goose chase?"

"Basically, yes."

"Do you think he was right?"

"It seemed likely, back then."

"And now?"

Boyd didn't answer. Joe prompted him with a stiff finger.

"Cut that out," said Tom.

"No."

"We know about the trunk," said Tom, as much to his brother as to the army man. "My brother gave you the markings and you identified them. We've all been out exploring together for more. It's not betraying a confidence to talk about what we already know."

"Talk," prompted Joe.

"Dad was wrong, wasn't he?"

Boyd said nothing.

"We're not going to be offended if you say our father was wrong, Sergeant. We've said worse ourselves."

Joe twisted the throat of Boyd's wet suit and brought their faces to an inch apart. He could have torn off the sergeant's nose with his teeth, and he looked ready to do it. "Talk!"

"Joe, stop it. We don't need the Sergeant to tell us that Dad was wrong. We know that already from the trunks. We know that they weren't empty either from the track someone made dragging them through the woods. And we know that to keep what was in them secret, someone shot at you and at the Dooley's. Presumably not to miss. We don't need the Sergeant to confirm any of that."

"Then come up with something we do need him for," said Joe. "Or he's going for a swim."

"Let's talk about that. It's three and a half miles from Pocket Island to the mainland. Do you swim those kind of distances regularly, Sergeant?"

Boyd shook his head.

"But there are people at the Fort who do?"

Boyd shrugged again.

"You have an amphibious unit there, right?"

"That's no secret," Joe grumbled.

"And I suppose they let them out of the swimming pool every once in a while?"

Boyd shrugged.

"Where are you going with this, brother?"

"Remember Hassad's Dobermans?"

"Hard not to."

"I always thought they were overkill, so to speak, if Hassad was just trying to keep picnickers off the island. He had some nasty stuff hidden there, but it was well hidden. No casual trespasser was going to stumble onto it. And setting killer dogs loose to patrol the shoreline certainly brought him a lot of attention. That's not something he would have done without serious thought, and unless he had a problem he couldn't fix with anything less...discouraging." Tom had the sergeant's attention now. "You guys don't discourage easily, do you?"

"We don't discourage at all." Boyd all but stuck out his tongue.

"Well, your 'swimming club' couldn't have gotten onto the island after the previous owner put Dobermans out there. Those dogs would have killed someone… or someone would have had to kill them."

Boyd smiled and a clot of blood slipped from his nose and splashed onto the deck. "He lost a few."

"And then what?"

Boyd shrugged. "The commander decided to use another island."

"For what?"

Boyd hesitated.

"This can't be an Army secret, Sergeant. Hassad is dead. The whole world knows what he had hidden out there."

"The Rangers used the island as a destination for long-distance training swims," Boyd answered. "Your dad knew about them. After that crazy professor put those Dobermans out there, they switched to another island."

"The next closest is Canopus," said Joe. "That's five miles out."

"Piece of cake," said the Sergeant.

Joe hooted. "You weren't out there training punk. You were half dead even before I bumped into you."

"I told you, Sheriff…I followed a jon boat from the lagoon."

"Swam after it?"

"I had a boat."

"Where is it?"

"I don't know. I followed two men onto the island and when I came back later, both their boat and mine were gone. I figured they took mine, or set it loose, or someone else did."

"So you decided to swim back?"

Boyd smirked. "Why not?"

Joe spat.

"I know this is where we probably get into army business," said Tom. "But bear with me. You weren't hanging out at the end of our local lover's lane because, as my brother suggests, you're a pervert. And you weren't there waiting there to catch two of our local poachers."

Boyd went silent again.

"The man who shot at my brother was Army. That's what the Dooleys said, and they met him. Haircut like yours anyway. Army issue sidearm and quick with it."

Boyd looked at Tom but said nothing.

"If you didn't follow somebody from the Fort, then you were waiting there for someone to show up. That means you have information about someone from the Fort doing something that involves going to that lagoon. Probably not to park with high school girls either. So somebody from the Fort is doing something that involves launching a boat from the lagoon. And if they're going somewhere in it, let's take a guess where. Pocket Island?"

"I'm not at liberty…"

SMACK!! Joe flung an open hand at the back of Boyd's head, knocking him to the deck.

"Joe! Cut it out!"

"I want to know what this piece of garbage knows about Dad's Colombian necktie!"

"He doesn't know anything! He never met Dad. Isn't that right, Sergeant?"

"What!"

Boyd's mouth tightened.

"Someone gave you that story as an intro to Mad Dog junior here, to get his help in whatever it is you can't talk about."

Boyd looked away.

"Bullshit!" said Joe.

Tom held up his hands.

"Some Army folks have been doing unlawful things on my property, haven't they Sergeant? Not garden variety unlawful. And not Army-sponsored."

Boyd said nothing.

"There're a lot of reservist coming through the Fort right now, aren't there? Some who've been stationed here before. Maybe one or two, like yourself, from fifteen years ago?"

Boyd shook his head, not in denial but in concern.

"There's your connection, Joe."

"What?"

192

"We can help, Sergeant."

Chapter Thirty-One

The Morgan brothers huddled in blanket-covered chairs facing the hearth in the main room of Joe's cabin. The hardwood fire had twice burned to coals while they argued.

"I don't trust him," said Joe. "And I don't think you do, either."

"It's free help, Joe. I can't afford to blockade my own island. And local law enforcement is kind of short-handed."

"That runt is trouble, not help."

"You think the Army's got it in for Frank Lloyd Wright?"

"I think the Army has some funny people in it. And some of them have a thing about Pocket Island."

"So why not use one of them to keep an eye on his own?"

"The Devil's Island trick only works if no one can get on or off. Here, they'll do god knows what to you in your sleep. You're better off with Brutus... even if he is a coward."

Tom stretched his lower limbs toward the dying embers. "Do you know yet when Bonnie and the kids are coming back?"

"Yes. And I told you, stay out of my business. You're heading back to the big city in a week, right? So stay here and go through the CDs I got from Karen Ryan and the stuff from her ex. I'm putting a tent on the island and staying there until I catch one of your night visitors in the act."

Tom turned his face from the fire. "And then what?"

Joe smirked. "We'll have a nice long chat."

"You crossed a line with Sergeant Boyd today, Joe. My guess is you would have gone farther, if I hadn't been there."

"And had the whole thing sewn up."

"I don't want that kind of help."

"I'm not talking about your torched house, Tommy. That army punk knows something about how Dad got killed and why. The next time I get hold of him he's going to... What's your word? Share?"

* * *

Tom parked the truck at the entrance to the Coldwater Commons. Three teenagers in hooded sweatshirts looked up from their lobby posts and ran into a stairwell. Tom opened the lobby door, and the sound of squealing tires and spraying gravel echoed behind him. Half expecting the elevator to be covered in artwork and ordure, he was surprised to find it relatively clean. Karen Ryan's apartment was on the third floor.

The woman who answered the door wore stained men's work pants and a man's button-down shirt open to the sternum. She was about five foot ten and a hundred sixty pounds, with hair and eyes the color of black pearls and as high as a teenager at a rock concert. Perhaps on account of that, she held herself momentarily like the package she must have been in her youth.

"Come in, handsome. I'm having a party."

Tom scanned the apartment through a filter that reminded him that this was Maggie Ryan's mother. This was where she lived, how she lived, and who she had become. Curiosity compelled advance; gut signaled retreat.

"You look like your daddy," said Karen. "Do you want a beer?"

"No thanks." Tom had not introduced himself, but apparently that wouldn't be necessary. He examined the bookshelves that lined one wall from floor to ceiling and perused the framed photos that screened most of the eye-level volumes, looking for one of Maggie. Karen disappeared into the kitchen and returned with a juice glass three quarters filled with a cold white wine. "Here." She put the smudged glass in his hand and placed a free paw on his forearm.

Turning away from the photographs, Tom found himself looking into pupils that opened wide onto nothing. He put down the glass and reached

195

into his pocket for the wallet of cd's. "My brother asked me to return these. They were helpful."

Karen tightened her grip on his arm and her button-sized pupils narrowed. "What's he going to do about them?" she demanded.

"He didn't say."

"Bullshit."

Tom shrugged and Karen pressed. "My ever-loving ex is not just a baby snatcher. He's a killer. Maybe twice. If your brother lets him get away with that, they'll eat him alive around here."

"I'll pass along the warning."

Releasing her grip, Maggie's mother slid hard into a deep vinyl chair. Her eyes treaded a spot midway to the wall and her lower jaw began to move from side to side.

"Can I ask you something about what's in those journals?" Tom asked. The woman swiveled her head slowly and slowed her chewing. "I take it Dee Dee Ryan was a very sick woman."

"Well, she married him."

"I mean her physical health."

"I wouldn't know."

"You didn't read the disks?"

"I read the parts about my daughter. I don't give a rat's ass about the rest."

"She had some pretty severe allergies. Did you know that?"

"You don't get fat from ragweed, honey." She raised her head to the shelf of framed photos. "It takes a lot of comfort food to go from that to this."

Tom took a step toward the photo Karen's nose was wagging at—a young, dark-haired woman in a black string bikini preening on a white blanket. The blanket was spread across the top of a large, flat rock and the woman in the bikini was doing something with her lips to the ear of a pale man with a jarhead haircut. "Do you date a lot of soldiers?" he asked.

"Used to."

"This is Pocket Island." He lifted the framed photo and brought it closer for inspection. "Washington's Head."

"There're some pretty spots out there. Private."

"Someone told me the island was popular with the Rangers before the last owner put Dobermans out there."

"What an asshole! We had some crazy parties out there back in the day."

"Where did you go to after that?"

"Oh, I don't know." She rolled her head, face-up, neck like a socket. "I think the Fort started to downsize around then. I don't really remember."

"You were in the hospital around that time."

"Says who?"

Tom looked at the photo and ignored the question.

"I have a recurring hormone imbalance."

"Do you remember a Coldwater policeman who was there at the same time?"

She laughed. "You take a roundabout way, don't you?"

"Do you remember him?"

She laughed again. "Your mama send you?"

"So you remember him."

"He's a *hard* man to forget. Even now."

"Do you remember what you told him?"

"About what?"

"About what you saw on one of your picnics." Tom held out the photo. "Or what Opie here let on after you finished swabbing his ear."

"I'm not following you, handsome."

"I think you follow me just fine. Crazy's not the same as stupid, is it? I'll bet people make that mistake with you a lot."

Karen reached for the glass he had neglected and drained it. "How about a hint?"

Tom stared hard into vacant eyes. "The same thing you told Burdock. The thing that got his skull bashed-in."

* * *

Tom eased the Grady White alongside the Ryans' dock and tied the bowline so that the boat faced away from the wind. A bungee-banded tarp covered a huddle of lawn furniture at the foot of the dock, and dust devils of leaf debris skimmed across the lawn beyond it. He looked up at the line of storm windows fronting the lake and assumed that someone was frowning behind one. He gave her time to make up her mind, then walked up to the house.

The only car in the steep, circular driveway was a leaf-covered Mercedes parked off to one side. He ran his finger along the hood. Rosemary Ryan stood at the opened front door and watched him. Her age-spotted hand gripped the inside doorknob. "She won't see you," Rosemary announced as Tom turned away from the car and came toward the house. "Or your brother."

"Hello, Mrs. Ryan. May I come in?"

"No."

"I didn't come to see Maggie."

"I said, no."

"And I didn't come *about* Maggie. *Or* her stepmother." He waved a hand at the unwashed car. "Or your son."

"I don't like riddles, Tommy Morgan. You should know that."

"I came to see you, Mrs. Ryan. To ask you a question about Karen Ryan... and my father."

Rosemary's hand slid from the doorknob and fell against her dress. Cold, rheumy eyes stared into Tom's. He pushed open the door. Rosemary followed him down the hall to a large, open room, separated from an enclosed wrap-around porch by a low divider inset with bookshelves. A couch and two wing back chairs formed a grouping of furniture in front of a stone fireplace. A mahogany credenza hugged the back of the couch. A lone candy bar lay at the bottom of a cut-glass bowl at its center flanked by two transparent, shell-filled table lamps at either end. In front of the couch on a low shin-smasher table, a beading can of Diet Pepsi pinned down on a pair of empty candy wrappers. "Sorry to interrupt your lunch," he said.

Rosemary grimaced. "It's the last of my daughter-in-law's exercise snacks. I don't like to throw away food, and no one else around here will eat them." She took a seat at one end of the couch and gestured Tom toward the wing-back chair beside it. Before his trousers touched the cushion she laid out the ground rules. "I told your mother years ago that this was something I didn't care to talk about. I haven't changed my mind."

"So she knew?" It was a confirmation rather than a question.

Rosemary pressed her lips.

"And you wouldn't talk to her?"

"I don't talk politics, religion, or husbands with my friends. Especially not Hellers. That's why I still have them."

"No exceptions? Not even when a friend needs a friend for support?"

"And I don't talk to their children behind their backs."

"This isn't idle curiosity, Mrs. Ryan. My brother is looking at a possible connection between our father's murder and some recent activities here in Coldwater. He's asked me to help. Neither of us care to embarrass or hurt our mother by asking her questions that could easily be answered by someone else."

"It's none of my business, Tommy. If your mother wants to discuss it with you, that's hers."

"I don't disagree with your principles, Mrs. Ryan. But in this case, they're misplaced. And my sheriff brother isn't going to give a hoot about what you do or don't want to talk about. So you might want to talk to me. I have better manners." When Rosemary didn't respond, he stood. "If that's your choice." He picked up the empty soda can and candy wrappers. "I'll dump these for you on my way out. Have fun with MadDog Junior. Don't say I didn't try to spare you."

Chapter Thirty-Two

T om found a post-it note from Joe stuck to a folder on the breakfast bar when he came out into the kitchen the next morning.

I downloaded Karen Ryan's CDs, scanned Burdock's and Ryan's autopsy reports, and loaded everything into a file named 'Smart Boy.' I left the hard copies in the folder. Weatherman says the temperature is supposed to drop twenty degrees tonight. Find something!

Tom made a pot of coffee and then started with the recent bank financials, comparing them to the spreadsheets Burdock had recovered from Ryan's personal computer. Once again there was a significant difference between the value of the bank stock reflected in Ryan's personal records and the roughly corresponding numbers in the most recent bank documents.

Ryan's own records showed the value of the stock corresponding to the loan he took against it falling substantially over the previous six months. It also showed a decline in the value of the investments he'd made with the loan money. The bank documents on Burdock's disks showed no similar erosion, but they were out of date. When Tom had visited Andrew Ryan, he had asked for the most recent financials to see if the discrepancy continued.

Comparing the documents in the folder with the ones on the screen, it was apparent that the gap between Ryan's numbers and the bank's was still there and still widening. If the personal records were accurate, both Ryan and the bank were steadily losing net worth. But the only evidence of it was in Andrew Ryan's computer. He didn't have enough money to pay back the bank loan with what was left of the investments he had made with it. A divorce this year would have bankrupted him. And if couldn't have prevented it, he would have been screwed.

Tom went back to the computer and screened the autopsy report for Dee Dee Ryan.

"Body Examination:

Initial examination at Coldwater Hospital revealed an adult female Caucasian seen supine on a steel autopsy table. The decedent has blond hair, blue eyes, veneered front teeth (top and bottom), and small scars in the crease of each breast near the chest wall, typical of cosmetic surgery. Multiple medical appliances are seen in place including an ET tube, IV sites, and a chest tube. A small laceration is noted on the palm of the left hand and another slight laceration is noted under the upper right arm as well. No additional external trauma is noted during the preliminary visual examination.

Identification:

The decedent was positively identified by her husband Andrew Ryan.

Opinion:

Asphyxiation by drowning. When found, the decedent was in a moderately advanced state of rigor mortis, placing the time of death at 10-14 hours before she was examined or anywhere from 8 p.m. to midnight on Sunday 9/10. Skin was wrinkled due to excessive exposure to water. Algae and water were discovered in the lungs and lumps of undigested food (lab results indicate corn syrup, whey, peanut oil, and chocolate) were discovered in stomach and esophagus. Froth was visible at the mouth and nostrils. Bleeding was also visible in the decedent's eyes."

Tom also read Joe's handwritten notes of his conversation with a Dr. Tran, which were also scanned and uploaded into the file.

"Hospital allergist notes that condition of body also consistent with non-aspiration drowning (i.e. decedent choked while in water or before entering water). Closed throat and small volume of water found in lungs atypical of aspiration drowning. However, no external trauma to throat area that would indicate strangulation."Tom translated. Basically, she drowned. Or she choked on something and then drowned. No one bopped her on the head and threw her overboard, or put his or her hands around her throat, or held her underwater. That didn't tell him much.

He went back to the other journal entries—the ones about Maggie that her mother claimed were the only ones she had read, and the ones about Maggie's stepmother that had made both Tom and Joe question Andrew Ryan's manhood. Tom spent an hour rereading the juicier bits and reviewing the autopsy material one more time. Then he took a piece of paper and made a chart.

Dee Dee Ryan			
If it wasn't an accident?			
Suspect	**Motive**	**Opportunity**	**Gut**
Andrew Ryan	Money Passion?	Yes	No passion in this guy. Even if he lost a fortune, he's the type that would earn it back or go without.
Maggie Ryan	Hatred/Revenge	Probably not. In hospital & probably in no shape to skip out	Maybe when she was a teenager, living at home and under her stepmother's thumb. But now?
Karen Ryan	Hatred/Revenge	Yes	**The journals.** Ample motive on every page. Burdock told Joe that Karen went nuts when she read it.
Burdock	For Karen Ryan?	Yes	Sleazeball. But would he kill someone he didn't know because some crazy woman told him to?
Rosemary Ryan	For Maggie?	Yes	-Maybe years ago, when Maggie was being abused. But now?
	For Andrew?	Yes	-No. Not the kind of person who would murder to save her son money.
Other			Dee Dee Ryan's reputation was she could piss people off without even trying. Maybe she swam into school of soldiers on a training exercise and flipped them off? Autopsy says no sign of a struggle. But would a Ranger(s) know how to make it look like accident?

Tom took a highlighter and ran it over Karen Ryan's name and over her ex-husband's journals as the catalyst. There was enough in those to make any biological parent, much less a crazy one, want to murder her step-successor.

And Karen Ryan was not the bloodless dullard she had married. Andrew was all about stoic, ineffectual self-sacrifice. Karen was about Karen. And her 'hormone imbalance', or whatever it was, clearly leaned toward the passionate, not the passive. She wouldn't need Burdock to do the wet work; though she might have easily bullied him into it.

Tom looked again at the chart. There were holes and a lot more to do—alibi's for time of death, a method of causing Dee Dee Ryan to drown without leaving evidence of a struggle. He would need some smart doctor to make progress, assuming there was really anything to figure out. Only Joe seemed to feel that Dee Dee Ryan's death may not have been accidental. And Joe's recent behavior made Tom question his state of mind.

Putting aside the chart, he opened the copy of Burdock's autopsy report. It followed the same standard Coldwater Hospital format: scene description, body examination, identification, and opinion. According to a Dr. Elliott, Burdock died of blunt force trauma to the head. Even in dry medical-ease, it was grim reading:

> "The distribution of cerebral contusions suggests that the majority are contrecoup injuries. That is, they are on the side of the brain opposite the site of the scalp trauma and skull fracture noted above. This pattern is typically associated with injuries produced as a result of a fall. However, multiple separate cerebral contusions are also present on the frontal portions of the brain in close proximity to the injuries to the face noted above. These frontal cerebral contusions are more characteristic of coup lesions, typically associated with an overlying blunt force blow(s) to the face, with direct localized force impact creating the frontal cerebral contusions."

In plain English, somebody didn't just bop Burdock on the head with a poker. They beat him thoroughly and with such force that every part of his head, front, back and sides had corresponding injuries to the brain. Whoever it was didn't just smack Burdock around, he (she?) went ballistic on him.

Tom took another piece of paper and made another chart.

Dwayne Burdock			
Suspect	**Motive**	**Opportunity**	**Gut**
Random computer store customer?	To keep secret something on hard drive that Burdock should not have read.		Burdock's hobby of reading stranger's private records was dangerous. People keep things on their computers that some would kill to keep secret. Someone probably did.
Karen Ryan	?	Why allow herself to be the one to find the beaten Burdock while he was still alive, and why bring a witness?	If she didn't kill her ex who "stole" her child and allowed her to be abused, why would she crack at anything Burdock could do? But if she killed Dee Dee Ryan, then maybe she turned a corner. Once you've done the first, the second is that much easier.
Joe?			

Tom put down the pen. He had not planned to write his brother's name. But it belonged there. Joe had more or less admitted that he had smacked the man around when Burdock had shown up at Karen Ryan's apartment and mouthed off about MadDog. Joe had been seriously out of control with that soldier on the boat. Too many wise guys seemed all of a sudden to know something about the former Sheriff Morgan's death. Joe had always had a tendency to emote rather than repress, and to do it with his fists rather than words.

The autopsy report made it clear that Burdock did not die quickly. If Joe were asking the questions and Burdock had the answers, then surely Burdock would have coughed them up. And if Burdock didn't have the answers, would Joe have beaten his brain to mush anyway? Tom didn't think so, or at least he hoped not. But how well did he know that side of his brother? A side that had undoubtedly matured with the temptations and tools that went along with a badge. Tom stood from the table and began to pace the room.

Joe had always had a temper. Starting in high school, people on the receiving end often got hurt. But Joe had always stopped when got what he wanted – victory, surrender. Maybe he didn't always stop soon enough. But he stopped. He'd never crossed the line where a message beating might have become permanent injury or fatality.

Or had he?

You've been gone a long time, Tommy. Joe doesn't appear to be mellowing with age. The autopsy lists Burdock as fifty-three years old. How many punches does it take to croak a geezer?

As Tom walked these troubling thoughts around the open room, the telephone in the kitchen began to trill. He let the answering machine take it. When he heard the familiar voice scream into the tape, he turned toward it and stopped. "Joseph! What the *hell* is going on! Rosemary Ryan just left here. I damn near strangled the woman! I told you to leave well enough alone! PICK UP THE GOD DAMN PHONE!!! ANSWER ME!!! FIND OUT WHAT THAT BROTHER OF YOURS IS UP TO AND PUT A SOCK IN HIS MOUTH!! I MEAN IT!! NOW!!!

Chapter Thirty-Three

Tom stared at the phone long after the machine had clicked off. Mary's temper had regularly stoppered her husband, even when he'd had a few, but it had been a while since Tom had been so close to a blast. When he thought about it at all, he had assumed that his were a kid's memories exaggerated by size and distance. They didn't seem exaggerated now.

He took Joe's truck and drove it to the Coldwater Senior Center, muttering thanks to Mrs. Ryan along the way and vowing to find an opportune means of returning the favor. The voice on the phone had sounded stoked on more than just Geritol. Tom found himself recalling the bromide "my country right or wrong," and the wag who'd compared it to "my mother, drunk or sober" and opining that no son or patriot would utter such words except in a desperate case. This was surely one.

The sound of screaming came through the door, but only one voice. The knob turned easily in his hand and he pushed it open. Glass in one fist and phone flattened against an ear, Mary whirled at the sound. "He's here!" She tossed the phone onto a cushion and closed the distance between them like a wolf on a kill. He reached to give her a kiss and his mother met him halfway with a roundhouse slap that made him hear tones.

"You idiot! You Ivy League numbskull! What right do you think you have to poke your nose into my marriage?"

CRACK! She slapped him again.

"Enough, Mom."

She raised her hand to strike a third time and he backed away.

"You're acting like a Heller, Mom."

CRACK!

He retreated behind a chair, but held her gaze. His mother spat more choice words and then left the room. A door slammed. Tom picked up the phone and pressed the redial button. "It's me," he said. "No, she's gone to her room. Why would she have a gun?" Tom held the phone away from his ear and grimaced. "Okay, I should have talked to you first. Stuff it, brother, you were the one who decided to go camping." He threw down the phone and went to his mother's bedroom. The door was locked. "Mom?"

"Get out!"

"Mom, let me in."

CRASH! Something large and audibly fragile shattered against the door. He went back to the other room and picked up the phone. Examining the keypad, he selected the button marked speed dial and then the first number that came up. A man's voice answered. "Hi," said Tom. This is Mrs. Morgan's oldest son. Are you in the same building as my mother?"

"I'm on the second floor."

"Is this Herbert?"

"Yes, What can I do for you, Tom?"

"I'm in a bit of a jam, Herbert. Could you come up to my mother's apartment? She's locked herself in her room and I've got an emergency on my hands. I'll be back later. But right now I have to find my brother."

"You've been very foolish, young man." Tom could hear the elderly voice struggling to find a steady range.

"I've just been told."

"A woman deserves her privacy."

"And the dead deserve…what? Tell me, Herbert, because they're starting to pile up."

* * *

Tom tied the boat to the stone dock at the back of Pocket Cove and then climbed the cliff-side steps to what was left of his dream house. A small tent was pitched beneath the pines facing the burned-out shell. Embers glowed inside a circle of stones in front of it. Joe paced beyond the fire with a cell phone pressed to his ear. Brutus followed him with his eyes but kept a safe distance.

"No, don't let her have anymore, Herbert. I know she's a grown woman. No. I'll check with you later. And thanks." He pocketed the cell phone and glared at Tom. "Spill it."

Tom took in the signs: left hand closed over right fist, lips pressed, brows narrowed to a tight wedge, chin up, eyes level. If this were a bar, he thought, it would be time to look for a door. He folded his arms and returned his brother's stare. "I went to see Karen Ryan, who was apparently a party girl with the boys at Fort Drum back in the day, and a regular at the Psychiatric wing of Coldwater Hospital. She met Dad when he ended up there after a binge. One thing led to another."

"I know all this, Tommy. It's not what I asked you to look into."

"But it leads there. Hot Karen Ryan used to spend time with her soldier pals out here on Pocket island, before Hassad and his Dobermans took up residence. We know now what the soldier boys were doing here. I think Karen Ryan found out, too, from hanging with them or maybe seeing something on one of her frolics. We know she told Burdock about Dad. You slapped him around for spilling that. My guess is she also told Burdock about what her army buddies had been up to back in the day. Maybe Burdock found something on one of the PCs that came into his shop, and that got the conversation going. Maybe she just told him for the hell of it. When I suggested to her that Burdock got killed on account of her putting him onto the same thing she got Dad onto, she almost had a stroke. But she didn't deny it."

"Is that all you've got?"

"No. But it's better than my other theory."

"I don't even follow this one. What's your other bright idea, bright boy?"

"That Dad and Burdock were killed by Hellers."

"Which ones?"

"You and Mom."

Tom watched his brother's eyes, so much like their mother's, glazed by the light of the embers. "This isn't good, Tommy."

"Did you know we were Hellers?"

"Long time ago, on Mom's side. So what?"

"And you knew about Dad and Karen Ryan?"

"Seems like everyone in town knew, except you brother."

"And you still beat the crap out of Burdock for just mentioning it?"

Joe shrugged. "Where are you going with this?"

"Fifteen years after the fact, you smack around a fifty-three-year-old man because he says something about Dad being a lady's man."

"So what?"

"So… what do you think Mom did when she found out in real-time? Not fifteen years after the fact, but in the heat of the moment?"

Joe glared.

"You would have beat Sergeant Boyd, too, or drown him, if I hadn't been there."

"What's your point?"

"You like smacking people around, Joe; and you get your temper from her."

"I said, what's your point?"

"That maybe you got carried away. Maybe she did, too."

"You're a son-of-a bitch."

"Did he talk, first?"

"Who?"

"Did Burdock tell you what he found on those PCs? Or was it all just from Karen Ryan?"

"You can quit now."

"He was beat to a pulp, Joe. Dad got his throat slit. They pissed-off people with serious anger-management issues. Are you telling me not to connect the dots?"

"I'm telling you to shut up!"

"Did Burdock talk? Did he even get the chance?"

All Tom remembered later was that it felt like a car crash and that the results were not dissimilar. Maybe he got his hands up and blocked a few. But it must have been a while before the beating stopped. Or maybe he just passed out. Probably the latter.

Chapter Thirty-Four

Tom was pried from a violent dream by a large wet tongue swabbing his face to the brink of suffocation. He could hardly feel the tongue, but he was keenly aware of the fetid breath that wafted over it. Gagging and spitting, he struggled to stand. The dog stood back and sniffed the patches of blood that smeared Tom's jacket. Tom could feel his teeth were somehow wrong, but his jaw was too swollen to open and probe.

Brutus tugged at Tom's trousers. Starlight and glow from a three-quarter moon seeped between gaps in the clouds. He could see ground, but little beyond. The fingers that splayed over his face felt like they were groping a pumpkin. Pressing one against what he guessed was an eyelid, he found that a tight salute made the landscape a little wider.

The dog led him to the edge of the cliff and to the sound of splashing and voices below. Tom held a finger to his eyelid and tried to focus on the shapes in the cove. An open boat rocked at end of the dock and, near it, two head-shaped spheres bobbed in the water. A large rectangular object surfaced between them, disappeared, and then surfaced again. One of the spheres rose from the water and became a man-sized silhouette that climbed onto the dock and hauled at the rectangular object until it, too, left the water and balanced on the edge of the dock. A dark arm emerged beside the other sphere and guided the boat toward the dock. Then sphere and arm rose from the water and became a second man-sized figure which emerged from the lake and helped the first load the long dark box onto the tethered boat.

Tom found his cell phone and dialed his brother's number. There seemed to be no injury to his hands, as there often was in a bare fist disagreement between grown men. He did not remember a fight exactly…just baiting his brother to the point of eruption, which had been the goal. But the face that met his hand had definitely been in a fight. He dialed the number from memory, adding to the evidence of unimpaired function, but what came out when he spoke was gibberish. The voice on the other end was groggy, irritated, and quickly gone. He dialed again, but could not make himself understood. He dialed a third time and a machine answered. He spoke into it slowly and urgently, describing what he was watching and the need for help. But the noise that came out of his mouth sounded less like speech and more like someone gargling through Jell-O.

He watched the two wet-suited figures reenter the water and emerge with another rectangular box that they hauled onto the dock and then loaded into a large Zodiac. A third man surfaced just beyond the rubber boat, and the two men on the dock jumped into the water beside him. The three figures struggled with something under the water and finally hauled it onto the dock. It looked like the trunk that Joe had described, and the two others in the boat were just like it.

Brutus growled.

Tom tried the phone again and got the answering machine. The dog tugged at his trousers and hauled him along the edge of the cliff toward a giant beech tree where a thick rope hung from a limb stretched far out over the water. Tom looked at the dog. *You're joking.*

The three dark figures scrambled into the Zodiac and assumed positions around the edge of the piled cargo. One man squatted next to the outboard motor and the others perched on the inflated pontoons and held onto boxes. Tom did not hear an engine start, but he could see the boat turn slowly away from the dock and head toward the mouth of the cove. A kid's instinct made him look for something to throw. *A big fat rock from this height into the middle of an overloaded rubber boat? Why not? Joe had almost sunk a Chris Craft from here once.*

Tom pried a discus-sized stone from the ground beneath the beech tree. He wound the Tarzan rope around his waist and then looped the end around the heavy stone. *You've done this a million times,* he coached himself. Then he put his weight on the rope, gripping it above his head. When the Zodiac was close enough for him to see faces, he pushed off with his legs and leapt into cold, clear space.

The arc of the rope carried Tom and his crude weapon far out over the water. A face in the Zodiac rose as he passed overhead fumbling with the loop of rope around the rock. Another figure in the boat reached for something beside the boxes. The Tarzan rope arrived at the end of its arc, slowed, and began its return. Holding the rock at his side, Tom gripped the rope with his legs and one overhead fist. A wet suit in the bow of the Zodiac crouched in the universal posture of aiming.

BOOM!

Tom dropped the rock.

BOOM!

His hand slipped from the rope. His body inverted and he fell end over end toward the Zodiac.

CRACK!

Torso bounced. Feet crashed against something hard and edged. A moment of simple pain was followed by cold, wet, and a different pain that completely obliterated the first. Freezing water seared Tom's mouth like a molten potion. Tongue clamped over a new car's worth of broken dentistry. Nothing he had ever experienced had hurt that badly. Not the mauling from Hassad's Dobermans, not even the dental grinding that had created the space for what was now apparently missing.

His body sank while he struggled with the zipper on a foam-filled jacket that had instantly sponged its weight in brain-numbing ice water, and with the laces on a pair of boots that had suddenly become water-filled anchors. *You've done this before,* he calmed himself. *Strip and get on with it.*

When his head broke the surface, he tried not to gasp. Sounds of splashing and engine reverberated across the water. Voices called to each other. Tom swam silently in the opposite direction... away from the dock and the stone steps cut into the side of the cliff that led to what was left of the Frank Lloyd Wright house. He stroked slowly toward the rope that circled innocently above the water and to the wall of rock beyond it where crevices and exposed roots, toeholds, and finger grips zigzagged up to the giant tree above it. He tried not to breathe through his mouth or think of his extremities.

At the top of the cliff, he could see that the Zodiac had run aground on the far side of the cove, and there sat empty with its engine running. The sky began to pale. One wet suit was still in the water. Another was almost at the top of the stone steps. As Tom looked for the third, a chunk of wood exploded from the tree behind his head, accompanied by a deafening CRACK!

Barefoot, heart-pounding and face aching, he ran through stabbing brush toward the pines. BOOM! CRACK!! Nearly three years ago he'd stood at the window of his Manhattan office looking down at a column of ash-covered people fleeing up Broadway. Where could so many thousands go, he had wondered? The mayor had immediately shut down the trains and subways and closed all of the bridges. Manhattan is an island and, at that moment, there was no way off it.

He ran toward the pines, hard and fast, but where was there to go to?

Soon he was running downhill. The first rays of sunlight had begun to filter through the trees. He looked at his feet, his wet trousers, torn shirt, and then ahead toward the water. There was no escape there. He was not a Ranger. He could not swim three miles to the mainland through fifty-four-degree water. He picked up his pace and headed toward the top of the island followed closely by the sounds of dry wood snapping under a heavy boot. He sprinted along its ridge toward the place where pines opened onto an oval of slag spilling from a dark wound in the side of a small hill. The sound of close pursuit grew louder. CRACK! BOOM!! A bough of pine at the far side of the clearing fluttered to the ground like a wounded bird.

Diving into the opening in the side of the hill, he scrambled fast until his face found a pool of water and his body piled in behind it. In the darkness, he felt for the lip of rock beneath the water, turned on his back, and pulled himself through and into the space beyond. When his lungs found air again, he gasped loud and long. There was no need for silence now. They knew where he was, and that he was cornered.

Spreading his hands across the cave floor, he searched the darkness for something that he could use as a weapon. Lungs and face were raw, and his body trembled with cold and exhaustion. But instinct screamed that if he did not meet with lethal force whatever next broke the surface of the pool in front of him, the game was over. He fanned his hands across the smooth dirt and found nothing.

* * *

Joe let the patrol boat drift toward the empty Zodiac that bumped the face of the cliff. He grabbed a boat hook and snagged a man's ski jacket floating nearby. Keys and a cell phone fell from a pocket. Tom's boat was tied at the far end of the dock. Before boarding it, he went to look at a scuffle of dark lines scratched on the cement. Something had been dragged to the edge leaving log, dark marks. He looked down into the water but saw nothing.

The Grady White looked undisturbed, its cabin door closed but not locked and the inside orderly but not tidy, like its owner. Nothing seemed missing or mishandled. Joe delayed trying the keys from the floating jacket until there was nothing else to check. The one that looked like a boat key fit easily into the ignition and when he turned it, the needle gauges leapt to attention and the engine rumbled. *"Shit."*

Grabbing the riot gun from the patrol boat, Joe sprinted up the stone steps to the top of the cliff. The campfire there was cold and the tent empty, but a familiar, motionless form lay beneath the skirt of a nearby pine. "Tsst!" The dog raised its chin but remained undercover. Joe reached through the boughs and grabbed its collar. "Where's Tommy?"

The dog whimpered. "Tommy!" Joe urged.

The Labrador shuffled toward the edge of the cliff, and from there to a tree where a thick rope swayed in the dawn breeze. Joe looked over the edge at the drifting Zodiac and at the hole in the dirt where something had recently been removed. *"Pearce's Chris Craft,"* he muttered. "Did Tommy sink a boat, buddy?"

The dog dropped his head and whimpered.

"Where's Tommy?"

Brutus folded his hind legs and sat hard on the dirt. Joe cursed and squinted across the dew wet grass that winked in the first rays of sunlight. Grabbing the dog by the collar, he pulled it to where the grass lay trampled in a direction that led into the pines. "Helen Keller could follow this, buddy! Come on, find Tommy!" The dog yelped and followed the flattened patches of grass. A few yards on, he howled at a splash of blood, and later at a partial print of toes and arch at the edge of a muddy hole. "No shoes, no jacket, no service," Joe whispered to the dog. "Tommy chasing a girl out here?"

The dog led Joe across the top of the island and then retraced an uphill arc that hugged the ridgeline north. It howled again at fresh boot prints in the soft earth. Joe pumped a shell into the chamber of the riot gun and trotted cautiously behind the Labrador. "Okay, buddy. Somebody else is following Tommy, too. But we know where he's going, don't we?" Joe slowed to a silent walk as they approached a slag-covered clearing. At the far end a pair of rubber-clad legs stuck out from the side of a hill, as if this were a place where the earth swallowed men and spat out rock. Nearby, a hooded wet suit worked a flat rock from the side of the hill and carried it toward the disembodied legs sticking out from the mouth of the low cave. Joe raised his riot gun and stepped out of the shadows.

"Don't drop it," he ordered. Joe approached the legs sticking out from the hole and brought a boot down hard on a taut Achilles tendon. A yelp echoed weakly inside the cave. Joe waved the shotgun at the wet suit holding the stone. "Step away." He turned the gun toward the side of the hill and fired.

"BOOM!"

Shards of dirt and slag blew over the man holding the rock. Joe pumped the gun and swung it toward his midsection. "That'll save explaining. Put down the rock and tell your pal there to pass out everything you shoved in." The hooded wetsuit dropped the rock and knelt at the mouth of the cave. "Shout it," Joe ordered. "So he hears it's you." The wet suit shouted into the opening. Joe prompted with his boot. One by one, out came a dozen, arm-thick pine boughs, and half a dozen pie-sized rocks. "Now haul him out of there." The wet suit tapped the rubber-sheathed leg and it began to toe backward. When it was almost out, Joe brought his boot down hard on an ankle. This time he felt something crunch. As he watched his boot press flattened ankle, the other wet suit used that moment of inattention to lunge at Joe's chest, knocking him to the ground and grabbing for the riot gun.

BOOM!

The shot exploded from the mouth of the cave. The hooded wet suit rolled from Joe's chest and staggered toward the woods. Joe lifted the riot gun by the barrel and brought it down on the pistol wavering from the mouth of the cave. He snatched the fallen weapon and ordered the man who dropped it to come out.

The answer was silence.

"I've got a shotgun, a dog, and an island full of firewood!" Joe shouted into the cave. "Which one do you want me to start with?" Joe took the recovered pistol and fired it into the side of the hill. "And you dropped this!"

When there was no response from the cave, Joe put fingers to his mouth and whistled toward the pines. Brutus slunk across the open ground and came to stand beside him. "You hungry, boy?" he asked loudly. Brutus growled uncertainly and yelped twice. Joe shouted into the cave. "How's that ankle, idjit? Tender enough to eat?" Joe leaned down and slapped the big black Labrador on the rump. "Get him, boy!"

Brutus yelped and thrust his face into the opening in the side of the hill. "Is Tommy in there, too?" The dog barked repeatedly, and the close stone walls amplified the sound as if the dog were barking into a metal barrel. But he didn't enter the cave. After a few minutes of canine bravado, Joe reached in and grabbed the dog's collar. "Guess soldier boy doesn't have anything else in there...or he would have used it on you." He pushed the dog to one side and stuck his own torso into the dark tunnel. *Shouldn't be able to kick much either,* he reasoned. He crawled forward until his fingers touched something to grab. A shank led to a foot and after some feeble kicking, the rest was just backing out and dragging the crippled wet suit behind.

Joe examined his catch in the daylight. "Burned yourself," Joe observed waving the riot gun at the captive's hand. "Pull back that hood and let's have a look at you." The wet suit glared and did nothing. Joe picked up one of the boughs that had come out of the cave and prodded the injured foot. "You

217

got a license for them canal boats?" He moved the crude club to a spot over the mangled ankle. "Pull back the hood," he suggested. The wet suit looked at the pine bough poised over his crushed ankle and then lifted a hand to yank back the rubber hood.

"Thought so." Joe grabbed the dog's collar and pushed him into the cave. "Get Tommy!" The dog howled. Joe prodded its rump with a boot to encourage sufficient noise making. A few minutes later came a splash and a whispered "Shush!" Out came dog, and behind it something that looked like a drenched scarecrow topped by a busted Jack-o-Lantern.

Joe removed his jacket and handed it to his brother. "You look like death warmed over. I'll get you out of here as fast as I can."

Tom wrapped his shivering torso in his brother's fleece. The short jacket did little for the rest of his frozen body, but it was a start.

"Can you hold yourself together until I find this idjit's boyfriend? I think Annie Oakley here may have shot him."

Tom held up a pair of fingers. "Ta-two," he chattered. The man on the ground dropped his head.

"Two what?"

"Bb-oy friends."

Joe picked up one of the pine boughs and poked the wetsuit in the ankle. "Do you know what Mr. Heller here was doing when I found him?" The man on the ground stiffened. "He was laying branches and rocks over that little pool in the cave. If you'd tried to come out while it was there, you'd have come up against a homemade lid and drown." Joe looked at his brother's broken face and shredded clothes. "He do that, too?"

Tom ran his tongue over a stubble of broken teeth. "Nn-ot all of it."

Joe closed his eyes and shook his head. "Sorry."

"Ta-talk la-later."

Joe nodded. "Where'd you see the other rubber freaks?"

"Ca-cove. Za-Zodiac. Bb-boxes. Da-diving."

Joe poked the Heller with the barrel of the riot gun. "Strip," he ordered. The military man glared. Joe shook his head. "Don't be stupid."

Joe took off his own clothes and gave them and the riot gun to Tom. Then

218

he pulled the wet suit off the injured soldier as if he were peeling a pelt from a dead rabbit, and with about the same amount of concern for the victim's comfort.

"Give me an hour," he said. "This one's not going anywhere, and if either of his pals shows up, just shoot them. We only need Mr. Heller here and trust me, he's going to tell us what we want to know."

* * *

Tom could feel blood returning slowly to his warming limbs. He sat in a patch of sunlight until his remaining teeth stopped chattering and then crawled back into the mouth of the cave until only his head and the gun Joe left behind were exposed and covered in shadow. The Heller said nothing. Tom focused his scattered thoughts on trying to forestall hypothermia. Stripped of his wet suit, the Heller sat naked except for a pair of dark swim trunks, his outsized hands alternating between slapping a torso rippled with goose flesh and supporting a swelling, purpled ankle. At least he's dry, thought Tom. As the cold retreated from his core he felt himself grow sleepy. It had been a long night and a longer morning.

"My brother says you're a Heller." Tom hoped that conversation would help him stay alert. The soldier looked away. "We're related. Did you know that?" The head swiveled, but the face remained expressionless. "My great-grandma or something was a Heller. They say most violence happens in families." Tom found the sound of his own voice warming. "Did you ever run into a Dee Dee Ryan when you were swimming out here?"

The soldier looked away again.

"Your pals ever mention a Karen Ryan or a Dwayne Burdock?" Tom chattered on about the recently deceased and his theories of how they might have gotten that way. It kept him warm and helped him think of something besides his broken face. The Heller held his ankle in both hands and watched the woods beyond the clearing. "Joe would really like to know who killed our father, too. Got any idea what you're going to say when he asks?"

The solder remained silent.

"You might want to think of something."

* * *

The Zodiac bobbed at the end of the dock. Beside it, a hooded swimmer struggled with something in the water. Joe watched the swimmer grab a boat line that dangled from the Samson post at the end of the dock, tie the other end to something under the surface, and then climb onto the dock and haul on the rope. He was a small man and the performance reminded Joe of a kid struggling with a greased watermelon. When the swimmer managed to get what turned out to be a suitcase-sized metal box onto the dock, he flipped it end over end into the Zodiac. Then he dove back into the water and did not come up.

Joe stood with Brutus at the top of the cliff near the beech tree that held the Tarzan rope. The dog tugged at Joe's trousers and pulled him closer to the edge. "What?"

The dog growled.

"Tommy jumped?"

Brutus pressed his nose to the back of Joe's calf and nudged him toward the rope. Joe slapped the dog on the snout. "There're steps, you know."

Someone had left a mask and a pair of flippers at the bottom of the stone stairs cut into the face of the cliff. Brutus lifted the strap of the mask and carried it to the end of the dock. Joe held the riot gun loosely in one hand while he squinted at the water and at a hooded head that rose rapidly toward the surface, its back to the dock and its attention on a large green box. When the head broke the water, Joe raised the gun and called out, "What's in the box, sport?" The man in the wet suit looked up, startled, his pale face a mask of anger and surprise. He let go of the box and then dove after it as it dropped. Joe called to the dog, "Get him, Brutus!" The Labrador yelped and jumped into the water. He was gone for a few seconds and then surfaced alone, barking excuses.

Joe picked up the dive mask and jumped into the water where the wetsuit had disappeared. A light flickered a few feet down from where the dock met the face of the cliff. He swam toward it. Then it was gone. Kicking hard toward where it had disappeared, he touched rock before running out of breath. When he returned to the surface, Brutus leaned over the dock and licked his face.

"Must be a cave down there, buddy. Filled with dog biscuits! You want to come?"

Brutus yelped and shimmied his body, spraying cold water like a garden sprinkler. Joe retrieved a box of flares from the patrol boat, lit one, and jumped into the water. It took four tries and two dropped flares to find the man-sized crack about six feet below where the dock met the cliff wall. Joe stuck a flare into the rock above the crack and returned to the surface for breath and a weapon.

Tommy had the riot gun and Heller's sidearm. There was nothing left in Tommy's boat, except a flare pistol and a diver's knife. He wasn't sure about the pistol working underwater, but he took both just in case.

Brutus lay at the edge of the dock with his nose hovered over the water. Joe lit another flare and jumped over him. Diving toward the flare he had left stuck in the rock wall, he found the crevasse and shimmied through it. The rock opened a little wider beyond that, angling back and up like a laundry chute. He kicked for the top. Seconds later he was breathing fresh air and staring into an Aladdin's cave of 1980's era military ordnance.

* * *

"Big Foot have anything to say for himself?" asked Joe.

"No," said Tom. "And I'm about out of small talk."

Joe dropped a wet suit in front of his brother's face. "You can come out of there now. Put this on, if you're not warmed up yet."

Tom crawled from the opening in the side of the hill and stood like an old man rising from an easy chair. He stuck his hand through a gash in the garment and then peered inside. "There's blood in this."

Joe shrugged. "Look. You'd better get yourself to the hospital. I found your keys and left them in your boat."

What about his friends?" Tom waved his chin at the silent soldier.

"One's sitting in an underwater cave in the dark, rubbing his skinhead tattoos to keep warm. I don't know about the other one, but he's not armed. I think Annie Oakley here winged him when he shot at me. There's a blood trail just up there."

"Do you want me to send somebody for you?"

"Call that Homeland Security jerk if you can find his number. His card's on my dartboard. But get yourself fixed first."

Tom dropped the shredded wet suit and stood with his arms wrapped around his chest. "We have to talk, you know."

"Let me finish with our pal here first. He and I have something to talk about, too."

"You and I..."

"Later, Tommy."

Tom made his way slowly along the hillside toward Pocket Cove. After a few minutes, he heard what sounded like a scream coming from the woods behind him. When he stopped to listen, he noticed another man-sized form slumped at the foot of a tree beside the path. Hobbling over, he prodded the inert figure with his brother's boot. When it didn't move, he turned the body over. The face of Sergeant Gene (Jenot) Boyd, the Fort Drum investigator, stared at the sky behind flat, glassy eyes, very much dead.

Chapter Thirty-Five

Tom sat in a hospital bed with his eyes closed and his hands on top of an open folder of notes and diagrams. Maggie Ryan moved a chair to his side and put her hand on his arm. Tom felt his eyes flutter and open. Swollen, ocher and eggplant face cracked across the middle with what might have passed for a smile among ghouls.

"You look like a hockey player," said Maggie.

"Feel like one."

She placed a stack of newspapers on top of the open folder. "The Morgan brothers made the front page again. The Coldwater Gazette ran a cartoon of you in a loincloth swinging from a Tarzan rope onto some tattooed guy in a dingy. The wire services picked it up. Jack Thompson's talking about a second Pulitzer."

Tom tried to laugh, but it came out a wince.

"The out-of-town reporters are talking to everyone who's ever met you, and somehow you're still a hero. But my father says they'll start looking for dirt if you don't give an interview to someone other than Jack Thompson. My father likes you," she added.

"My brother hasn't been taking advantage of my idleness?"

"He's been around asking questions about the bank. Dad says that at least you know what you're talking about."

"And Sister Judith hasn't guilted you back to the classroom?"

Maggie pressed her fingers gently onto Tom's arm and held his gaze until he dropped the flippant tone. "I'm not meant to be a teacher, Tom. Or to live in Coldwater. As soon as I can get professional help to figure out what's causing me to space out and what I can do to control it, I'm leaving."

Suddenly, Tom felt empty.

"Dee Dee left an insurance policy. A lawyer from Atlanta sent it along with a lovely letter from her dated about five years ago—apologizing for being such a lousy stepmother and telling me to use the money to 'escape.' Her words. When I'm well again, I intend to use that money to travel."

Tom turned his face toward the window and spoke as if to his own reflection. "How do your father and grandmother feel about this 'escape' idea?"

"Grandma Rosemary says it's good. She's been spending a lot of time at the Senior Center with your mom, who thinks it's a good idea, too. I'm sure if I asked Father Gauss, he'd agree. Dad's kind of wistful. I didn't ask Sister Judith."

"How *is* my mother."

Maggie took a moment to answer. "Happy to know who killed her husband. But wishing everyone would just leave it alone. She hasn't been here?"

"No." Tom gestured at his swollen face and explained how he got it.

"But that soldier confessed. The papers say that a reservist who was here during the first Gulf War killed your father."

"Accused conveniently dead. Not to mention how someone could have gotten MadDog down an unlit, overgrown cul-de-sac and then taken him by surprise. Pinning everything on some dead soldier isn't the same as credibly solving for who and how."

"But you have a theory."

"My family wishes I didn't. That's why they're not here."

Maggie looked away. "I shouldn't say this. I don't know your family well. But since I'm leaving Coldwater and won't be back, I'll say it anyway."

"I'm listening."

"You could stop."

"Thinking?"

"Thinking you have to know everything." She lifted her hand from his arm. "Do you know why Christ's parents decided to have only one child?"

"I don't think that's historically accurate, but I'll bite."

"Because the first one turned out to be such a know-it-all."

* * *

Tom leaned back in the pillow and tried to make sense of what had just happened. Too brief, too flippant, too unsatisfying. But he was wired. He tried to remember if the hospital had given him steroids. Thoughts scattered and then snapped into focus. The edge of a cell phone peeking out from under a fold of blanket caught his attention. He picked it up and dialed Tanner Hartwell. "I'm in," he said, without preamble.

The managing partner at his former law firm took an audible breath. "Wonderful. Can you start today?"

Ignoring the question, or perhaps not even hearing it, Tom kept talking. "But the exchange has to launch in Europe, not the States. None of the big U.S studios need an alternative source of financing. They're doing fine, and the current sources will have knives out for anyone who tries to poach their business."

The scratch of Montblanc pen on a yellow legal pad was the only sound on the other end of the line.

"Europe's a different story. The film production companies there don't have access to reliable financing. Every project is a one-off combination of private bank, distributor, and government support. If we offer an efficient, low-cost source of alternative financing, I don't see a government or industry group with an incentive to stop us."

The busy scratch of pen on paper momentarily paused, "I don't know, Tom. This client made a huge investment in supercomputer capacity at the top of the market. Management is looking for a mega-project to use the capacity and cover its costs before the company has to put out its annual shareholders' report. Are the European studios big enough to take that on? Can it be done this year?"

"Just get me a meeting, Tanner."

* * *

Father Gauss arrived as Tom was finishing his call. "Just the man I was hoping to see," said Tom.

"You look more in need of a medical healer than a spiritual one."

"I don't know what I need, Father. Everyone seems to have an opinion on that, and few compunctions about sharing. But I do want to talk to you about how we might get our school project back on track."

Gauss bowed his head and then gestured at Tom's bedridden posture, IV drip, and other medical paraphernalia. "In the middle of all this? Sometimes you astonish me, Thomas."

Tom kept talking as if he hadn't heard. "The Pearce estate will come up for sale as soon as Susan's will is probated. We could buy it and put the school there instead of on Pocket Island. Cheaper to renovate, easier to access, no environmentalists, no smugglers, and no Homeland Security."

Gauss moved a plastic chair to the side of Tom's bed and took a seat facing him. Tom started to explain about the film futures exchange and his intent to leverage his equity in it to kick start an initial round of fundraising for the school. Gauss held up a hand to stem the torrent. "Thomas, you're talking a mile a minute and I have only the vaguest idea of what you're saying, except that this movie business must mean that you'll be leaving us. You look feverish, by the way."

Tom paused, as if momentarily disconnected from his power source. A sound like a kid's pocket whistle vibrated in his ear. "Forgive me," said Gauss. "I'm not sure that this is the time or place, or if you're in any state to hear what I have to say. But if you're leaving us, I'll have to take that risk.

"You have a wonderful gift for making money. But until you figure out why you have it and discover your life's purpose, you'll remain as you are: vaguely discontented and spiritually unfulfilled. To put it simply, you're lost, ass backwards, upside down, and heading nowhere to be proud of. You've been that way for some time."

Tom found his voice again. "But you'll take my money."

Gauss looked at his former altar boy who, in the almost three decades he had known him, had never said a sarcastic or disrespectful word. Something was clearly wrong. But the priest felt the need to hammer home the point while his audience was in no position to escape. "Money is not the root of all evil, no matter how often the Apostle Paul is misquoted. Love of it is. Though that doesn't seem to be your problem. In some ways, I think you could care less. You have a talent. Charitable institutions like the church will always be happy to make good use of whatever you care to share. But the wisdom traditions, both religious and secular, are about souls, not shekels. I once thought the secular path might be the better one for you: art, literature, philosophy—to make up for all the silly catechism you had to endure early on. But I can see now that I was wrong."

"So no you're going to whack me with the theology stick?"

"You're not ready. And I wouldn't presume to know which one might penetrate that arrogant intellectual armor. It's not what you believe, anyway; it's how you live. Theology can come later, if you need it. Cart after the horse."

"So what's my cart? Or horse? I'm not following you."

"I doubt that. But let me be clear, just in case. You're lost. You don't know where you're going, or why. You don't have a vision for your life that makes it meaningful or you happy. Until you find one, you'll remain an aging, self-absorbed, unconscionably rich, vaguely dissatisfied skirt chaser."

"Ouch."

"Money can be useful servant, Tomas, but it's a terrible master."

"More Paul?"

"PT Barnum." If Gauss expected a laugh, he didn't get one. "All I can do is point you in the right direction. It's up to you to find your own path. But you can't do that with a head full of financial babble and nary a word getting in from anywhere else."

"Voices now? You mean like God?"

"Something beyond ourselves is always trying to communicate with us, Thomas. Call it what you like: Him, Her, It. Most are too preoccupied to listen. You especially right now. I wouldn't say 'time's running out.' I don't believe that. But you're not getting any younger."

* * *

The lake was calm…almost pastoral. Tom stood at the end of the church dock looking through clear, cold water at discolored patches of mud and sand where the under-dock residents had fanned their spring nests some months ago. He had learned to dive from this spot, jumping over the outstretched arm of Monsignor DiMaggio, who stood in the waist-high water backing slowly away from the dock until there was no way for young Tommy to get over the outstretched arm except head first.

Holding a manila folder over his head to shade his eyes from the sun, Tom watched the heavy equipment working on Pocket island and wondered if he'd have a house or even a single tree once they were finished. The Homeland Security people were being grimly thorough this time. They told him that he could have his island back once they'd finished taking it apart and crazy-gluing its various hidey-holes shut, which wouldn't be soon.

Lowering the folder, he flipped through the notes and charts inside. He was sure of the answer. Less sure what to do with it. Closing the folder and tucking it under his arm, he strode up the lawn to the steps of the church to keep an appointment there.

"Nice teeth," said Joe, the tone of his voice conveyed as much of an apology as Tom knew he was likely to get. He ran the back of his hand over a still painful stretch of discolored jaw. The brothers stood awkwardly while the occasional, mostly elderly parishioner trickled in for Saturday afternoon confession. Tom recounted what the Homeland Security people had told him about the multiple caches of stolen military ordnance on the island, and how his restoration of the Frank Lloyd Wright house on it would have to wait until they were sure they had found everything. Joe filled him in on the parts of Heller's confession that had not made the papers, including the frightening revelation that one of the missile buying groups had tested their purchase by firing at a commercial plane during the recent 4th of July fireworks. "It missed," said Joe. "But not by much. They came back to buy more once they knew the old stingers still worked. That was them you ran into."

"Nice detective work," said Tom, not intending sarcasm, but hearing it come out that way. He didn't care. "Did the Heller say how they got MadDog to drive down Beaver Lane alone and then surprise him?"

"He said Dad somehow got wind of one of the stinger exchanges and was there watching when they did the transfer."

"Karen Ryan could have told him. She'd been on the island a few times with the boys from the Fort. They might have gotten careless. But that doesn't explain how they jumped him. You wouldn't think he would have dozed off."

"I know the papers are saying that Boyd did it," said Joe. "But the Heller wasn't there, so take his story for what it's worth. He did say that Boyd had 'family' in Canada and that the tongue thing was Boyd's idea to lead the trail away from the Fort."

Tom tapped the folder under his arm. "There was a Boyd on the list of computers in for repairs at Burdock's shop… with a Fort Drum address. Maybe there was something in his hard drive that he didn't want anyone to read. Inventory of what they had left on the island maybe. He might have killed Burdock just to make sure."

Joe shrugged. "Sounds right. That could explain the condition of the body, if they needed to know if he had read whatever it was he wasn't supposed to. Big Foot and I didn't get around to chatting about that."

"Boyd could have done it to muddy that trail too… if he knew about you hammering Burdock before that. Once an improviser…"

Joe sighed. "Don't start with me, Tommy. I would have thought you'd had enough."

Tom ran his tongue over his new teeth. "It served its purpose."

Joe shook his head. "It served no purpose, brother, unless you like taking a beating. We had this talk a year ago. Remember? Outside Frankie Heller's garage. You didn't listen then, either."

"Lock up the dangerous. Let God take care of the guilty?" Tom quoted.

"That's right. And what did you do? Went and got yourself mauled by a pair of killer dogs. You're not cut out for this game, brother. Not the part people need, anyway. Sometimes I wish I had your talent. I really do. But you're missing the common sense to go with it. You think I'm dangerous? I think you're lethal."

Tom folded his arms across his chest, "You're the third person this week to tell me I'm in the wrong line of work, and none of you are talking about the same thing. Fine. I'll figure it out. But before I put away the Watson cape, just tell me this: Are you going to let her get away with it?"

"With what, Tommy? You're fishing. Not even Dooleys go tossing dynamite willy-nilly at family."

"Are you going to ask her?"

"Ask her what? 'Mom, did you kill your husband?' That was your last theory, wasn't it? Boyd did it, Tommy. Heller may not have been there, but he didn't make up that story just to help out the widow."

Leave it, said a little voice. But Tom took a breath and plunged anyway. "MadDog was too smart to go alone down a dark cul-de-sac and not take precautions when he was expecting trouble. He might have gone down there with a girl, though. Or to wait for one. Someone could have got the drop on him if he had something else on his mind."

"You're making yourself crazy brother."

"Tell me I'm wrong and I'll stop. Tell me that you don't want to know the truth, too. Not just part of it."

Joe pointed at the folder in Tom's hand. "'Meet me at Our Lady of The Lake for Saturday confession hour.' he quoted from the message on his answering machine. What are we doing here, Tommy? You think you're going to get Mom to go to confession and wash her soul clean or something? If you're going to quit, then quit. Now, before something else gets broken. Something that can't be fixed."

Tom handed the folder to his brother. Inside was a copy of Dee Dee Ryan's autopsy report, notes on some follow-up conversations with the hospital anesthesiologist, and interviews with Dee Dee Ryan's girlfriends. "It's not about Mom. It's the other dead body you said didn't pass the smell test. You were right. What you do about it is up to you. I'm finished here."

* * *

Father Gauss moved his ear closer to the opaque cloth screen. The voice on the other side came through as a hesitant whisper. "I was just mad at her, Father. You didn't know Dee Dee Ryan, but that woman could make anyone want to kill her. She fed off drama. It was like fuel to her."

"But did you intend to cause harm?"

"I thought it would just make her sick. I knew about her allergies, of course. She made sure that everyone in town did. And her bowl of energy bars. No one who went into that house could miss it. It wasn't hard to add one more."

"One that you knew she'd be allergic to."

"Yes. But there was no way I could have known she would take that one just before going swimming and then drown."

"Was it a possibility you'd thought of?"

"Not when I put it there. I was just angry. I thought it would make her sick. A childish impulse. But she had such a gift for making people angry."

"And when did you make the connection between that childish impulse and Dee Dee Ryan's death?"

"The thought crossed my mind after they found her body. I guess I didn't want to go there, so I stopped thinking about it. Then yesterday I found an envelope in my mailbox with a protein bar wrapper inside, a receipt from Kellogg's Grocery store, and a copy of this week's church bulletin with a circle around today's confession hour."

"I don't understand. Do you know who put the envelope there?"

"There was no note. But the Coldwater sheriff is standing outside with his brother. I don't think they're here for confession."

"I see. Well your intent, as you describe it, was venial, not mortal. And intent is what matters in my business."

"I suppose that should be a relief."

"It should. Though what matters to the Morgan brothers may be different."

"What should I do, Father?"

Gauss sighed. "Send in the one with the Smokey The Bear hat. I'll have a word with him. The other one's a bit on edge."

"Thank you, Father."

The priest made a sign of the cross in front of the faded linen screen and intoned the absolution. "Go in peace, your sins are forgiven, Rosemary."

A Note from the Author

I come from a family of unabashed storytellers. Great uncle Gil, acrobat, minstrel, and neighborhood raconteur set a certain standard by the regular recital of ribald poetry at family gatherings. Cousin Jimmy Ross, aptly named, continues the tradition of laugh out loud entertainment. My contribution consists simply in applying the fig leaf of literary respectability to uninhibited tradition. By taking the tall tales out of the back yard and exposing them to a wider and more critical audience, I've tried to do for my loved ones what Tom Morgan, in the Coldwater Series, has so far been unable to do for his. We may both be kidding ourselves. You can take the boy out of Coldwater...

Acknowledgements

I would like to thank the Rose Bar, Cowboy Coffee, the Teton County Public library, and all the other Jackson Hole, Wyoming, venues that have graciously allowed me to linger, scribble and tell tall tales.

Excerpt from COLDWATER ENDGAME

Book 3 of the Coldwater Mystery Series due out April 2023

Prologue

Luke sat alone in the tree stand, silent and unmoving, his face randomly streaked with green and black camouflage paint. The worn brown wood of an ancient Browning compound bow that had belonged to his dad when he was a boy was large for Luke's ten year old grip. But his other hand, strapped firmly to the bowstring by a Velcro strap and mechanical release, would launch a lethal arrow at 300 fps at the slightest pressure from his sweaty index finger. He was excited, and for the first time in a long time, happy.

Scanning the thorn filled gully below the tree stand for sign of movement, he reminded himself that his dad was down there somewhere, stalking slowly up the hill. Not quite silent, the sound of his footsteps and cloth scraping against brush would push the deer, if there were any, uphill toward his son in the tree stand. "Don't shoot unless you see horns," were his final instructions. Luke wouldn't. He'd practiced. He could hit the center of a pie plate at thirty yards nearly every time. But he felt jittery and the sound of his breath was loud in his ears. It took him a long time to settle down.

Eventually there came the telltale sound of hoof on dry leaf and then movement behind a dense thicket of bush thorn. A doe and two yearlings appeared below his stand, feeding on fallen acorns. Luke's heart began to churn like a cake mixer and the wood under his hand felt moist. Opening the hand to admit dry air was a rookie mistake. Three pairs of soft brown eyes flickered toward the movement followed by three snow white tails wafting high in graceful bounds back into the thorns. Luke let go his breath. *Wow!*

For the next few minutes thoughts and feelings combined and recombined as if passing through a kaleidoscope: red and ocher fall woods, dappled deer and the happiness Luke felt being back in Coldwater. Living in Canada with grandma and grandpa had been hard. They were nice; but their house was small and grandpa was old. Mom had been quiet most of the time and still was. Dad seemed okay. He didn't get angry with Luke or his sisters much, or even with Mom anymore. Luke was happy to be back at his old school, with his friends, and to be out in the woods with his dad. He hoped his parents would stay together.

He had heard them talking in the kitchen last night when Dad got home. It was late and their voices woke him. Luke didn't understand what they were saying and he was afraid that they might be arguing again about whether he was too young to go deer hunting. But after a while he could tell that they were not talking about him, or deer hunting, although he heard his name once. They weren't fighting. Maybe they would stay together.

Another sharp, sudden *Crunch* broke into his reveries. Hooves? No. The sound was too loud. A voice? Dad said he might use a grunt if he needed to. "If you think you hear me," he'd said, "be patient. Sound carries in the woods. I might be close by, or I might not. Don't lift the bow until you see horns. Be sure."

Crunch. Clash. Not hooves. But what? Could it be two bucks fighting! Or was Dad carrying a set of rattling horns? Luke couldn't remember. No, it was voices. Dad said he might use his voice to move the deer if they stopped too long. Luke cocked his head and strained to hear. Adrenaline surged through his slim, pre-adolescent body. Without thinking, and almost as if he were watching someone else, he felt himself stand, lift the bow and pull the bowstring back to full draw. His dad had said to be still. Be patient. Don't lift the bow until you see horns. But it felt right to be ready, though his thin, unmuscled arms began to quiver and the bow shake. He quickly realized that he would not be able to hold the bow at full draw for long, and that he would have to put it down. But partway down the gully, he saw brush move and something pass behind a tree. Horns? Dad had warned him that branches can look like horns. Luke's arms trembled and the bow vibrated like a tuning fork. He could not hold the bow steady. Easing his grip was the second rookie mistake. The tension simply transferred from the hand holding the bow to the fingers of the opposite hand crimped to the bow string; and just like that, he felt and heard the *whoosh!* of an arrow escaping into air. He could not have held it back.

Instantly there came a shout, or more accurately a man curse. Luke felt frightened and sick. Dropping the bow, he unbuckled the harness, scraping hands and face against the rough tree bark as he scrambled out of the tree and ran toward the sound of the cursing. Up ahead a man lay on his side, a hand covered in blood pressed to his lower back and the other clamped to his front. Luke was afraid to go closer. The snap of dry wood sounded nearby and Luke turned in time to see someone in green camo running downhill, head covered in a tan fishing cap with a flap in the back like the Japanese soldiers wore in WWII movies. Whoever it was must have seen what had happened and was going for help, or the police. Luke tried to shout, but no sound came out. He started to run after the fleeing figure, but then fell, his face ploughing the soft earth. He thought he heard another voice. But he wasn't sure. He couldn't see his dad anymore, or hear him. He called to his dad, but got no answer. Then he stood up and ran toward the voice or voices. He was scared. He had accidentally shot someone and they needed help. But he was all turned around now and he didn't know where he was. He didn't know where his dad was. All he knew was that he was scared and needed to get away.

About the Author

James A. Ross has at various times been a Peace Corps volunteer in the Congo, a Congressional staffer, and a Wall Street lawyer. His debut novel, *Hunting Teddy Roosevelt*, won the Independent Press Distinguished Favorite Award for historical fiction and the American Fiction Award in the Adventure/Historical category. It was also a finalist for the National Indie Excellence Award and the American Book Festival Award for historical fiction. Ross's debut mystery novel, *Coldwater Revenge* won the Firebird Book Award for legal thrillers, the Maincrest Media Award for Mystery/Suspense, the American Fiction Award for Hard-boiled Crime, and the Pencraft Award in the Thriller-Terrorist category. His short fiction has appeared in numerous literary journals and his short story, Aux Secours, was nominated for a Pushcart Prize. Ross is a frequent contributor to, and several times winner of, the live storytelling competition Cabin Fever Story Slam, and he has appeared as a guest storyteller on the Moth Main Stage. His live performances, online stories, newsletter sign-up, and more can be found on his website: https://jamesrossauthor.com

SOCIAL MEDIA HANDLES:
  FB: https://www.facebook.com/james.a.ross.author
  Twitter: https://twitter.com/JamesARoss10
  Instagram @jamesrossauthor

AUTHOR WEBSITE:
  https://jamesrossauthor.com

Also by James A. Ross

Hunting Teddy Roosevelt

Coldwater Revenge

CPSIA information can be obtained
at www.ICGtesting.com
Printed in the USA
BVHW030228260422
635357BV00003B/25